The Fool's Gambit

Len Boswell

Black Rose Writing | Texas

ISBN: 978-1-68513-137-1
PUBLISHED BY BLACK ROSE WRITING
www.blackrosewriting.com

Printed in the United States of America
Suggested Retail Price (SRP) $21.95

The Fool's Gambit is printed in Calluna

To all I love without condition
To all I love without omission

Never doubt

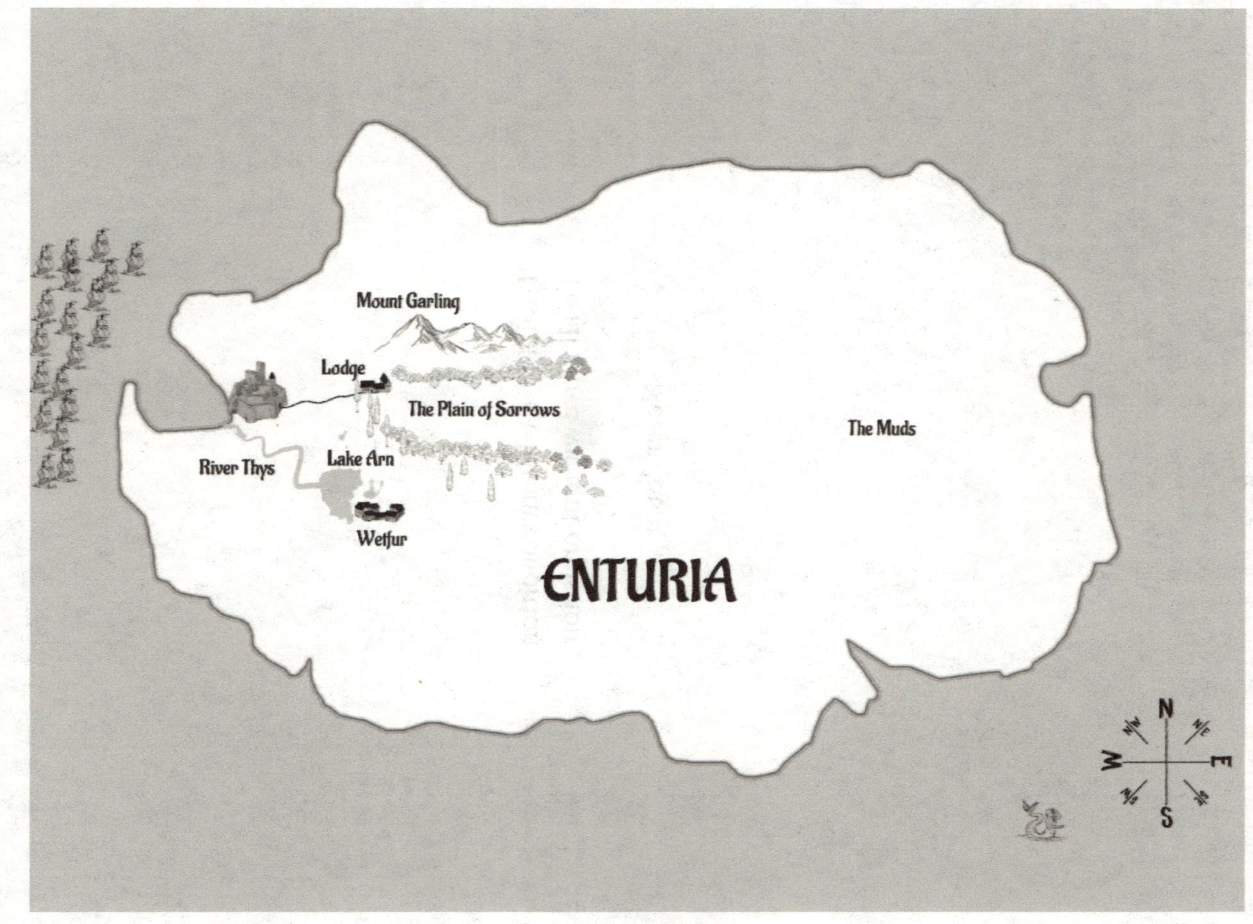

Mount Garling
Lodge
The Plain of Sorrows
River Thys
Lake Arn
Wetfur
The Muds
ENTURIA
W
N
E
S

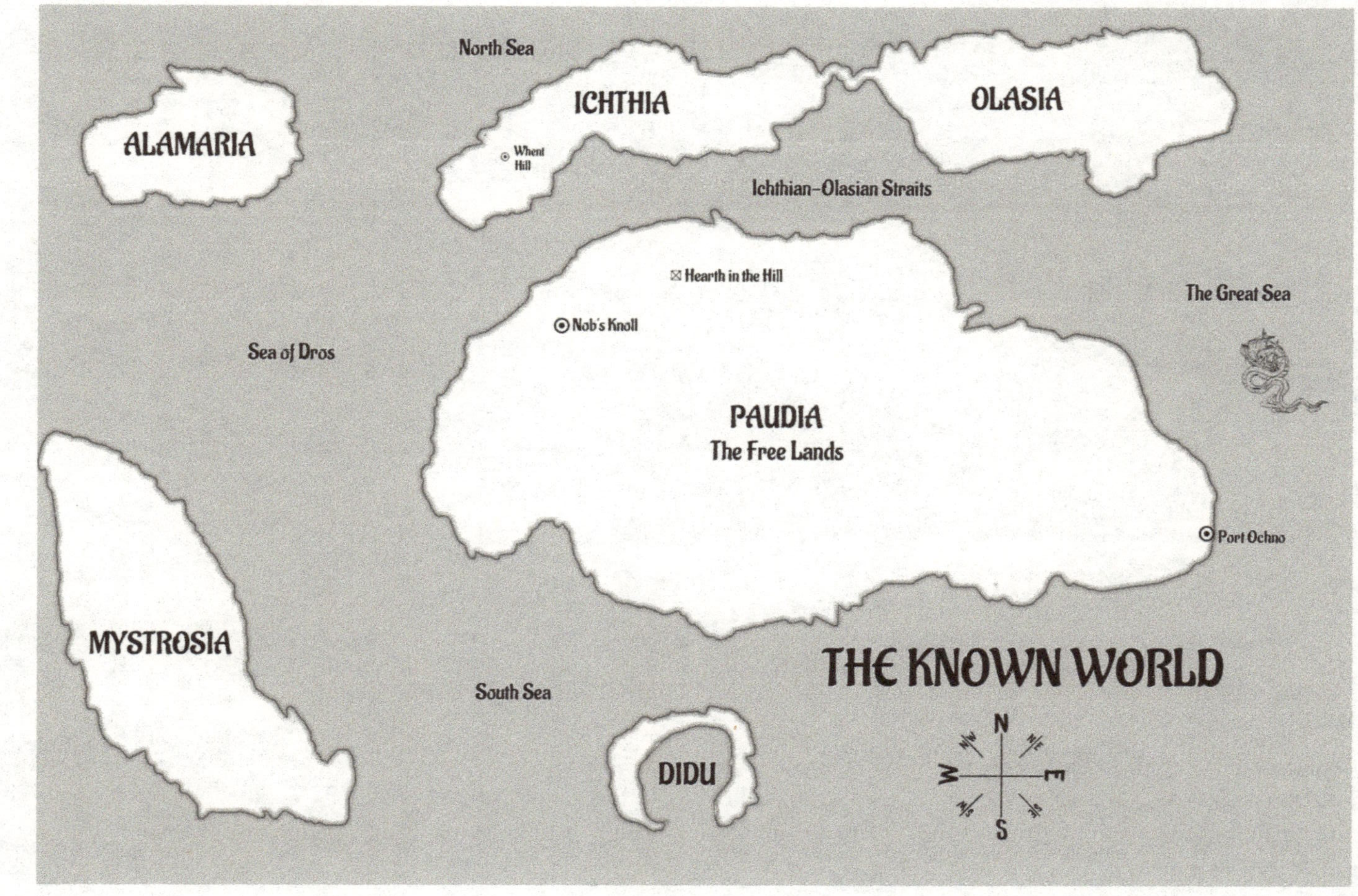
THE KNOWN WORLD
ALAMARIA
ICHTHIA
OLASIA
North Sea
Whent Hill
Ichthian–Olasian Straits
Hearth in the Hill
Nob's Knoll
The Great Sea
PAUDIA
The Free Lands
Sea of Dros
Port Ochno
MYSTROSIA
South Sea
DIDU
N
NE
E
SE
S
SW
W
NW

THE FOOL'S GAMBIT

List of Characters

Enturia

Queen Rhynt
Baron Bookins, formerly the king's fool
Lord Braque, formerly King Braque
Calax Halfhand, a sellsword, Supreme Commander of the Armies
Gash, Calax Halfhand's warhorse
Blusk, a sellsword, Master of Foot
Phendour, a sellsword, Master of Archers
Zyrx, a blacksmith and armorer
The Red Monk, d'Abo Pourcrey
Bebo, a Paudian troll
Orthor "Dreedle" Billibuck, Language Meister to the Queen
Priss, a handmaiden and archer
Cresh, Bookins' manservant
General Boh, former High Commander of the Forces of the King
Besbo d'Arc, Chancellor of Coin
Marthe, captain of the good ship *Marthe*

Mystrosia

King Merek the Mighty
The White Monk, d'Porto Saleen

The Gods

Whelan the Wanderer, Randall Himself, God of Gods
Abo, the Red God
Porto, the White God
Canto, the Blue God
Bedo, the Green God
Dado, the Gray God
Indo, the Black God

"The cleverest of all, in my opinion, is the man who calls himself a fool at least once a month."
—Fyodor Dostoevsky

"I wasn't planning to lead, I was standing in the back and then everyone turned around."
–Avery Hiebert

"How ill white hairs become a fool and jester!"
—William Shakespeare

"The best laid schemes o' mice an' men gang aft agley."
–Robert Burns

Part I

"Gods! We are such a fickle lot. One day we're for you, the next against. And let me tell you, there's nothing like a war to bring out the worst in us—and sometimes, on rare occasions, the best. So you see, this war between the Enturians and the Mystrosians was like the nip of the cat to us. We just couldn't resist getting involved, playing one side against the other, even within the same camp, where loyalty and common cause are everything. And yes, there was strife even between and among the gods. We all had our favorites and used every ploy to support them and undo the other side. But I get ahead of myself. Sit now by the fire, enjoy my wine— it is quite the vintage, from times long past, and said to cause the wildest dreams—and I'll tell you all I know, from start to finish, for I know everything."

Rhynt's first sunset as queen of Enturia should have been more uplifting. Not that it wasn't spectacular. The sun had conspired with the air and clouds to paint a sunset rich in swirls and swaths of every color, all highlighted by streaks of gray. The ocean had chipped in as well, its waves sparkling in the fading light. Her armor, too, had something to say about the sunset, the rainbow of colors swirling on her shiny green armor as she moved, making her appear to glow from some strange internal fire.

There was just one problem: the Mystrosian fleet arrayed in a seemingly unending line of ships from north to south. And they weren't making a single move to fall into the trap foreseen by the king's fool, Bookins. Instead of sailing straight into the harbor, where they would have been ambushed, they had stopped and struck their sails. Now they bobbed in the light chop two hundred yards offshore, their masts gleaming perhaps too beautifully in the fading light.

What were they up to now? she thought. She pushed the crown back on her head once more—it was just too big for her head—and turned to her constant companions. "This can't be good."

She was small, even for a fifteen-year-old. Under her impressive armor, she was a small-boned yet lithe little girl, with red hair, a freckled face, and deep green eyes, a coincidental match to her armor, which also covered a withered leg supported by a mechanical calf and foot made from a strange metal called merilium, the invention of Zyrx the Dwarf.

"No, this can't be good at all."

No one was there to answer but her hill tigers: Mela, Mila, and Spook. The tigers, bigger even than a dire wolf, just sat there, staring back at her, hoping that she would signal the end of day so they could get some sleep.

"I'll have to have a talk with Bookins. Perhaps he has another gambit that might work."

Mela, a male and the largest of the tigers, offered a noncommittal grunt, but the female Mila and her now-grown kitten Spook continued staring at her.

Rhynt's crown used this moment to slip down over her eyes, forcing her to rip it off entirely. King Braque had given it to her earlier in the day, when he had stepped down following her victory at the Gathering. She'd have to have Zyrx make it smaller somehow or forge a new one intended just for her, perhaps one that matched her green armor, also forged by Zyrx. "Damnable crown!"

The hill tigers jumped to their feet, trying to make sense of what she had just shouted. She was clearly upset. Perhaps they could help.

She recognized their concern. "There, there, nothing to get excited about—*yet*. No, what we need to do is call a meeting, see if anyone has a solution."

She glanced back at the ships. "We have to have an answer for them. They won't sit there forever."

She tried putting her crown back on, but it slipped back down almost immediately. She yanked it off and put it on the head of Spook, who tried to slap it off with his paw. Rhynt laughed and took the crown back.

"Sorry, Spook, looks like I need a smaller crown. Or a bigger head."

She turned back to the bobbing ships once more. "What are they up to?"

Merek the Mighty, King of Mystrosia, was livid. *What are they doing? Striking our sails when we should be attacking? What are they thinking?*

The king turned to the White Monk, d'Porto Saleen, who had already begun rolling his eyes, knowing what questions were about to come from this fool, his king.

Merek and d'Porto were polar opposites. Where Merek was short and plump, d'Porto was tall and gaunt. Merek's eyes were black and dead, d'Porto's icy blue and very much alive. Their clothing could not have been any more contrary, the king dressed in multicolored capes and robes of the finest fabric, the monk dressed only in a white robe, cowl, and hood of coarse cloth.

"What's going on? Why aren't we attacking?" said the king, his whole body shaking with anger.

The White Monk shrugged, showing no concern whatsoever. "As you can see, we've lost the sun. We don't dare attack in darkness. Too much is unknown."

The king flapped his arms against his sides. "But the element of *surprise*."

The White Monk offered an even deeper shrug. "Yes, a pity, but we still have the numbers. And most important, we avoided an ambush."

"What?"

The White Monk tried not to roll his eyes, but was only partially successful. "The ambush, the ambush. If we had sailed into their harbor, we would have been trapped."

A light seemed to go on behind the king's eyes. "Oh." He thought about it a bit more. "Oh, oh, I see what you mean."

"Yes, Majesty."

The king puffed out his cheeks. "So what do we do now?"

"We rest, we sleep."

"That's it?"

The White Monk sighed. "No, there's a bit more. As soon as the sun sets, I will send out scouting ships. We have no idea about the size of Enturia or its defenses."

"But it will be dark. What can they possibly see?"

This time the White Monk could not resist rolling his eyes. It was like talking to a small child. "Majesty, they will position themselves at intervals around the entire circumference of Enturia. We will then know everything at first light."

"But how will we know? I know that the scouting ships will know, but how will you and I know?"

The White Monk turned away from the king briefly—*how could this man be so dense?*—and then turned back with a smile. "Majesty, as always, I will send out gelas. My eyes will see what they see. I will know everything—*everything.*"

The king smiled, and then his smile broadened. "Your gelas, of course. I wish I had such powers. To see through the eyes of phantoms at great distances would be quite the thing."

The White Monk cringed. Thankfully, the king would never have such powers. "Yes, Majesty, that would be wonderful indeed. Alas."

The king frowned. "Yes, I know. I will never have such powers. Still, it is fun to think about." His eyes brightened. "And speaking of fun, I shall leave you to it and return to my cabin and my concubines."

The White Monk bowed. "Yes, Majesty." *Oh, blessed relief,* he thought.

The king turned to go, then stopped. "Oh, and have someone send food and wine."

"Already arranged, Majesty, including several bottles of Alamarian wine."

The king's smile could not have been broader. "Wonderful, wonderful!"

The White Monk bowed again, hoping this final bow would signal the king to finally leave.

The king interpreted the bow correctly. "Well, then, I'm off for an evening of pleasure. But make sure you brief me at first light. I would know about their defenses and our plan of attack."

"Yes, Majesty." He watched the king walk away, then turned to view the battlements of the enemy's castle, which glowed orange in the fading light. *What would they be thinking now that their ambush had been foiled? What would they do now to deal with his superior force?*

The White Monk smiled. "They will have a meeting to discuss what to do. Well then, perhaps a gela or two would be just the right thing." He laughed to himself. "We'll know everything—*everything*—by morning."

3

Baron Bookins, the king's former fool, was crestfallen. His gambit had unraveled quickly.

"We are doomed," he said, but it was barely a whisper, meant for his ears only.

"What?"

Bookins glanced over at King Braque, or rather *former* King Braque, who was now known simply as Lord Braque, as he awaited a more fitting title from the newly risen Queen Rhynt. They were quite a pair, he and the king, each frail and weak, though the king was a bit taller. If their hair had been a color once, you would never know now. Both had white hair, or rather wisps of hair, Bookins' long and wild, the king's equally long but combed flat with the help of lamb's fat. Though now a Baron, Bookins continued to wear his brightly colored and noisily belled costumes. Today's was a bright yellow with red stars. The king also clung to the clothing of his former job, his robes a shimmering gray with bright green diamond sigils. The only sign of his now lower rank was the absence of a crown.

As for his new rank, there was talk of designating him the Queen Father, but Lord Braque didn't like the sound of that. That sounded like the principal accomplishment during his reign was the widespread sowing of his seed. Bookins had to chuckle at that—perhaps it was.

"My plan, Majesty. My ill-fated gambit."

"Oh, you mean the trap."

"Yes, the *failed* trap."

Lord Braque scoffed. "Oh, but it was a brilliant plan, I have to give you that. Just because the rabbit didn't cooperate, don't blame the trap."

Bookins smiled. "Perhaps, but then again, now we have to deal with a powerful rabbit, or rather thousands of powerful rabbits."

Lord Braque shrugged. "Or perhaps we overestimate them and underestimate ourselves."

"Ourselves? Majesty, the one strength of our army is their ability to march in parade."

Braque laughed. "Indeed, but don't forget our reinforcements. We have Calax Halfhand, the hero of the Battle of Whent Hill, plus his battle-hardened comrades, Phendour and Blusk."

"Yes, but they are just three."

Braque rolled his eyes. "You forget the thousands of elves that have just arrived on our shores to help, along with that horde of trolls. I mean, think what those trolls alone can do to our enemy."

Bookins began to feel somewhat better. "True enough, but still, will that be enough?"

Braque slapped his knee. "My goodness, how you fret, when we have not even engaged the enemy."

Bookins sighed. "I do not like the unknown."

"Oh, relax, we'll know soon enough."

"Yes, that's what I'm afraid of. I've heard it said that you should never wander into a battle, and I fear that is exactly what we're about to do."

Braque shook his head in disbelief. "Listen to you, the man with a plan. Surely you can't give up now, at the very start."

"No, of course not, but we need a plan—and soon."

Braque nodded. "And *that*, I suspect, is why Queen Rhynt, in her infinite if untested wisdom, has called us to a meeting in the council chambers. We will thrash this out, come up with a plan, and be ready by morning. I just know it."

Bookins sighed, then stood. "Perhaps you're right. Come now, or we'll be late."

4

Queen Rhynt breathed a sigh of relief when Bookins and the former king, Lord Braque, finally appeared in the doorway to the council chamber and made their way slowly to the conference table, Bookins pushing Lord Braque's roller chair, its wheels squeaking as they came.

"Ah, at last," she said. "Welcome Bookins, welcome Lord Braque. Here, we have saved you places by me so your words do not get lost by the length of this table."

Bookins nodded and tried to pick up the pace, but his knees screamed at him to take care. "In time, Majesty. I have always found this room too large, even for a table as immense as this one." Finally, he rolled the chair up to the table, positioning Lord Braque at the queen's right hand, and sat down next to him with a grunt.

Lord Braque smiled at the queen, then noticed the crown sitting on the table in front of her, and frowned. "Is the crown too heavy for you, Majesty?"

Rhynt laughed and turned to the others at the table. "I will know the weight of it soon enough with the Mystrosians at our gates, but for now, it is just a little large for my tiny head."

No one laughed except Bookins, which took Rhynt by surprise. "Here, gentlemen, though it is a time for all of us to keep our wits about us, it is also a time to retain our good humor."

There were a few chuckles, but no more.

Rhynt rolled her eyes. "Perhaps Bookins will tell us a few jokes as we proceed." She turned and nodded in his direction. "Along with whatever new gambit he may have in mind."

Bookins nodded back. "Perhaps one that *works* this time, Majesty."

Smiles grew to titters, then to chuckles, then to belly laughs around the table.

"Good," said Rhynt. "That's more like it." She scanned the table. "Now, I see several people I do not know—at least not yet—so if you don't mind, I'd like to go around the table. Please introduce yourself. Name and title and anything else you'd like to say. But save your battle ideas for now or we'll be here all night just saying hello. Here, I'll begin. My name is Rhynt, age fifteen, risen this day to queen by dint of hand-to-hand combat and the largesse of the king, and still searching for a crown that fits."

5

Calax Halfhand patiently waited his turn to introduce himself to a queen who already knew him well. Like her, he wore the bright green merilium armor crafted by Zyrx not that many days ago. Like her, he also had a mechanical device to assist him. Hers was a leg and foot, his was a forearm and a hand with finely articulated fingers. If not for the armor, no one would have guessed he was Calax Halfhand, hero of the Battle of Whent Hill and berserker extraordinaire. He was just not that imposing a figure, being neither impressively tall nor demonstrably wide and muscular. His dark brown hair and wild matching beard might fit the bill, however, along with the velvety scar that ran from one ear down to his chin. Still, his pale blue eyes and knob of a nose could have belonged to anyone, from a king to a peasant. They were just ordinary, unremarkable.

He settled in, waiting his turn. Those introducing themselves before him—he was about twentieth in line around this huge table—kept to the queen's edict, mostly. Some, like General Boh, former High Commander of the Forces of the King, wanted to go on and on about themselves. Others, like Besbo d'Arc, Chancellor of Coin, wanted to praise her to the heavens. But Queen Rhynt, bless her, was quick to cut them off with a cock of her head and the words, "Thank you, *next.*"

Calax wondered whether so large a group could come up with a sensible battle plan. Most had never seen battle—or planning for that matter. The troops he now commanded were a mix of native Enturians with no particular skills other than marching, a collection of trolls who could be relied on for nothing more than brute strength, and many thousands of elves trained by his comrades, Blusk and Phendour. If anyone could save Enturia, it was probably the elves, but even they were untested.

Training can only take you so far. The question is what will you do when you see a man swinging a bloody sword at you?

Finally, it was his turn. He gave the new queen a nod and a wink and said, "Calax Halfhand, Supreme Commander of the Armies." Then he had just turned to the general to his right, signaling that it was now his damned turn to introduce himself to the queen.

And so it went, from each person to the next, round the table until it was time for the former king to introduce himself.

He cleared his throat as if to give a long speech, and many at the table rolled their eyes, knowing the former king's predilection for verbosity. "Ahem," he began, looking up and down the table. "I think you all know me. I am your former king, King Braque, now happily in retirement. You may have heard of my illness and imminent death, but I have to say, all things considered, I feel like a man reborn. The mantle of leadership is a heavy one and wears a man—or a woman—down. Once relieved of that burden however, the world, even in grave circumstances, is light." He turned to Queen Rhynt. "I guess what I'm trying to say, Majesty, is that I am feeling much better and would hope to serve you more closely, as a counselor or ambassador or in any capacity you wish. I seek only to serve."

"Thank you, Lord Braque, I will take your request under advisement. Perhaps we can talk more when we break fast tomorrow morning."

She turned to Bookins. "Now, last but far from least, our good Baron Bookins."

Bookins gulped and looked around the table. Everyone was looking at him as if he had done something wrong. And he had. His gambit had failed. Miserably.

"As the queen says, I am Baron Bookins, newly raised from my position as king's fool by former King, now Lord, Braque. My plan, my stratagem, failed of course, which is why we sit now at this table. I would hope that between us we can come up with a new plan, a new gambit that will see us through to ultimate victory."

He stopped and turned to the queen, who returned the nod with a smile.

"Thank you, Baron Bookins, and thank you all. Now, who would like to start things off? Bookins, do you have a new plan?"

Bookins nodded, then shook his head. "Yes, no, I mean I might, but I'd like to hear from the rest of you. I know most people at this table would like to hear any idea that didn't come from me just now. So . . ."

"Understood," said Rhynt. "So, what do we do, gentlemen? The enemy is just offshore and there are only so many hours left to this night."

A great silence ensued. Standing alone at the door to the room, a guard smiled to himself, suppressing a chuckle. *They have no idea what to do.*

Finally, the queen spoke. "I sense some reluctance to share. Very well, in that awkward silence, I realized that several people are missing from this meeting. Where's the Red Monk? Where's Phendour and Blusk? Where's Zyrx? Where's Whelan the Wanderer? And that ship's captain, Marthe? I specifically asked that he be here. His knowledge of ships and the sea could be invaluable."

Calax raised a hand. "Majesty, Phendour, your new Master of Archers, and Blush, your Master of Foot, are seeing to the defenses and keeping an eye on the Mystrosian ships. We think they'll be quiet this night, but we're not sure."

"I see," said Queen Rhynt. "And the others?"

Calax continued. "Zyrx, as you may remember, is in the floating tower, manufacturing armor and training blacksmiths. While a day has passed in our time, Zyrx has been at work for almost two years in the tower. We expect a major delivery by daylight."

"And what of Whelan, the monk, and the captain?"

Calax shrugged. "I don't know."

Bookins raised a hand now. "Majesty, if I may respond."

"Of course."

Bookins hesitated. He should have told her sooner.

"Bookins, why the frown?"

"Majesty, um, Majesty, it's just that—"

"Come on, out with it."

"Majesty, the good ship Marthe has sailed, and with it Captain Marthe, the monk, and that Whelan the Wanderer fellow."

Rhynt was incredulous. "What? Why? And how could they get by the Mystrosian fleet?"

Bookins shrugged and lifted his hands palms up. "I don't know why they left, Majesty, but as for getting past the Mystrosians, I suspect that was rather easy."

"Oh, and why is that?"

"Well, Majesty, the ship was there one moment and gone the next."

Rhynt nodded. She should have realized sooner. "Of course, the Red Monk and his invisibility trick." She shook her head. "But why did they leave and where are they going?"

Bookins shrugged. "I was trying to ask them that very question, but they pushed past me, boarded the ship, and set sail without so much as a word, despite my entreaties."

"That's the Red Monk for you," said Rhynt, turning back to the men at the table. "All right, we'll parse this out later. For now, let's keep to the topic at hand. Someone, anyone, tell me our best course of action?"

Silence.

"Come, gentlemen, the Mystrosians are at our door. What shall we do?"

Calax spoke up. "Majesty, as a sellsword, I've sat in on many councils like this, and most always start with an assessment of the enemy, their strengths and weaknesses. Once we know that, we should be able to come up with a plan to parry their strengths and take advantage of their weaknesses."

Rhynt smiled at him. "Of course, perfect." She turned back to the others. "So what say you? Strengths? Weaknesses?"

Silence.

Rhynt closed her eyes and tried not to scream. It was going to be a long night.

The guard could no longer suppress his laugh, so he opened the door a crack and slipped out of the room. The booming laugh that followed could be heard even through the closed door. But no one was aware that the guard then disappeared.

6

The White Monk, d'Porto Saleen, laughed uncontrollably for some minutes before finally regaining his composure. *They have no idea what to do. Developing a plan by committee? Assessing our strengths and weaknesses when they have no sense of either? Victory will be ours, and soon.*

One important piece of information, along with the Enturian's complete disarray, was the fact that additional weapons were expected the next morning. *We will have to strike quickly, take them by surprise on multiple fronts.*

But the most significant development was that the Red Monk, the most powerful monk in the known world, was gone. His presence alone could have swung the balance of power, but for whatever reason, he had apparently sailed away from the coming battle. The White Monk wondered whether to give chase, but decided against it. The Red Monk's skills included invisibility, so all attempts to find him in the vast ocean would be fruitless.

He also wondered whether to wake the king, but decided against it. The king would be angry, even with this wonderful news, and might interfere with d'Porto's new plan. He also wondered whether he should send another gela to monitor the enemy's meeting, and decided against that, too. Even if they came up with a plan—which was extremely doubtful—they would not have time to execute it. The surprise attack would put them on their heels and chaos would surely ensue. Besides, sending a gela always sapped his strength. It was not an easy thing to do, particularly for extended periods of time.

No, what he needed to do now was gather his lieutenants and lay out the plan. The scouting ships would have to be told when and how to manage their attack at first light. The attacks must happen simultaneously. That alone would have the effect of splitting the enemy's defensive forces. He'd have to send gelas to each of the scout ships, which would be taxing, but doing so was far more important than going back to that pathetic meeting.

He looked up at the moon. The night was rapidly disappearing, and they had to work quickly. He treated himself to one last chuckle. "Those fools!"

7

The Red Monk strode into the conference room, followed by Marthe and Whelan. Each was so unique in appearance that the eye didn't know where to rest, except in the case of Marthe, who was arguably the ugliest person in the known, or perhaps even the unknown, world. In his case, the eye quickly moved on, hoping to avoid the bulbous wandering eyes and misshapen nose of a black-bearded man so stout he did not appear to have a neck.

The eye much preferred to rest for a time on Whelan the Wanderer, the strange minstrel who had accompanied Rhynt and Calax to Enturia. His bright red tunic with yellow sleeves was a sight for the eyes, as was his red feathered cap. He was shorter than Marthe by a head, and much thinner. His green eyes didn't wander like Marthe's, but danced from person to person, seemingly assessing everyone at the table. The blond hair tucked under his cap matched the thin, upturned blond moustache that sat wormlike above his lips. His broad smile, which seemed to be fixed on his face no matter the situation, suggested he knew things you didn't.

The Red Monk, d'Abo Pourcrey, though smaller than Marthe and Whelan, was the most imposing figure of the three, despite his frail appearance. He was short and thin and walked in a way that suggested pain, a grimace accompanying each step. And yet this red-robed, white-bearded man was the most powerful monk in the world. He could disappear, bring storms, even stop time if he had a mind to. And you knew that without asking, just because of the way his steel blue eyes met yours. Here was a man to be reckoned with—or avoided at all cost.

"Did it take the bait, the gela?" he said.

Queen Rhynt smiled broadly. "It did, d'Abo." She turned to Bookins. "Just as you said it would, Baron."

Bookins returned the smile and gave her a little nod. "Nothing is more enticing than news you hope to hear, Majesty."

"Indeed," she said. "Now we just have to back up your latest gambit with steely resolve and action." She turned to Calax. "Are the defenses ready?"

Calax nodded. "We could withstand an attack if it came even now, in the darkness."

"But we won't have to," said the Red Monk. "If I know the White Monk—and I do—he will wait until first light and then attack with his full force."

"What about the scouting ships you detected. He'll surely have them attack as well. Can we manage three fronts?"

The Red Monk nodded. "Our ruse only gives them a few hours to travel along our coastline. That means the ships to the north and to the south will be faced with 200-foot cliffs, along with enough of our troops to make climbing impossible."

"Excellent," said Queen Rhynt. "Well then, gentlemen, I suggest we get what sleep we can."

General Boh raised a hand. "Majesty, should we not continue the meeting? I mean, what if the gela comes back and finds an empty conference room?"

"Not to worry," said the Red Monk. "First, the White Monk's gelas will not be back. He has convinced himself that we are ill-prepared and weak— to his peril, I believe. And second, I will keep watch throughout the night. No gela can get past me."

"Fine," said General Boh, "but won't blocking a gela be a concerning sign for the White Monk?"

"A fair point," said the Red Monk. "The good news is that any gela entering this room will see what I want it to see, namely every person at this table, struggling to come up with a plan."

General Boh laughed. "How wonderful!"

"Indeed," said Queen Rhynt. "Now, gentlemen, you all know what to do when the Mystrosians attack. For now, to your beds."

Everyone rose from their seats and began filing out of the room.

The queen called after Calax. "Calax, I would have a word."

8

Rhynt slumped back in her chair. "This queen business is exhausting."

Calax laughed. "You seem a natural, though. I would never have been so, so royal if I had been made king."

"Yet most still look at me as if I am no more than a child."

Calax smiled and sat down in the chair next to her. "It has been but a day, Rhynt. And I'm sure each day will make them more comfortable with you and you more comfortable with them."

Rhynt shrugged. "I wonder whether this will be the shortest reign in Enturian history."

"You are uncomfortable with the plan?"

"Yes, no, maybe—this is all so new to me. I've never fought in a battle. I don't know what to believe, what to have faith in, and what to think about our chances."

"As anyone in your position would." He reached out and put his hand on her shoulder. "Listen, it's not about the plan—all plans change at the sound of the horn—it's about will, resolve."

"But you've said it yourself. We are largely untested. And I wonder at our confidence when we see their warriors land."

"I cannot promise you anything, but one thing I do know. We are ready, and the enemy no longer has the advantage of surprise. We may win or we may fail, but my coin this night is on a win. We will beat them back, easily I think. They're not expecting much resistance from us, which can only lead to overconfidence and mistakes. Plus, we have the high ground."

Rhynt sighed. "I hope you are right. I hope Bookins is right—this time. I just wonder whether we shouldn't have pushed the issue. Perhaps if we waited a week, we would be stronger, better prepared."

Calax shook his head. "No, Majesty. I saw that once. A battle between Ichthia and Olasia. The Ichthian king decided to delay a week, and it didn't go well."

"What happened?"

"His army grew nervous, fearful. Demons filled their heads. Doubts. Mistrust. Rumors. When the time came to fight, they had already beaten themselves. Their lines broke, and Olasia overpowered them in half a day."

"You were there?"

"Yes, on the wrong side, and was lucky to come out of it alive."

Rhynt nodded, then grew silent.

"What, Majesty?"

"I wonder about myself. In this coming battle."

"You worry that you will not meet the moment."

"Yes."

"Rhynt, you are the queen. Your place in this battle is to stand above it all, watch the battle unfold, and make changes in the moment to assure victory."

"I would fight."

"If we are overrun, yes, but otherwise, no. You cannot lead effectively while dodging arrows and swords. When you're in hand-to-hand combat, you can see no farther than your next opponent. The sweep of battle is lost in swinging steel."

"But what will my subjects think of me? Won't they expect me to fight alongside them?"

"Not if they are smart. The last thing we need is for you to be killed in battle. That does nothing but ensure defeat. The Mystrosians would like nothing more than to see you enter the fight. They would be on you like flies on a cave rat pie, Majesty."

She sighed. "Very well, I will do as you say, but know this. If I am needed, I will not hesitate."

"Yes, of course, Majesty." He puffed out his cheeks. "Go now, get what sleep you can. I'll wake you before the cock crows."

Rhynt stood, gave him a nod, and walked from the room, leaving him sitting at the table.

Calax waited for the door to close behind her and then slumped back in his chair. They were taking a big risk, an incredible risk, even for a trained army, which they definitely were not. Bookins' latest gambit would work nine times out of ten with an experienced force, but this lot of unbloodied marchers and untested elves made one out of ten the best bet.

He pushed back the chair. He'd check the defensive positions once more, have a word with Blusk and Phendour, and then manage whatever sleep he could.

9

Rhynt only had to turn one corner in the vast castle to be confronted by the last man she wanted to see: the Red Monk. "You! What do you want?"

The Red Monk bowed, which startled Rhynt. Their previous relationship was master and servant, or perhaps master and *slave* was a better description. He ordered. She obeyed, albeit reluctantly. "My dear, or should I say *Majesty*, I would have but a word with you."

There was something about the way he said *Majesty*. "You make fun of me?"

He looked surprised. "Why, no, Majesty, I just wanted to apologize for my part in the ruse that brought you here."

Rhynt cocked her head. "Apologize? You?"

"I misjudged you, my, um, Majesty. I thought if I told you the truth, you would never agree to face the dangers of The Gathering."

"Well, I'd say you were right about that. Travel to a mythical land to fight for my life? No, thank you."

"But it all worked out. You survived and are now queen."

"And I could have been lying here in a pool of blood."

He shook his head. "But you had the skills to succeed, Majesty. I made sure of that. And Zyrx did the rest, providing you with weapons and armor for your journey."

She snorted. "I thought it a great kindness at the time, but now I see it was all a part of your plan. Tell me, was Calax part of your plan, too?"

"No, no, Majesty, Calax was just a happy happenstance. And he fit perfectly with our plan to get you safely here to Enturia."

"And you weren't worried about my chances against a right berserker, a man who killed for a living?"

"Yes, he's a killer, true enough. But he has a weakness, and that is his heart. Zyrx and I were certain that he'd never raise a sword against you, even if it meant his own death."

"Ha! So you thought I would kill him in the end?"

He shrugged. "We weren't certain, of course, but are happy nonetheless with the outcome: a new queen, a new head of the army."

"I fear I may be queen for only a day."

"The Mystrosians."

"Yes."

"Well, I think you are giving them too much credit. Their king is an imbecile, and the White Monk has nowhere near my power."

"Speaking of which, how do you plan to use those powers? We've spent hours coming up with a plan—another Bookins gambit—that doesn't involve you, *at all.*"

The Red Monk chuckled. "Bookins included me in his plan. I am what he refers to as the wild card, or the joker if you will. If things go wrong, I will be there to help."

Rhynt shook her head. "I don't see any humor in our situation."

"No, of course not. I just meant—"

"I know what you meant. It's just that, if you have all these powers, why not use them now? Bring forth a mighty storm to smash the Mystrosian fleet on the rocks. Send invisible gelas to kill the king and his monk. Stop time itself for the Mystrosians and then let them awaken just before our swords lop off their heads. Do, do—*something!*"

The Red Monk nodded. "I wish it were as easy as that, Majesty. The fact is, while the monk is not as powerful as I am, he does possess enough skill to thwart me in many ways. For now, I must save my strength, my powers, to counter his magic in the battle to come."

Rhynt shook her head. "I would have thought you could overwhelm the monk with ease."

He shrugged. "When I was younger, perhaps. Now I must guard against using all my powers at once. No, it is better to follow Bookins' plan, part of which is that I have fled Enturia. If it works, there will be ample opportunity for me to use my power to finish them forever."

"And if the gambit fails?"

He put a hand on her shoulder. "Then I am your last best hope."

Calax moved along the battlements, from torch to torch, looking for Blusk and Phendour. Men and women he didn't know nodded at him and smiled as he passed. *I hope they can smile tomorrow night,* Calax thought. *Tomorrow will be a long, bloody day, and if these untested warriors survive, they will never be the same—for good or ill.*

Finally, he spotted his fellow sellswords under a torch at the center of the defenses. Phendour saw him first and motioned him over with a wave of her hand. "Here, Calax."

Calax never ceased to marvel at this warrior, the best archer, some said, in the known world. She was taller than Calax by a head, with dark, almost black skin and hair the color of scorched wheat, swirled around her head and held firm by a strand of animal teeth, as was the custom on her home island of Didu. Dressed in fine silks, she would make a fine princess, but dressed as she was now, in the green merilium armor made for her by Zyrx, she was an imposing figure. Her green eyes leveled on him. "We'd have a word, Calax," she whispered.

"Yes," said Blusk, "perhaps more than a word."

Unlike Calax, Blusk looked the part of a warrior. He was tall, broad, and heavily muscled, with a thick black beard striped with blue dye. He had but one eye, and it was icy blue. The other was nothing but a hole covered by a brown leather patch. Adding to his fearsome aspect was a large nose covered with warts and the scars of battle. "This plan of ours seems to be ill-advised, at least to me," he said.

"And me," said Phendour.

"Oh, and why is that?" said Calax.

"We are too few and spread thin," said Phendour. "Once the Mystrosians land, we'll be hard pressed to hold this position."

Calax chuckled.

"This is not funny," said Phendour.

Calax shook his head. "Of course it isn't, but you have to understand that this lack of warriors is intentional, at least until dawn."

"Wait, am I missing something?" said Blusk.

Calax nodded. "You are, you both are. What were you doing when we laid out the plan? Tonight our defenses will be light, on the chance that the Mystrosians will send a gela or two to check us out. The rest of our troops will pour forth from the great hovering tower just before daylight, boosting our ranks by thousands."

Phendour smiled and gave him an apologetic grin. "I must have been distracted by my new armor. It is so bright and shiny."

"Aye," said Blusk. "If nothing else, we will blind them when the sun rises."

Calax laughed. "Every weapon is a good weapon."

"Indeed," said Phendour.

Calax looked out at the Mystrosian ships bobbing in the waves. "You'd best get whatever sleep you can. They will be upon us soon enough, in full force, I suspect."

"Right," said Phendour, Blusk nodding in agreement.

"All right, then," said Calax. "I have to check on Zyrx and the trolls." He reached out his hand. "Be safe on the morrow, and we will toast a victory."

They shook his hand in turn, then turned back to their watch.

Calax knew exactly where to find Zyrx. He'd be in or at least near the floating tower. One day in Enturia was the same as many months within the tower, allowing Zyrx and the blacksmiths he had trained to manufacture thousands of weapons and sets of armor. Each morning, the door to the tower would open and tiny wagons drawn by little oxen would emerge from the tower and instantly grow in size, the wealth of new weapons and armor shining brightly in the morning sun.

But now, in darkness, the tower was closed to all. Calax rapped softly on the little door, knowing that to knock hard would be like a thunderstorm within. After a few moments, a tiny figure—an elf—appeared at the door. "Ah, it is you, Calax Halfhand. What business do you have here this night?"

"I would speak to Zyrx, if you please."

The elf nodded and slammed the door shut. Minutes passed and then more minutes, but finally the door opened once more and a tiny version of Zyrx appeared in the doorway. "Oh, it's you. What do you want? I'm very busy."

"I don't suppose we could talk face to face."

"You want me to be the giant dwarf, eh?"

Calax couldn't help chuckling. "It would be better, yes. I can barely see your lips move or hear your voice."

"Very well." Zyrx stepped outside the door and immediately grew to his full stature, which meant the top of his head barely reached Calax's belt. He was small, to say the least, but years of pounding hammers on metal had made him broad and muscular. His face was ruddy from the heat of the forge and just slightly less red than his close-cropped hair and beard.

As always, he was dressed in a simple charcoal-stained tunic and a well-used brown leather apron. His icy blue eyes fixed on Calax. "Is this better?"

"Much. Now, where do we stand with the armor?"

Zyrx shook his head, annoyed. "Well, with this interruption, we've lost a few days at least, so please, please, get to your business."

"Will we be ready by morning? The armor, that is, and the weapons."

"I think so, but every word we speak delays my efforts by hours, perhaps days."

"Okay, if you're satisfied, I'm satisfied. One thing, though."

"Yes, yes, what?"

"The armor and weapons for the trolls."

Zyrx rolled his eyes. "Oh, that, yes, delivered this morning, and let me tell you, I have never faced such a daunting task. They are all so different, one from the other. Some are merely twice as tall as a man, others ten times that. Every piece of armor had to be custom made. It was nightmarish."

"But it's done now, right?"

"As I have said."

"And is Bebo satisfied?"

Zyrx rolled his eyes even harder. "Oh, that one. That one is near impossible to work with. Demands a joke before he will do anything, that one. And you know I don't know any jokes."

Calax nodded and tried not to smile. Bebo was difficult to work with, and only Rhynt seemed to be able to tell jokes that tickled the troll's sense of humor. "Yes, yes, but is he satisfied?"

Zyrx nodded. "More than satisfied. In fact, I think all the trolls are happy about the armor and the weapons, particularly the bows and arrows. Oh my, wait till you see those arrows." He spread his arms as wide as he could. "A single tree was used for each shaft. They are immense and will do great damage at great distances. If I were you, I'd place them at the front of the fray. One arrow could take down an entire Mystrosian ship."

Calax smiled broadly at that. "Really? And have they been trained well enough on their new bows?"

Zyrx waggled his head and frowned. "Somewhat. Some are better than others. You can't expect them to hit a ship every time, but the sheer size of the arrows should strike terror in the Mystrosians as they fly by."

"Good, good. Well, I'll leave you to it, then. But be sure to make your next delivery about an hour before sunrise, so we have time to distribute the weapons and such."

Zyrx nodded. "Understood." And with that, he walked back to the door, grew tiny, and disappeared, the door slamming behind him.

Calax puffed out a sigh. "Well, then, now I just have to find Bebo." He wondered whether the joke Rhynt had provided him would be sufficient to get Bebo and the others to fight come morning, but he nonetheless strode off toward the trolls' camp with a smile on his face. *Arrows as big as trees!*

12

Queen Rhynt, free now from the Red Monk, made her way through a maze of corridors and vast, cavernous rooms that seemed to have no purpose. Bookins had told her the same and had further warned her of the difficult ascent up the staircase to the king's bedroom, now her bedroom. But the climb was easy, so easy she took the steps two and three at a time until she burst into the hallway on the king's landing.

She turned and looked back down the staircase. She couldn't help but feel that she was being followed, by someone, perhaps a gela sent to kill her even before the battle. After drawing a dagger from her boot and listening intently for a few seconds, she decided her pursuer was nothing at all, just her imagination.

She slipped the dagger back into her boot and turned back to the long hallway, which was lined with portraits of past kings. Rhynt was hoping to see a queen or two in the mix, but there was none. Portrait after portrait of just men, some young, some old, some bearded, some bald, all looking worried about something, escorted her down the hallway. Their eyes seemed to be following her with a deep curiosity. *What, a queen?*

She startled at a sound behind her. A young boy, perhaps no older than twelve or thirteen, stood in the hallway, attempting to juggle three wooden balls. He was brightly dressed in a yellow and blue harlequin and wore a matching belled cap that jingled as he moved. The balls dropped from his lunging hands, hit the floor with a clunk, and rolled away from him. "Oh, bother!" he screamed.

Rhynt laughed. "And who might you be?"

The boy attempted a bow, but it seemed he was better at juggling. "Um, your new fool, Majesty, name of Dreedle."

The name seemed to be perfect for a fool, but the boy standing in front of her did not. There was nothing athletic or comely about him. He was so thin his costume engulfed him, and his pallor was ghostly. Not even fool's paint could cover up that pasty face, which seemed to be pinched in the middle, making him appear to be the number eight in the flesh. His hair was mouse brown and shaggy and drooped in a wave over a nose thin enough to cut parchment. Thin lips turned down into what appeared to be a permanent frown. In fact, the only thing that identified him as living were his eyes, which were a blue deeper than the ocean and seemed to dance.

"Dreedle? That's quite a name, perfect for a fool, but is it your real name?"

Dreedle frowned even deeper. "No, Majesty, my real name is Orthor Billibuck, but everyone calls me Dreedle."

"But why? How did they get from Orthor to Dreedle?"

Dreedle sighed. "It is said to be a combination of *dither* and *needle*. They say I am indecisive but persistent to the point of being a pest."

"A strange combination to be sure."

"Not so much, I think. I don't really dither; it just looks that way. I just want to make sure I'm right before proceeding or claiming something is true or false."

"And the needle part?"

Dreedle sighed. "I am very passionate about what must be done, at least at times. And I will champion a cause, no matter the objections, if I feel strongly about it."

"I bet you would, I bet you would." She looked him up and down. "Well, then, Master Dreedle, your name alone is worthy of a fool, but your juggling skills seem, well—you don't have juggling skills, do you?"

He sighed and looked down at the floor. "No, Majesty."

"And yet you would be my fool?"

"It was a thought, yes, Majesty."

"Well, then, what fool-ish skills do you have?"

"Um . . ."

"Can you tell me a funny story?"

Dreedle shook his head. "No, Majesty, I know none."

"But you can dance, can you not?"

Dreedle cringed. "Um, not really, Majesty."

"Are you witty, then?"

Dreedle puffed out his cheeks and sighed. "I sometimes think of witty things to say, but it is usually well after the moment where wit is needed or appreciated."

"So you have no skills other than this bright costume of yours."

He looked down at the costume. "Well, I've heard that clothes make the man, Majesty."

Rhynt shook her head. "Well, you have heard wrong. Words, and more often deeds, make the man, not some silly costume." She gave him a serious look. "Tell me, who put you up to this?"

He shrugged and gave her a sheepish look. "No one, Majesty. It were my own idea. I just seek to serve."

Rhynt put a finger to her nose and considered the foolish fool in front of her. "I have need of warriors."

Dreedle looked crestfallen. "Majesty, as you can see from my juggling skills, my eyes and my hands are at odds with each other. The same is true of me with a bow or a sword. When it comes to fighting, I make a far better juggler."

Rhynt frowned. "I see. Well, then, before you decided to put on that ridiculous costume, what did you do all day? What skills, if any, do you actually *have?*"

"I am an apprentice librarian in the king's—I mean the queen's—library. I sort books and scrolls, mostly, and put them back on shelves. A little dusting as well, so if you need someone to clean or—"

"So you can read?"

"Yes, Majesty, never been a word that could stump me, in pretty much any language."

Rhynt raised an eyebrow, intrigued. "Many languages, you say? What about ancient languages?"

"You mean like the Corple Tongue or the Runes of the Blind Dwarves?"

"The what?"

"Runes, Majesty. Little scribblings said to convey secret messages. I've parsed those out. Not difficult, but time-consuming. The Corple Tongue took me—"

Rhynt interrupted. "And do you think you could read *any* language, even one you've never seen before?"

Dreedle shrugged. "I think so, Majesty, though I hear that there are tongues more difficult than those in your library."

Rhynt smiled at him and waggled her eyebrows.

"What, Majesty?"

"Master Dreedle, I have a job for you. A very *important* job."

"Majesty?"

"There's a language I would know."

"Then I am your man, Majesty. If you but show me the manuscript, I will solve the riddle for you."

Rhynt cocked her head and smiled. "The manuscript? No, there is no manuscript. It is all scribed on a wall, in a cave, in a land far across the sea. Are you up for that?"

Dreedle gulped. "Um, I have never been to sea, Majesty."

Rhynt nodded. "Nor I till quite recently." She thought about her time heaving over the rail of the good ship Marthe. "You'll absolutely love it."

"Yes, Majesty. Well, then, I'll do it."

She slapped him on his shoulder. "Good, good, Dreedle. Gather what you think you might need for the journey and your time in the Cave of Randall."

Dreedle's eyes grew wide. "The Cave of Randall? The cave of the gods, said to contain the Teachings? Why, Majesty, there is no such place. It is nothing but a myth."

"No, Dreedle, I have been there. Some call it Randall's Reach, and I have seen the strange runes, and I would know what they say."

Dreedle beamed. "True, then. How wonderful!"

"Yes, I thought you'd think so. Now, off with you. Make your preparations. Your ship sails at first light."

"First light? But, Majesty, the Mystrosians."

Rhynt scoffed. "Don't worry, they will see neither you nor the ship."

"What?"

"The Red Monk will cast a spell on the ship. No one will see you set sail."

Dreedle wasn't sure about the truth of what she was saying, but he gave her a shrug and a smile. "Yes, Majesty. I'll go gather my things."

"Good, but hold a second. There is one last thing."

"Majesty?"

"You may call yourself Dreedle and answer to that name, but when we speak and when I speak of you, your name will be Orthor Billibuck, and your title will be Language Meister to the Queen."

Dreedle gulped. "Yes, Majesty." He attempted a bow but failed. "Um ..."

Rhynt stifled a laugh. "That's fine, Orthor. Go now, and I shall see to the ship."

Orthor raced away, dancing in a way quite worthy of a fool.

13

The joke didn't work. Bebo, a bridge troll and friend to Queen Rhynt, stood there frowning, arms crossed. "Not good. Not even joke. Sad, so sad."

"Really?" said Calax. "Maybe I told it wrong. Believe me, it's a joke sent to you especially by Queen Rhynt."

Bebo shook his enormous head. "Not possible. Little Rhynt knows jokes. Good jokes. Make me laugh. Make all trolls laugh. This one not joke. Not anything."

"Let me tell it again."

Bebo put his hands over his ears. "No! No tell again. Hurts ears. Hurts heart. Defiles the air."

"But—"

Bebo waggled a finger at him. "No, you go now. See Rhynt. Get new joke."

"But—"

"No joke, no fight."

"But—"

Bebo roared and stormed off. "No joke, no fight."

Calax called after him. "But she's asleep."

Bebo yelled something back at him, but the words were lost in the wind coming off the ocean. His violent gesture was message enough, though. *No joke, no fight.*

14

The knock on her door—first soft, then hard, then harder, persistent—was actually a welcome sound to Queen Rhynt. This new bedroom of hers, the former king's, was far too large to be cozy. Even her hill tigers, who had taken over most of the bed, were restless and uncomfortable.

Despite fine tapestries hanging from each wall, including one depicting the final moments of the Battle of Whent Hill, and thick carpets in colors designed to suggest warmth, the room was just too big to retain heat. The white marble floor may have been the cause, or perhaps it was the negligence of her servants. No fire had been set in the vast hearth, which made Rhynt even more certain that she could see her breath floating over the vast bed that, had it a sail, would have made a wonderful ship.

Steeling herself against the cold, she threw back the covers and sat up. She was still in her armor, a fact that had caused her new handmaids much consternation. She should take it off, they said. How could she possibly sleep in armor? they said. But she had insisted on keeping it on, and had sent them away.

She turned to the tigers. "Come, let's see who seeks our attention in the middle of this endless night."

She jumped down from the bed, her tigers following, swirling around her protectively as she walked quickly to the door. She had to walk on her toes to see over their backs. "Who is it?"

"It is I, Calax."

How wonderful, she thought. *He is calling me to the battle.* "A second, sir."

She tugged at the heavy door, which swung and creaked on its hinges enough for Calax to put his hand on its edge and push it open faster than Rhynt could manage.

"Are we ready for battle?" she said.

Calax groaned and rolled his eyes. "No, Majesty, we have a reluctant troll, or trolls. They're refusing to fight."

"What? But you told him the joke, right?"

Calax shrugged. "It didn't work. I must have told it wrong."

Rhynt sighed. "Where is he, then?"

"At the troll's camp, near the floating tower."

"I'll go to them, set things right." She put a finger to her nose. "And you told the joke, the one about the entrails of the golden ox?"

"Golden ox? What golden ox? I mentioned the entrails, of course, but weren't they from a squirrel?"

Rhynt laughed. "No wonder Bebo's angry. Trolls love squirrels. A joke about their entrails would be far from funny. It would be sad, very sad." She shook her head at the thought of Bebo's reaction to the joke. "He must have been horrified."

Calax cringed. "Well . . ."

"Come, let's go find him."

She turned to her tigers. "Mela, Mila, Spook, to me."

"We must hurry," said Calax. "The sun will be upon us soon—and the Mystrosians."

She nodded, then sighed heavily.

"Don't worry, Majesty."

"Worry? Believe it or not, I'm ready for the Mystrosians." She rapped a fist on her breastplate. "No, what I'm worried about is Bebo. I just hope he and the trolls are still here."

Calax stopped in his tracks. "You don't think they'd actually *leave*, do you?"

She shook her head. "I don't know, but you actually told them a joke about the entrails of a squirrel? I'm surprised he didn't kill you on the spot."

"Majesty, I-"

"Enough words, just try to keep up." She turned and sprinted away, her tigers loping along beside her. Calax lagged behind them, just hoping to keep her in sight.

15

A ship can either rock you to sleep or wake you from a deep slumber, depending on the course of the ship and the height of the waves. Any change in either will usually startle you awake, which is the condition King Merek the Mighty found himself in. Something had changed. The ship that had been at anchor, rocking him to sleep in a low chop, was now slapping its bow on higher waves as it picked up speed in full sail.

This sudden change confused the king. *Are we attacking? Fleeing? Or am I just having another dream brought on by the mysteries of Alamarian wine?*

He carefully extricated himself from the arms and legs of his concubines, who somehow remained asleep, pulled on a robe, and made his way out of the cabin onto the deck, the rising sun forcing him to shield his eyes. After a moment, he spotted the White Monk standing at the rail. When the White Monk caught sight of the king, he beamed and motioned the king forward. "We've got them," he shouted over the wind.

"Got who?" said the king, further confused. And then he remembered they were here in Enturia for a fight. "Oh, wonderful, are we attacking, then?"

The monk shook his head. "Not yet, moving into position, but we will *have them!*" He thrust his arm in the air for emphasis.

The king joined in. "Yes!" Then he looked more closely at the course of the ship and had a sudden thought, which can be taxing for a king who rarely uses his brain.

"Wait, what?"

16

Rhynt ran as fast as she could, her new metal calf and foot crafted by Zyrx doing its work flawlessly. She would have to thank him again for giving her this new skill, running, something she could not do with her old wooden device.

She glanced at the sky, which was brightening rapidly. *I must make sure Bebo does what needs to be done.* A hundred yards ahead she could see Bebo walking slowly down one of the many piers that served the harbor, scratching his head

She glanced back. Calax was running as fast as he could, but he was more than fifty yards behind her and clearly struggling to breathe, let alone keep up. She turned her attention back to Bebo, who had disappeared from view. He was either at the end of the pier or already in the water.

She ran faster.

Then she caught sight of him again at the end of the pier. He was just standing there, shaking his head. When Rhynt finally saw what he saw, or rather what he wasn't seeing, she came to an abrupt stop.

There were no Mystrosian ships in sight. Nothing at all from horizon to horizon. Bookins had said it might be so when they had spoken in private earlier, but she had not thought it possible.

She bent over, put her hands on her knees, and struggled to get out a single word.

17

King Merek the Mighty did not understand—in the least.

"Majesty," said the White Monk, "our attack will come, yes, but for now take courage in the fact that we have avoided yet another trap laid down for us by the Red Monk, the new queen, and that fool of theirs, Bookins."

King Merek shrugged. "But why did we not just attack?"

The White Monk rolled his eyes, for about the twelfth time in this conversation. "Majesty, majesty. It. Was. A. Trap."

King Merek blinked and blinked again. "A trap?"

"Yes, they would have won the day."

"That would not have been good."

"No, Majesty."

The king giggled. "Wonderful. So what now? Where are we going and when will we get there?"

The White Monk sighed. Now that his king had finally understood, he could lay out what came next, which was a good plan. Perhaps a brilliant plan. "Majesty, I have split the fleet into two groups. One group has sailed north and will make its way around the island. Another group—ours—is now sailing south around the island. When each group catches sight of the eastern coast of Enturia, we will each split our forces into three groups, making six groups in all."

"Six groups? Is it wise to split our forces?"

"In this case, yes, Majesty. Each group of more than a thousand men will land at different locations along the eastern coast and then proceed inland, making their way to Queen Rhynt's castle on the western coast."

"Where we first arrived."

"Yes."

"And how is this better than our original plan to just storm the beaches near the castle?"

"Again, majesty, it was a trap. They would have been ready for us. We would have lost the element of surprise, and since they hold the high ground, the advantage would go to them, even though their numbers are less than ours."

King Merek frowned. "If you say so. It seems an extra bother to me. And if we're not landing on the western shore, as we planned, won't they figure out we have to land elsewhere and spring another trap on us?"

The White Monk blinked now. The king for once had made an excellent observation. "They will, and I'm counting on it."

"Counting on it? I don't understand. Tell me how this is a good thing."

The White Monk took a deep breath and smiled. It was a smile reeking of arrogance and pride, a smile that obviously delighted in what was about to be said, a smile that foretold mischief and stratagems and a victory for the ages.

"Majesty, the explanation is a long one. Perhaps we should go to your cabin and break fast."

The king beamed. "With wine!"

18

Queen Rhynt drummed her fingers on the long council table as she waited for the last of her so-called advisors to find their seats. She was frustrated—and angry—even though Bookins had said it might go like this. The plan should have worked but didn't. Why?

Finally, the last person, the minstrel Whelan, took his seat, and after a brief flurry of greetings, the assembled advisors grew quiet, all eyes on Queen Rhynt and her drumming fingers.

She lifted her fingers from the table and looked around the table. "Gentlemen," she began, her voice quavering from anger. A thousand questions came to mind, so many that she could only shake her head and say, "What just happened?"

Several people began speaking at once, but then the Red Monk slapped a hand on the table, silencing them. "It is my fault, Majesty. It seems I have either underestimated the White Monk or he has access to some new power."

"And what new power would that be?" said Rhynt. "Making his ships disappear?"

The monk shook his head. "The ships are not invisible, Majesty, they have just moved."

Rhynt scoffed. "I know that, d'Abo. The first thing I did was far-see. The ships are halfway around Enturia, some to the north and some to the south."

"And will no doubt meet on the eastern shore, where conditions for landing are best, and then proceed inland," said the monk, adding "*without opposition.*"

Calax jumped to his feet, seemingly as angry as Rhynt. "Well, *I'll* have something to say about *that*. Majesty, with your permission, I will lead a force to meet them at once."

Rhynt smiled at him and motioned him to sit back down. "We will certainly do that, Calax, but not at once. Rushing headlong into a battle without a plan is not something we should do." She glanced at Whelan, who was nodding. She couldn't help wonder what song or story he was working on to describe the current disaster.

Calax huffed. "Majesty, every second we wait gives the Mystrosians an advantage. They will land, and if there is no opposition, they will be upon us in short order."

"I fully understand that, Calax, but didn't you tell me once never to wander into a battle? No, I would first know how they came to know our plan." She turned back to the Red Monk. "Did we miss a gela? Is that what happened?"

The Red Monk shrugged; he didn't seem to have a clue. "It's possible, but only if the White Monk has increased his powers."

Rhynt began drumming her fingers again and looked around the table. "A question for each of you, for all of you. Last night, did any of you discuss our plan with anyone else?"

Everyone began shaking their heads and looking from left to right to see if anyone else might have discussed the plan. General Boh neither shook his head nor looked around. He just stared down at the table.

Rhynt noticed. "General Boh, do you have something to tell us?"

General Boh lifted his head, then sighed. "Majesty, I did, but I assure you, it was done so in *complete* privacy—in fact, in *whispers*—and with my trusted colleague here, Besbo d'Arc, Chancellor of Coin."

The chancellor looked stricken. "What? We did no such thing! I never spoke to you outside this room." He turned to the queen. "Majesty, I must object—that is a lie!"

General Boh looked stunned. "What? But Besbo, we talked for hours, in my chambers. Surely you remember."

Besbo shook his head, emphatic. "No, no we didn't."

General Boh began to object again but the queen cut him off. "It was a gela, general, a gela."

General Boh's eyes grew wide. "A gela? But he looked and spoke like the chancellor."

Queen Rhynt rolled her eyes. "Of course he did. That's what gelas do."

The general looked crestfallen. "Majesty, I had no idea. I thought—"

"Yes, I know what you thought. The result, however, is an army about to land on our eastern shore."

Calax slapped the table. "We must meet them with force, and soon. Countering an assault is not *wandering*, Majesty."

Queen Rhynt nodded. "I know your opinion, Calax. What about the rest of you? Is attack our best option?"

Baron Bookins, only a day removed from being the king's fool, raised a hand, prompting the queen to roll her eyes. "Baron Bookins, I will hear your idea, but only after others have weighed in on our situation."

"But Majesty—"

"No offense, Bookins. Your gambits have been remarkable, even if both have failed. And yes, I know you told me in private that this action by the Mystrosians might take place. And yes again, I would hear your next plan, but I think even you would benefit from the counsel of the rest of this table."

Bookins nodded and folded his hands together. He would bide his time. "Very well, Majesty."

Queen Rhynt turned back to the others. "Now, out with it. Any idea. Any stratagem. Any caution. By the gods, what should we do?"

Former King Braque raised a hand in a way that suggested he was unsure whether he should contribute. He did not want to appear to undercut the queen or to question her power. "Good Queen Rhynt, if I may offer whatever wisdom remains in this old noggin of mine."

Rhynt nodded. She couldn't help notice the sparkle in his eyes. Just hours ago, he was near death, but if anything, his decision to raise her to queen had given him new energy. No one would have thought he was robust, of course—he was a frail old man with near translucent skin—but he certainly was far from death. "Of course, Lord Braque, we would all love to hear your thoughts on the matter."

"I keep coming back to the Red Monk's comment about the possibility that the White Monk has increased powers."

"Yes, and?"

"Perhaps that power is not coming from him."

Queen Rhynt looked confused. "Not from him? Who else would have such power?"

Whelan cleared his throat and spoke up. "My dear queen, have you forgotten what I told you in the Cave of the Six Arrows?"

Many people around the table began to laugh, some loudly. General Boh spoke for them. "Majesty, there is no such place. It is a myth, one perpetuated by monks." He turned to the Red Monk. "No offense intended."

"None taken," said the monk. "But I think you'll find that Whelan and the queen have seen that cave and know it well."

"Indeed," said Whelan. "It is as real as you and I." He looked around the table and added, "Assuming neither you nor I is a gela."

"He speaks truly," said Queen Rhynt. "And if I hear them correctly, Lord Braque and Whelan are referring to the six gods."

"Yes," said Whelan. Perhaps the White Monk is receiving aid from the White God, Porto."

The Red Monk slumped back in his chair. "By the gods."

The queen turned to him. "Is it possible, d'Abo?"

The Red Monk shook his head, then nodded. "None of the gods has been seen in eons, not since the Great Unraveling. Most people think them a myth, a few think them dead and gone, and an even smaller number, I among them, retain faith that they are not only real, but that they will return."

Whelan seemed particularly troubled. "Majesty, if this is true, we will need more than an army to defeat the Mystrosians."

"Yes," said the queen. "We will need a god."

19

The White Monk, d'Porto Saleen, paced back and forth on the deck, not because he was concerned about their course or what lay ahead, but simply from impatience. He wanted to land his ships and defeat the Enturians. Now.

A white crow sitting on the rail followed the monk's movements with interest, then transformed into a man, or rather into a god in the shape of a man. "Stop your pacing. All is well."

The White Monk sighed, then nodded. "With your help, yes."

Porto, the White God, smiled. "It is the least that I can do, and besides, we gods love a good battle." He raised his hands and flexed his fingers. "It has been hundreds of years since I took the form of a man. It is so—how do you say it?—*restricting*. Far from the grace and elegance of a bird."

The White Monk didn't know what to say. Porto had transformed into a godlike man. Tall, handsome, strong, with a regal bearing. Only his white hair and beard gave any indication of aging. Shaved of each, he would have appeared to be a young warrior. "Um . . ."

"Oh, I'm sure you are happy with your form, but trust me, if you could be a bird but for a minute, you would quickly trade places."

"If you say so, your, your—what do I call you, anyway? Majesty? Holiness?"

Porto rolled his eye. "Porto, just Porto. These haughty appellations you give to your kings and queens just underscore how small and weak they are—*you* are. A name should carry its own weight. Porto will do. Porto says everything."

The White Monk bowed. "Yes, Porto, your, your, um—yes, Porto."

Porto sighed. "So, we will be at the landing site in thirty-three of your minutes. Perhaps you should warn his thickness, the king, so he can extricate himself from sleep or, more likely, his concubines."

"May I tell him about you?"

"No, not yet. In my experience, he will think you've lost your senses."

"As you wish."

"Indeed, and always. Now go, wake the king." He turned back into a crow, squawked loudly, and flew off toward the shore.

The White Monk watched him go. "We will win, I know it."

He watched until the crow was but a speck in the sky, then turned and headed for the king's cabin.

20

Queen Rhynt began drumming her fingers again. *Was it even possible? A god helping the Mystrosians?* "Tell me, d'Abo, if the Mystrosians have managed to bring back the White God, Porto, can we not bring back the Red God, Abo?"

The Red Monk knew she would ask this and had begun preparing an answer the second she began drumming her fingers. "Majesty, I have tried to bring him back many times. Many, many times, to no avail. He is lost to me." He shook his head and looked down at the table.

Whelan the Wanderer, minstrel extraordinaire, cleared his throat and raised a hand. "Um, Majesty, if I may."

"May what?" said the queen.

"As a minstrel in good standing with the Minstrel Guild—"

The queen rolled her eyes, exasperated. Whelan made a habit of long introductions to every topic. "Yes, yes, get on with it."

"Songs, Majesty. Lore. Tales handed down mouth to ear over the eons. We of the guild know them, sing them, *remember* them."

"And?"

"There is a song, 'The Calling,' said to be among the oldest, on how to summon a god, or rather *each* god."

The Red Monk brightened. "Really? But I have never heard of such a song. And we just have to sing it?"

"Yes, and no. The song must be sung, yes, but by the right person, in the right place, surrounded by the right things."

The Red Monk now rolled his eyes in frustration. "Out with it! How do I summon the Red God?"

Whelan ignored the anger in the monk's voice. "It may only be sung in its entirety, from start to finish without interruption."

"So sing it for us," said the queen.

Whelan cocked his head. "Majesty, as with most things, it is not that easy. If I sing it here, it may bring back the wrong god, or even all the gods except Abo. And I assure you, each god has its likes and dislikes. No, to sing it here might be our undoing."

"So where do we sing it?" said the Red Monk.

Whelan smiled. "Not we, d'Abo, *me.*"

"You?" said the monk. "But I am his faithful servant, the *Red Monk.*"

Whelan smirked at him. "Indeed, you are, but I'm afraid the song may be sung only by a guild member, namely me."

"But not here?" said the queen.

"No, majesty, I must sing it along the banks of the river that flows by the Cave of Randall, at Randall's Reach."

Queen Rhynt shuddered. "I remember it well. You said there were monsters in that river, beasts."

"Indeed, Majesty, and that is where the Red God resides as well. I must stand on that river's banks and sing my song."

"But the beasts."

"Yes, Majesty, one of the risks, I'm afraid. Calling the god will call the beasts as well."

The queen suddenly looked crestfallen. "It is of no matter, anyway. The Mystrosians are about to land on our shores. There is no time."

Bookins, who had remained quiet but restless during the discussions, raised a hand. "Majesty, a question."

The queen seemed startled by the interruption. "Um, yes, of course, Bookins. What is your question?"

"How long would it take for Whelan to travel to the cave and retrieve the god?"

Whelan raised his eyes to the ceiling, calculating. "Let me see. It's a two-day voyage to Paudia. Then, with fast horses, we could get to the cave in a day, perhaps two, so . . . six to eight days in all, there and back."

The queen frowned. "Enough time for the Mystrosians to traverse this island and take us down."

"No, Majesty," said Bookins.

"No? What do you mean *no?*"

"If you follow my plan, my gambit, all will be well. We can retrieve the Red God and defeat the Mystrosians."

"Really? What plan can buy us a week?"

"Yes," said Lord Braque, who had to this point appeared to have returned to his natural state: asleep. "And more to the point, if the Mystrosians have a god working for them, why does he not strike us down this instant? He has such power, does he not?"

The queen blinked. "It is a good point."

Whelan chuckled. "The answer is in almost every god song, Majesty. If there's one thing universally loved by the gods, it's a good battle. A protracted battle. Life, death, intrigue." He turned to Bookins. "Gambits."

"Then there's time," said Bookins.

"I believe so," said Whelan.

Bookins looked around the table and smiled. "Majesty, I will need a faithful map of Enturia, one that shows the depths and elevations of the land. Then I can explain it to you all."

The queen turned to General Boh. "Do we have such a map?"

General Boh nodded and pushed back in his chair. "We do, Majesty, and I shall retrieve it for you."

"Excellent," said the queen. "Fetch it at once."

Boh nodded, then stood and walked quickly from the room.

"Now," said the queen, turning to Whelan. "There is no time for you to hear the plan. Make your way to the docks and set sail with Marthe."

Whelan stood. "At once, Majesty. But knowing Marthe, he will require good coin for such a voyage."

Besbo d'Arc, Chancellor of Coin, leaped to his feet. "I can deal with that."

"Come then, we must make haste."

The queen raised a hand to stop them from leaving. "Wait, I would have you take three others with you."

"But I can move faster alone," said Whelan.

"And yet you will be accompanied by Calax—for protection—and the monk here—to deal with the god—and a third person, a young man I have challenged to unravel the mystery of the runes within the Cave of Randall."

Calax was on his feet. "But I have an army to lead."

"No," said Bookins. "There will be no need of an army for at least ten days."

"So you will go," said the queen. "I will hear nothing more from you. Prepare the horses and get them to the docks."

Whelan looked troubled. "Majesty, I am with Calax. I must object. I need none of these men. And who is this young man. No one can solve the riddle of the runes."

"You may be right, Whelan, but I am sending him anyway."

"Who, then, Majesty?"

"His name is Orthor Billibuck."

The Chancellor of Coin began laughing. "Oh, Majesty, what could he possibly do? I know him. He is but a boy known by all as Dreedle. Not very bright in my estimation."

The queen slapped her hand on the table. "If I am not mistaken, it is *my* estimation that counts."

The chancellor bowed. "Yes, Majesty."

She looked at Calax, Whelan, the Red Monk, and the chancellor in turn. "Go, now, and collect Orthor on your way. You will find him in the library if I am not mistaken."

She watched them go, then turned back to Bookins. "Do we need the map to begin? I would know your plan, *now.*"

21

King Merek the Mighty, now extricated from sleep and his concubines, stood at the rail of the ship with the White Monk, his eyes fixed on a small spit of land coming into view. "Is that it? Is that where we land?"

"Yes," said the White Monk.

"And why, among all the spots to land along this vast coastline is that the spot?"

The White Monk thought to tell him about Porto, but decided a believable lie was best, at least for now. "Majesty, I have sent many gelas into the land, and they have assured me that this is one of the two spots where we must land this morning."

"Two spots? I thought we were talking about six."

"Yes, Majesty, but first we land at two spots—then we split the forces into six. We hit them from many directions at once, Majesty. It will confuse and split their forces, assuring our victory."

The king sighed. "And how long will this take, monk?"

As long as it takes, thought the White Monk. "But days, your Majesty, a week at most."

That was not the answer the king was looking for. "A week? A whole week? Can you not send a thousand thousand gelas to win the battle in a day?"

The White Monk couldn't help chuckling. "Majesty, I wish I had such powers, but I am but a monk. And besides, the Red Monk could block me at every turn."

"So he is more powerful than you?"

"No, no, Majesty. I am more than his equal, as you will soon see." He looked at the spit of land, which was now just a hundred yards away. "We're here, Majesty. You'd best change into your armor now."

"Armor? Why would I need armor? I will be at the rear, watching, um, sometimes."

The monk sighed. He knew the king would only see the aftermath of the battle, not the battle itself. "A precaution, Majesty."

The king huffed. "Precautions be damned. That armor is heavy—and hot—and I'll have none of it."

"Then you may stay at the rear, in your tent."

The king sighed. "A whole week sleeping in a tent?"

The white monk knew the king would be doing more than sleeping. His other modes were eating, drinking, and dallying. "Perhaps less, Majesty."

The king grumbled. "So you say." He turned on his heels and walked away. "Just make sure I have food and wine."

The White Monk didn't answer. Instead, he turned to look for the ship's captain. He spotted him standing at the wheel of the ship with a crew member. "Captain, strike the sails. We land here."

22

Calax, the Red Monk, Whelan the Wanderer, and Besbo d'Arc, the Chancellor of Coin, were on their way to the docks, reducing the number of people in the council chamber to ten. On the advice of Bookins, however, that number had been reduced to just four, to assure the secrecy of Bookins' gambit: Lord Braque, General Boh, Queen Rhynt, and Bookins himself.

The four gathered around the end of the table, the map spread out for all to see.

"How old is this map?" said the queen.

General Boh shrugged. "Not too old, maybe ten years."

"Does it include everything?"

General Boh seemed confused. "Everything?"

"I mean, are there any new towns, villages, or any new landmarks at all that we must account for in our plan?"

General Boh stared down at the map intently, then looked around the room.

"What are you looking for?" said Bookins.

General Boh didn't answer, instead walking to the middle of the table and retrieving a bowl of fruit that had been set out for the meeting. "There are a couple of changes, yes."

He moved back to the map and put a grape down along what looked like a winding river. "Here, just below Lake Arn, on the River Thyss, there's a small town, Wetfur. No more than a village, really. About forty people, mostly trappers."

Queen Rhynt giggled. "Wetfur? As in *wet fur?*"

"Indeed, and once you see it, you'll think the name apt. The smell of wet Ahnk fur is, um, remarkable." He shuddered for emphasis.

She turned to Bookins. "Were you aware of this?"

Bookins shook his head. "No, but it will not interfere with my plan."

"Good." She turned back to Boh. "Any other changes we should know about?"

Lord Braque interrupted. "Wait, what about those poor people in Wetfur? We must warn them, evacuate them."

Bookins nodded. "Yes, we can send one of the fishing boats. They often go there to haul fur back."

"No," said the queen. "That will take too long. I'll send a gela."

"You can do that?" said Lord Braque.

"Yes, the Red Monk taught me earlier in the day; thought the skill might come in handy. And apparently . . ."

"Yes, okay," said Lord Braque. "Sorry, I didn't mean to interrupt." He turned to General Boh. "So, anything else out there? I seem to recall an outpost on Mount Garling, or am I misremembering?"

General Boh was nodding vigorously. "Indeed, indeed, right here." He placed another grape on the map, atop Mount Garling. "We use it for training new recruits in the art of climbing. But they're all on their way back here now."

Bookins seemed concerned for the first time. "Back? All of them? No, no, no, we need someone there—to *observe*. It is the highest point in Enturia. On clear days, you can see all the way to the east coast. In this case, we'll be able to follow the approach of the Mystrosians. The gambit, in fact, depends on it."

General Boh puffed out his cheeks. "Oh, my. I didn't realize." He turned to the queen. "Majesty, a gela, perhaps?"

Queen Rhynt shook her head. "I am new to this. The Red Monk said with experience, I'll be able to hold a gela in place indefinitely, but for now, no more than a few hours."

"That won't work," said Bookins. He turned to General Boh. "General, how many men are on their way back?"

The general looked at the ceiling, thinking. "Um, as I recall, with staff and trainers included, about two hundred men."

Bookins beamed. "Good." He turned to the queen. "We must send a gela to turn them around, give them instructions."

The queen nodded. "Very well. Gentlemen, if you'll give me a moment, I will do just that."

"No, Majesty," said Bookins. "Not quite yet. You'll need to hear my plan first, and that shouldn't take too long."

"All right," she said, "what is this gambit of yours?"

Part II

"There are four kinds of people in the world: those who believe in gods, those who don't believe in gods, and those who aren't sure to one degree or another. What are you saying? That's only three kinds? Yes, you're right in a way, but to get to four, you have to take the believers and split them into two groups: those who think gods listen to their prayers and act upon them, and those who think gods couldn't care less about listening or helping. No, wait, I don't want to hear your ideas about fifth kinds or sixth kinds. I am Randall, after all, the all-knowing, all-powerful god of gods. What you think or feel is of no importance to me, so settle down by the fire once more and sip the mead I have provided. There are surprises ahead for you, no matter your beliefs—or mine for that matter. Yes, yes, we'll get back to the war and that little gambit of the fool. Will it work? Will it fail? And what in Randall's name is it? We'll see in good time, I assure you, but first we need to focus on a young man with special skills: Orthor Billibuck. No, do not call him Dreedle. Oh, no. Not now. Not anymore."

23

Orthor stood at the rail of the good ship Marthe, staring back at the coastline of Enturia, which was rapidly disappearing as the ship raced away in full sail.

What had he gotten himself into?

He never thought he'd miss the dead air of the library or the dismissive grunts of the librarian, but now, with his world disappearing before him, he began to miss both. And his new companions, if you could call them that, had done nothing to make him feel welcome. In fact, they had ignored him completely.

He glanced over at them. They seemed to be in a heated argument with the captain of the ship, a man named Marthe who was arguably the ugliest person Orthor had ever seen, a man who rightly belonged in one of the old scrolls in the dark corner of the library, where the librarian stored books and scrolls about monsters.

Where Marthe was monstrous, the warrior Calax Halfhand was merely ordinary. Save for the look of determination in his eyes, he could have been any shopkeeper. *How in the world*, thought Orthor, *could this man have been the hero of the Battle of Whent Hill?* True, he had the armor for it. Green and shiny and said to be made by the dwarf Zyrx, a man Orthor had never laid eyes on.

The Red Monk, of course, was far from ordinary. His red robe and cape and cowl made him look like a wingless redspin. Not that he had the energy of a bird. He seemed ever about to fall down, so thin was his frame and so frail was his nature. His white hair and beard fluttered in the breeze as he made his arguments to the others, including the strangest of them all, Whelan the Wanderer.

Orthor had read about minstrels, including the famous Edvard of Didu, who was said to have created the first song. Orthor wondered what that would have been like, to hear the first song. If he remembered correctly, the *Annals of Didu* reported the response of the listeners: pure panic that turned from fear to anger. They had reportedly hanged Edvard on the spot. And yet his songs live on. Orthor made a mental note to ask Whelan about the first song.

Of all his new companions, he was worried most about Whelan. The man kept glaring at him for some reason. *What have I done to provoke such a reaction in a stranger?*

Orthor turned his attention back to the rapidly disappearing coastline of Enturia. How quickly the ship moved and yet he would have to endure a voyage of two days in close quarters with these strange, unfriendly men. He couldn't wait to reach Paudia. At least then he would be on a horse and could keep more to himself.

He glanced back at the men again. The argument had apparently ended. Calax and the Red Monk had moved away and were now in a whispered conversation. Marthe was waving his arms, trying to get the attention of the first mate, leaving Whelan the Wanderer standing there. Staring at Orthor. The look was unmistakable: menace.

24

Calax and the Red Monk moved along the rail toward the ship's bow, trying to put as much distance as possible between them and the others. Finally, the Red Monk held up a hand and motioned Calax to stop. "This should do. I doubt that our words will carry too far now."

Calax looked around in all directions. That strange young man Orthor Billibuck was near the stern of the ship, locked in what looked like a staring contest with Whelan. The captain, Marthe, was not far away, standing at the wheel of the ship with several seamen. He seemed to be issuing orders. "This news is not what I was hoping for."

The Red Monk nodded. "Nor I, but the currents are the currents, and besides, an extra day to reach Paudia is not the end of the world."

Calax scoffed. "Oh, really. What do you think is at stake back in Enturia right now?"

The Red Monk rolled his eyes. "I did not mean the end of the world *literally*. Now look, Marthe said they will add a sail—that should help— and I'll do what I can to call strong, favorable winds. In short, I think our delay will be but a few hours, not a whole day."

Calax sighed. "I don't like it, this whole thing. We should be back in Enturia, helping defeat the Mystrosians."

"But Bookins' plan—"

"Is the plan of a man who was just the king's fool a couple of days ago."

"Calax, Calax, his first and second plans should have worked—they were brilliant in my estimation. Save for the White God—"

"They would have worked. Yes, I know that, but now we have the White God to deal with. How can any plan work against a god?"

"Never fear, we shall soon have the Red God to help us, assuming the minstrel really knows how to call him back. Do you trust him?"

Calax seemed surprised. "Trust him? Of course. That man helped Queen Rhynt and I get to Enturia safely."

The Red Monk glanced over at Whelan, who was still locked in a staring contest with Orthor. "I hope you are right."

"I don't worry about *him.* I worry about your Red God. How do you know he will even help us?"

"He will. I'm sure of it." Something in his voice suggested the monk was trying to convince himself.

"You're not sure, are you?"

The Red Monk threw up his hands. "How can anyone be sure of anything in this world? I *feel* he will help, but I do not know that for sure."

Calax furrowed his brow. "Do you think we should bring back all the gods, then? You know, five gods against one?"

The Red Monk startled. "All? No, no, *never* that."

"But—"

"No, bringing them all back is far too dangerous. The Great Unravelling was caused by an argument among the gods, and I think bringing them back would just open old wounds and rekindle old rivalries."

Calax sighed. "I see what you mean, but what about the Green God, what's his name."

"Bedo, his name is Bedo, and no, I don't think we should bring him back, either."

"But is he not the god of Enturia?"

The Red Monk laughed. "He was the god of the Green Monk, and no more. Gods do not recognize borders or even have an interest in countries."

"But are they not subject to *flattery?* Surely, knowing that an entire country of people worships you would tend to make you think on them favorably."

The Red Monk cocked his head. "Interesting point. I will think on it."

25

Orthor Billibuck had been hovered over by an expert, his former boss, the librarian, so when Whelan the Wanderer hovered over him like some god looking at a mouse, he did what he always did: he smiled. He knew it would infuriate Whelan, just as it had infuriated the librarian. People who hover don't want you to smile, they want you to cringe and shake with fear.

He could see the fury in Whelan's eyes, but there was something else: curiosity. Whelan simply did not know what to make of Orthor.

Whelan blinked and took a step back. "This mission of yours will be for naught. No one has been able to decipher the runes at Randall's Reach."

Orthor shrugged. "So you said, but you don't know me or the skills I bring to the challenge."

Whelan scoffed. "Skills? What skills? Filing books and scrolls all day? Dallying? Needling? *Dreedling?*"

Orthor smirked. "More like reading, researching, parsing, analyzing. I have read every text known to Enturia, including many written in runes intelligible only to me."

Whelan laughed at him. "What runes you have seen are nothing to the ones you will see in the Cave of Randall. Be prepared to be amazed, puzzled, and ultimately defeated."

Orthor laughed back. "You know songs, I know runes. You'll see—and soon."

Whelan sighed and shook his head. "Just stay out of my way."

Orthor rolled his eyes. "It will be my pleasure."

Whelan jabbed a finger into Orthor's chest. "Just. Stay. Out. Of. My. Way." He turned to leave.

"Wait, a question."

Whelan stopped and turned back. "What?"

"This ceremony of yours, to bring back the Red God."

"Yes?"

"Is it the same as the one written in the *Paudicon?*"

"The what?"

"A book, very old, filled with ceremonies and incantations for every purpose."

Whelan was taken aback. "There is such a book?"

"There is."

"I would like to see it."

Orthor shook his head. "Sadly, it's back in Enturia, in the library. I know many of its sections by heart, so if you are uncertain about yours, I'd be happy to review it with you."

Whelan laughed. "Ha! I need no help from you where the gods are concerned."

"Very well, but if you change your mind, I'd—"

Whelan screamed at him. "I won't change my mind!"

Orthor backed away. "As you wish, as you wish."

Whelan thought to say something else, but instead just shook his head and stormed away.

Orthor watched him go. He wasn't sure why he had lied about the whereabouts of the *Paudicon*—it was packed in a large chest in his cabin, along with a dozen books and scrolls on runes—but he sensed that showing the book to Whelan would be a mistake. There was just something about Whelan that made Orthor uncomfortable.

He turned back to the rail for one last glimpse of the coastline of Enturia, but it was gone. There was nothing but the sea now, and the waves seemed to be growing higher. His stomach suddenly went sour. "Oh, no."

26

Marthe did his part, adding a sail to catch more of the wind, and the Red Monk did his, mumbling words and raising his arms to bring on a wind just strong enough to fully fill the sails, but not strong enough to raise the waves or endanger the ship.

The good ship Marthe, like Marthe himself no thing of beauty, then did its part, lurching forward at great speed, overcoming the current pushing against it. The trip from Enturia to Port Ochno on the eastern coast of Paudia took but one day and half of another.

The port town had changed considerably since the last time Calax and Whelan had seen it. Most of the homes and businesses had been burned to the ground by the departing Mystrosians, leaving only a boarded-up brothel and a tavern offering nothing more than mead and stale bread. The tavern keeper, a man of wide girth, ruddy complexion, and bald head, said meat would be available "tomorrow, maybe the next day," but Calax and the others were in no mood to wait. They bought flagons of water and mead and a few loaves of bread, and packed them away in their saddlebags. If they wanted meat, they would hunt it along the way.

The tavern keeper, not a friendly sort, didn't wave goodbye when they left. He just grunted, shook his head, and walked back into the tavern, offering but one word to the empty tavern: "fools."

After a brief argument about who should lead the way, Whelan relented and let Calax take the lead, with Whelan second, the Red Monk third, and Orthor trailing far behind, slowed by the extra horse carrying his trunk and additional supplies, including a small cage containing two pigeons. Bookins had encouraged him to send a bird if he needed help or if he discovered anything worthy of the queen's attention.

They made their way up the bluff near the port and onto the Plain of Morthos, which seemed to stretch on forever.

"Can we make it to the cave today?" said the Red Monk.

Whelan chuckled. "We could, but descending into the chasm would be too dangerous. And there would also be the river beasts to deal with."

Calax nodded. "Which is why we'll stop before the sun sets, set up camp, hunt some rabbits—or molfrumps, if we're lucky—and get some rest."

Whelan turned in his saddle and looked back. Orthor and his pack horse were barely visible. "And we have Dreedle slowing us besides."

The Red Monk sighed. "Very well. I'm just eager to get this done. I worry about Enturia. I can far-see, but not that far."

"The queen has faith in Bookins and his gambits, and I have faith in the queen, so I do not share your worry. Still, we must be as quick about our business as we can."

"I'll drink to that," said Whelan. "Now, enough dallying." He looked back at Orthor, who seemed much closer now. "So long as we leave him far behind, we'll know we're making good progress."

"Don't be so hard on the boy," said Calax. "He is just doing the queen's bidding. She thinks his job—those runes—is important, and that's good enough for me."

"Aye," said the Red Monk. "I talked to him briefly on the ship. He is much brighter than I thought and seems to have a good heart."

"Good heart, bad heart," said Whelan. "It makes no mind to me. Come on, let's go, the darkness waits for no man."

They rode on, the sun seeming to arc toward the horizon faster than their horses could trot.

27

By the time Orthor rode up with his packhorse, Calax had started a fire and begun roasting two freshly killed and dressed rabbits.

"It's about time you showed up," said Calax, giving the rabbits a turn on their spits. Whelan and the Red Monk, who were sitting by the fire with him, nodded.

"Aye," said Whelan. "Not that we would have missed you."

The Red Monk chuckled. "And there would have been more rabbit for us."

"Very funny," said Orthor, dropping down from his horse and rubbing his backside. "And I'm here no thanks to any of you. If I hadn't smelled the rabbits, I would have probably never found you in this darkness."

"Even with our fire?" said Calax. "Surely you would have seen that."

"No, I wouldn't have. I was riding in a depression between two small hills, out of sight of the fire. The smell alone drew me in."

Whelan poked at the fire. "Perhaps I will never think fondly of the smell of roasting rabbits again."

The Red Monk rolled his eyes. "Leave the boy alone. I for one am glad he found us. Otherwise, how would we explain his loss to the queen?"

"Aye," said Calax. "His mission is different from ours, but it is no less important."

Whelan couldn't believe what he was hearing. "No less important? Our work will save Enturia. His will only be a failed attempt to understand a language beyond our ken."

Orthor started to defend himself, but Calax interrupted him. "Here, let us put an end to argument. We are all here on missions for the queen, and

I for one would rather spend our time preparing for and carrying out those missions."

"Well said," said the Red Monk, nodding vigorously. "And while the boy unpacks his horse and these rabbits make their way to done, I suggest we discuss the calling of the gods."

"Fine with me," said Orthor. He grabbed the reins of his horses and led them toward the other horses. "I'll just see to my horses, the pigeons, and my trunk."

Whelan watched him go, and sneered. "Fine with us. Take your time." He turned to the Red Monk. "You know, there's really nothing to discuss about the calling of the gods. You just get me to Randall's Cave, and I'll take care of the rest."

The Red Monk squinted at him. "I do not question your role in this, Whelan, and it is much appreciated. However, it would be good for all of us to know how this will play out. We need to know what to expect in case anything should go wrong."

Whelan scoffed and poked at the fire, hard. "All you need do is watch—and be amazed."

"I for one seek nothing more," said Calax. "I'm sure it will be a wonder to behold."

Whelan smiled. "It will be."

"But what if it isn't?" said the Red Monk. "What if something goes wrong? How will we know?"

"Nothing will go wrong," said Whelan as forcefully as he could. Frustrated, he threw his poking stick into the darkness.

Calax shook his head. "How many times have I heard those words before a battle? Nothing will go wrong? *Anything* could go wrong, and in my experience, something *will* go wrong. No, the monk is right. We need to know what you will do, what you plan to say, what we should expect, and how we should react."

Orthor plopped down beside them. "If he won't tell you, I will. I know exactly how it should go, what should be said—in fact, *everything.*"

Whelan laughed. "What, from these books of yours. The books that slow us down and endanger our mission?"

"Yes," said Orthor. "These books and many others I have studied over the years."

Whelan laughed even harder. *"Over the years?* You are but a boy."

"Admittedly," said Orthor, "but I am a fast reader and an even quicker study." He looked at the others. "I know things, and one of those things is the summoning ceremony."

Whelan grumbled. "All right, all right, I'll tell you how this should go, but could we at least eat first?"

The sizzling reply from the rabbits seemed to suggest *yes.*

28

Whelan picked his teeth with a bone one last time, made a few sucking noises as he attempted to free the last morsel of rabbit from his teeth, and let out a satisfying—to him—burp. "I never tire of rabbits—or cave rats, for that matter. So good."

The Red Monk groaned. "On the other hand, I tire of your delay. Are you going to tell us about the ceremony, or not?"

"Yes," said Calax. "Come on, I'd like to get some sleep if you don't mind."

Orthor chuckled. "If he won't explain it, I will."

That got Whelan to his feet and his lute in his hands. "Perhaps a song first, to set the mood?"

All three of the others bellowed, "No!"

Whelan took a step back. "Very well, I'll tell you." He looked at each of them in turn. "You're not exactly my kind of crowd. So demanding. So— what should I call it?—negative."

The Red Monk grumbled.

"All right, all right. Here we go. The ceremony. As ceremonies go—"

"No preambles," said Calax. "Get on with it, man."

Whelan sighed. "A tough, tough crowd, indeed. So, as I was saying, the ceremony lacks in complexity what it makes up in brevity."

"What in the gods' names does that mean?" said Calax.

"I think he's trying to say that the ceremony is short and sweet," said Orthor. "Simple, really. Not complicated at all. Anyone could do it."

Whelan huffed. "*Not* anyone. Me, only a person like me." He began thrusting his arm out again and again, pointing at each of them. "Not you, monk. Not you, warrior. And especially not you, Dreedle. You are the last person to do it."

Orthor just rolled his eyes. "Go on, then. Explain it to us—if you can."

Whelan turned away from Orthor and began pacing. "I must stand by the river and call the beast."

"Wait," said Calax. "I thought we were calling a god, not a beast."

"He's right," said Orthor. "Calling the beast is the first step."

"Could everyone please stop interrupting? I, too, would like to get some sleep this night. Now, where was I?"

"The beast," said the Red Monk, "the watzel."

"Ah, yes," said Whelan, rubbing his hands together with delight. "A fascinating creature, unique among creatures. In fact, unique in itself. There is only one."

The Red Monk seemed to let out a low growl.

"A little patience," said Whelan. "Now, this beast is a river beast, as most of you know. And the thing about river beasts is that they are reluctant to appear during daylight."

"So we perform the ceremony at night?" said Calax.

"Oh, no, no, no," said Whelan. "That's when the beast feeds. No, the ceremony must be performed in the light of day, when the beast is both sated and groggy from sleep."

"This makes no sense to me," said the Red Monk.

"No," said Orthor, "he is correct. The words must be said before the sun climbs to its zenith. Then, and only then, will the words take effect."

Whelan squinted at him. "You seem to know the ceremony—at least a little bit. What about the words, then. What are they, Rune Master?"

Orthor was taken aback. "You want *me* to tell them?"

"Yes, if you know them."

"Very well." He stood and began to speak.

"No," screamed Whelan. "Not here, fool. Not now." He turned to the others. "You see, the dolt knows some of the ceremony, perhaps even the words, but he forgets the cautions, first being never to say the words anywhere but the place of the ceremony, and only at the appointed hour, by the appointed person."

Orthor blinked and sat back down. "It is as you say, Whelan. I had forgotten. Please continue on—um, without the words."

Whelan sighed. "We could have been in big trouble if Orthor here had uttered but a single word of the ceremony. Now I'm at a bit of a loss. Where was I? Ah yes, the words. We can't say them, but let me tell you about their effect on the beast and ultimately the god."

Everyone listened, their attentive smiles turning to furtive glances, one to the other, as Whelan's words took hold and they began to understand the danger.

"By the gods," said the Red Monk. "By the gods!"

29

Orthor's dream was filled with beasts of every kind. Some slithered, some hissed, some dove at him from the clouds, the sound of their wings growing louder by the second. And then came the beast from the river, the one that Whelan had described as the cook fire turned from flame to coals to ash.

He awoke screaming, startling the others in the early morning darkness.

Calax reflexively leaped to his feet, drew his sword, and spun around to search for the invisible attackers. "What the—"

The Red Monk did the same, though he used his staff, not a sword. He was halfway through a defensive charm when he realized that Orthor's scream was prompted by nothing more than a nightmare. "By the gods, Orthor. You near scared me to death."

"I'm sorry," said Orthor. "The dream just felt so real."

Calax nodded. "Aye, you'll find that true whenever you sleep beneath the sky. It does things to a man."

"Then I hope ever to sleep beneath a thick roof," said Orthor. "Oh, the monsters I saw."

"Well, you'll be safe from such nightmares when you sleep in Randall's Cave. I can't think of a thicker roof than the one that cave provides."

Orthor nodded, then looked around the camp, puzzled.

"What?" said Calax.

"Where's Whelan?"

They all looked around, but there was no Whelan to be seen.

"Perhaps he's taking care of necessary business," said the Red Monk. "I know the older I get, the more urgent my stream."

Calax chuckled despite his concern. Had Whelan abandoned them? If so, why? "I have no reason to think anything's amiss. I do know he takes his meals seriously, so my guess would be that he's out there somewhere hunting molfrumps."

"Is it true they're better than rabbits?" said Orthor.

"The plump ones, yes," said the Red Monk. "But in my experience, most of them are lean and stringy, and don't cook up well."

"The same can be said of the rats in Randall's Cave, Orthor," said Calax. "Most are stringy and either have a foul flavor or no flavor at all."

"More to the point," said the Red Monk. "What should we do, do you think?"

"Normally, I'd say give him another minute to show up," said Calax, "but minutes are precious now. No, if you will, could you far-see for us?"

"Of course, of course," said the Red Monk. "I should have done that immediately. Getting too old, I guess. Okay, let me see what I can see."

He seemed to go into a trance and then broke from it quickly. "This is impossible. There's no one out there for as far as I can far-see, which is all the way to the sea back there and Randall's cave ahead. He's vanished."

Calax looked over at the horses. "And so has his horse. Could anyone really ride that fast on a tired horse?"

"No," said Orthor. "By my calculation, he could only make it halfway, at best."

"Perhaps he knows speed charms," said the Red Monk.

Calax shook his head. "I'd have to say no to that. We could have used such charms when Rhynt, Whelan, and I made our way to Enturia."

"Maybe my calculation is wrong," said Orthor. "Perhaps he is this minute *inside* Randall's Cave. Monk, could you see him then?"

Orthor's explanation seemed to calm the Red Monk. "Why no, no I couldn't. That must be it. He's inside the cave. But why? Why would he leave without so much as a word?"

Calax looked at the horizon, which was beginning to brighten. "I don't know, but the sun will be upon us soon. We should gather our things, saddle and pack the horses, and make our way to the chasm and the cave. The ceremony must be done this day, with or without Whelan."

Orthor gulped. "Do you mean by me?"

Calax nodded. "You said you could do it, did you not?"

"Yes, I know it well, but what of Whelan's caution that he alone must perform it?"

The Red Monk smiled down at him. "I think that is but jealousy."

"Indeed," said Calax. He scanned the plain, looking for any signs of Whelan. "If he's not already there or fails to come at all, you will perform the ceremony."

Orthor wasn't so sure. "But—"

"Say no more," said the Red Monk. "I think it wise you practice the ceremony in your head as we ride. When we descend into the chasm and face the river beast, you must be prepared."

Orthor puffed out his cheeks and sighed. "I will do my best."

"No," said Calax. "You will do it *right*. All of Enturia is counting on you."

Orthor gulped, his eyes widening.

"No pressure," said the Red Monk, laughing and slapping Orthor on the back. "Come, my boy, we must to horse."

30

The horses seemed to be moving through a sea of tree sap. Even Calax's warhorse, Gash, was slow and lethargic and resisted all of Calax's attempts to coax more speed out of him. Orthor's horse, slowed even more by the packhorse trailing behind, was barely walking and far from any notion of a trot.

No one was more frustrated by their slow progress than the Red Monk. He had tried charm after charm, but to little effect. The horses would trot briefly, then fall back to a walk. Finally, he could stand no more and slid out of the saddle and down to the ground. "Enough! Get down, we can make better progress walking, I think. The horses just can't bear our weight today."

Orthor and Calax followed suit, dropping down from their saddles and tugging the horses to a faster pace.

"How far, monk?" said Orthor.

The monk closed his eyes but continued walking. "Another hour I think."

Calax looked up at the sun. "That will be cutting it close."

"Too close," said Orthor. "I am the lightest here. Perhaps I should ride ahead, get the ceremony started."

"You don't know the way," said Calax.

"That is easy," said the Red Monk. "It's just a straight shot that way to the chasm. I think we should give it a try."

"All right," said Calax. "Take Gash, he is the strongest of the horses, and I think he'll appreciate someone so light in the saddle."

"Very well," said Orthor, handing the reins of his horses to Calax and climbing quickly into the saddle atop Gash. "My word, he is so tall."

"He is that," said Calax. "Now, don't baby him. Give him a good kick. He understands the words *fast* and *faster*, so don't be shy about using them." He glanced at the position of the sun. "In fact, I think you should use those words now."

Orthor nodded, gave Gash a forceful kick, and shouted, *"Fast, faster!"*

Gash reared up briefly, then bolted toward the horizon, Orthor hanging on for dear life.

Calax and the Red Monk watched him go.

"I like that lad," said the monk.

"Aye," said Calax. "Now, let's follow as best we can. Perhaps we can make it to the chasm in time to see the ceremony unfold."

The Red Monk shook his head. "I hope the boy knows what he's doing."

"I hope the boy is not needed and that Whelan is there even now, ready to bring forth the Red God."

"Indeed," said the monk, "indeed."

31

Whelan glanced up at the rim of the chasm. *They must still be asleep,* he thought. *Good. Very good.*

He turned back to the river, which was full and raging from a recent rain, took a deep breath, and began . . .

"*Bahdja lichthe kahlko meunch.* By the river of the watzel, in the land of the free, within sight of Randall's Cave and the seventh god's Teachings, I summon you . . ."

He paused to see if the beast had surfaced. *Nothing.*

"Hear me now, oh gods, and hear me truly, the time has come to return, to arise, in a broken world requiring your presence. Hear me, I plead, from the depths come, from your sleep come, from the infinite come, oh mighty ones . . ."

He caught sight of the beast swimming toward him through the swift currents. Hideous in aspect and striped in white, blue, green, red, gray, and black—the colors of the six lesser gods—it swam with a speed unknown among reptiles. Its orange eyes focused on him, its mouth opening to reveal long fangs.

Whelan knew he'd have to talk quickly now.

"I, Randall, God of Gods, summon you. Heed my call and rise now. Rise!" The last word was shouted, which caused the beast to shriek and writhe in the water.

"Rise!" he shouted again, lifting his arms toward the sky. "Come forth!"

The beast began to move faster, its head pursuing its tail, churning the water into a pale froth. And then with a roar, it was flying straight up into the air, splitting apart as it rose, into six beasts, each the separate color of a god: Porto white, Canto blue, Bedo green, Abo red, Dado gray, and Indo black.

Whelan watched the beasts rise, writhe, and then plummet back into the river. Seconds later, six gods surfaced and swam to the banks of the river, rising to stand a few paces away from Whelan. Some smiled when they saw him, others frowned, wary of what was to come.

Each wore godly robes in their chosen color and with their chosen sigils: Porto in a white robe with the off-white sigil of a crow; Canto in blue with the sigil of a jay; Bedo in dark green with a light green sigil of a diamond; Abo in scarlet with the sigil of an eagle; Dado in gray with a lightning bolt sigil; and Indo in Black with the sigil of a crescent moon.

Whelan was happy they had each chosen a human form rather than those suggested by their sigils. Birds were one thing, but lightning bolts were something else entirely. He had tried to carry on a civil conversation with Dado when he was in his lightning form, but that did not work out, at all.

No, human forms were best, and each of these gods could have been exemplars of the human form. Five represented themselves as men, each more handsome than the next; and one, the Red God, Abo, took on a female form, though she was capable of presenting herself in any form. She just preferred the female form, and to Whelan's mind there was no woman alive who could match her beauty. Today she had chosen long red hair and green eyes and a shape that even under her robes could clearly be seen to be statuesque. Her smile was disarming, her voice deep and sultry. But she chose to give Whelan only a brief smile as she emerged from the river.

Porto was the first to speak. "Why have you summoned me, Randall? I was busy with . . . *other things.*"

Whelan nodded and gave him a wry smile. "It is those *other things* that have brought you here." He turned to the others. "All of you."

32

Orthor saw the chasm a mile ahead and gasped. *What a wonder,* he thought. He urged Gash forward, but the horse, already spent, could only respond by slowing down from a gallop to a trot to nothing more than a walk.

Frustrated, Orthor climbed down from the saddle, took Gash's reins, and tugged him toward the chasm, which now seemed impossibly far away. He trudged on, head down, concentrating on moving one foot in front of the other. Every few steps he would stop and rub a hand along his aching rump. "I will never make a horseman, Gash, even astride a specimen such as yourself."

Gash seemed to nod and whinny in agreement.

Orthor laughed. "Oh, so you agree with me? Well, I won't hold that against you. I am a man of letters, not saddles."

He continued on, each step harder than the last, until the chasm began to widen in his eyes. "It is wider than I thought, Gash. I shudder to think how deep it might be."

He slowed his pace, easing up to the edge of the chasm. Its depth made him back up and fall down. "Oh, my. We have to go down *that?*"

He turned and looked away from the chasm, searching for any sign of Calax and the Red Monk. He wanted to wait for them, let them lead the way down, but with no sign of them at all, he knew he'd have to attempt the descent on his own.

He walked back up to the rim again and looked down. He could see the river but nothing more. No gods, no Whelan. He kept looking, searching for the way down.

"Ah, there it is, Gash. Our path down. Come, it is not far."

He began walking west along the rim until he came to a notch that led to a narrow path that led down to the chasm floor. He wondered whether Gash could handle his weight on the descent and decided he couldn't. He'd have to walk him down.

He turned to Gash. "Follow me, and mind your hooves."

He took one step onto the path and looked down. The world seemed to spin briefly before he gained control and focused on the movement of his feet along the path. Gash seemed more eager than Orthor, and nudged him forward.

"Stop pushing me," said Orthor. "Do you really want me to fall?"

Gash said something in horse that seemed to be, *Well, move then, slowpoke.*

"All right, all right. I'll go faster. You just keep your distance."

They continued down, step after tentative step, until they reached the bottom. Orthor wasn't sure who was most relieved, him or Gash.

He looked back up at the rim of the chasm, now a line in the sky. "I don't think I could do that again."

He looked around. The river was roaring, sending up a spray that was quickly drenching them. Orthor tugged on Gash's reins. "Come on, let's get away from this spray. The cave's ahead. See it? Up there." He pointed at a black hole in the side of the chasm.

Then he remembered his mission. The ceremony. "No, wait, the cave will have to wait." He let go of Gash's reins and walked back to the edge of the river.

He wondered whether his words would be heard over the roar of the river. *"Bahdja lichthe kahlko manchette . . ."*

33

Whelan and the Red God, Abo, stood at the mouth of the cave, peering out at the river and the chasm wall. Whelan spotted him first. "There he is, near the bottom of the chasm, the young lad who thinks he can decipher my runes—and conduct the calling ceremony."

The Red God laughed. "He is much too young to do either. He is but a boy, albeit a boy with a fine warhorse. I recognize it from the Battle of Whent Hill. Is it not the warhorse of Calax Halfhand?"

"It is, indeed. Gash is his name, and there is none finer."

The Red God shook her head. "I have tried to kill that man so many times, and have always failed."

Whelan smiled wryly. "He must be under the protection of another, *stronger* god."

The Red God chuckled. "Yes, yes, I know you like him. Why, I can't imagine. I find him brutish and dull."

"And I find him heroic and brave."

The Red God shrugged. "No matter. It is to your credit that you have set in motion on this day events that may kill the man you so admire."

Whelan sighed. It was true. The calling of the gods had led to a lengthy discussion of the looming war between the Enturians and the Mystrosians, and to the gods' part in it. The solution could have been easy, if only Porto, the White God, had not already taken the side of the Mystrosians.

At first the argument had centered on the need for balance. If the Mystrosians were to be supported by Porto, who among the gods would support the Enturians? Bedo, the Green God, offered to take on the task, but Whelan thought him angry, perhaps too angry to defend Enturia and its queen. After all, his monk had been killed at the hands of Calax and the new queen. Could he really support her kingdom?

Canto, Dado, and Indo volunteered in turn, but Whelan turned each one down, turning instead to the only goddess among them. Abo had accepted the task readily, and was eager to meet Orthor and Calax and her powerful monk, d'Abo Pourcrey.

The argument had then shifted to the roles of the other gods, including Whelan himself. Each thought they should have a part in the war's outcome. Finally, Whelan relented and assigned each a task. He alone would determine the outcome, of course, but keeping the other gods happy and engaged would only make things go smoother.

Something happening outside the cave caught the Red God's attention. "Look," she said with alarm, pointing down at Orthor. "The young lad is trying to call the gods."

Whelan couldn't believe what he was seeing. Orthor was raising his arms, exactly as they should be raised, in the very spot they should be raised. He ran from the cave and began shouting at Orthor to stop, but the river was already churning.

Whelan ran faster, reaching Orthor just in time to pull him back from the banks of the river and shout, "What are you doing?"

Orthor struggled to free himself from Whelan's grasp. "Calling the gods, something you should have already done. Now let me go, so I can finish."

Whelan tugged him farther away from the river just as a snake-like beast emerged from its depths, surfacing and bursting into the air. It was striped in many colors and huge, bigger and longer than ten horses end to end. Its open maw was filled with fangs as long and sharp as swords.

Orthor gasped as the beast began its descent toward him, its mouth opening wider still. Terrified, he cringed and closed his eyes. They would both be killed, he knew it. And then what would the queen think of him? He had come to decipher the runes and become famous in doing so. Now all that would be lost, and his life in the bargain.

But as those thoughts flashed through his mind, the Red God stepped forward and thrust her arms toward the beast, shouting, "*Manklasdo baweelo*, begone!"

The beast closed its mouth and slid back down into the waters, barely missing Orthor.

Orthor opened his eyes and stared drop-jawed at the woman in red. "Oh, my."

34

Orthor couldn't help staring at her. For her beauty, yes, but also because he had seen her before.

"You know," said the Red God, "if you stare at me too long, you might just turn to stone."

Orthor blinked. "Oh, sorry. It's just that I know you."

"Yes, I believe Whelan just introduced us."

"No, I mean from *before.*"

"Before? I've never seen you before, and at your young age, there's really not much before, is there?"

Orthor shook his head. "No, I'm not being clear. I have seen you in a book, specifically *Admok's History of the Gods and Their Peculiar Nature, Volume Two.*"

She rolled her eyes. "Oh, him. What a bore. He's been dead, what, a thousand years?"

Orthor tried to do the calculation in his head. "Um, thereabouts, I think. Anyway, there's a fine woodcut illustration of you. On page 637, as I recall."

She nodded. "Yes, I seem to recall that one. The artist was Blazdon Cordoll. Like you, a fine young man looking to get ahead. Did you know he died a month after making that woodcut?"

"Truly?"

"Yes, he attempted an image of King Wazza the Second."

"The king of Ichthia?"

The Red God clucked. "Well, you know your history."

"I read a lot."

"I bet you do. Anyway, Blaz—I called him Blaz—presented the woodcut to the king, expecting a fine reward, perhaps an annual stipend to continue his work, but . . ."

"But?"

"But the king was—how should I say this—*displeased.* He hated the woodcut so much, he snapped it in two across his knee and then had an aide set fire to it. All as Blaz watched, mind you. He was horrified."

"I bet."

"But not for long."

Orthor smiled. "He got over it, then?"

The Red God chuckled. "Over it? Oh, my, no. They lopped off his head right then and there." She frowned. "What were we talking about?"

"The woodcut of you. You know, Admok's book."

"Oh, yes. Well, I think that Blaz captured my feelings and aspect precisely."

Orthor seemed taken aback. "Really? The woodcut shows you killing a warrior. The look on your face was, was—horrifying."

She shrugged. "I was angry back then. No patience for anything. But look at me now. Have you ever seen a woman more beautiful?"

Orthor shook his head vigorously. "No, you are a wonder."

"Good answer. Perhaps you'll amount to something after all."

Whelan's shout startled them both. "Behold the Red Monk and the berserker Calax Halfhand, here at last, if more than a little late."

The Red God and Orthor turned to see Calax and the Red Monk coming down the chasm trail, leading their horses by the reins.

The Red God was not impressed. "That's my monk? Oh, that will not do. That will not do at all."

35

Orthor stood apart from the others in Randall's Cave. He had no interest in their argument, which seemed to be centered on what to do next. The Red Monk wanted to "rest his bones" in Randall's Cave for a night and spend time getting to know the god he had worshipped all his life. He had been astounded that the god was female, or at least presenting herself so. This just made him more determined to spend time with her, to ask her myriad questions about the Teachings and her role among the six gods.

The Red God had other ideas. She stood there, shaking her head at the monk's every word, suggestion, and appeal. She had her secret instructions from Randall himself, and she was not about to deviate from them. There would be hell to pay if she did.

Calax was eager to return to Enturia. The queen was counting on him—and them—to turn back the Mystrosians. Every second they delayed was a problem for Calax, so he forcefully entreated them to do the right thing and start their journey home at once.

Whelan was uncharacteristically silent throughout the argument, nodding in agreement to each of the other's words. It was as if he was disinterested in the outcome and sought only the end to all argument.

Orthor, if asked, could not have told you the exact words of their conversation; he was just too distracted by the runes on the walls of the cave. He had seen runes before in many a book and scroll, and solved each language, but this—*this!*—was something else entirely. The runes he was used to had form and order and followed a logic unto themselves. Randall's runes seemed to be runes of runes of runes. There appeared to be no logic to them at all, and their form and order varied from rune to rune, as if each had been chosen from some different, unique language.

A shout from the Red God brought his attention back to the argument. "We will do as I say," she screamed.

Calax and the monk stood there, stunned.

The god calmed herself. "I appreciate your argument, Calax," she said, then turned to the monk. "And yours. Pourcrey, I would love to spend time with you, and will when we're in Enturia, but Calax is right, we've a battle to fight and any delay risks the outcome."

All three nodded, Whelan with more vigor than the others.

"I have assessed the situation as it stands in Enturia and can only conclude that my presence is required there this very minute. The White God is up to mischief, so whether you start your journey back today or wait until tomorrow when your steeds are rested is your choice. Mine is already made."

She stepped away from them and walked over to Orthor. "I must go now, but I would have a word with you."

"Yes?"

"In private." She glanced over at the others, who were now debating whether to take to horse now or after a night's rest.

Orthor stood and walked with her deeper into the cave. "What is it?"

The god stopped and pointed at the runes. "These runes, the Teachings, have been forgotten for eons. Bringing them back to life will be a difficult task, and I fear it may take more than your lifetime or many lifetimes to do so."

Orthor shook his head. "They are as difficult as they are mysterious, yes, but I am up to the challenge and plan to surprise you and the queen with a full translation—and soon."

She smiled down at him. "I like your confidence, but do not wish you well in your task."

Orthor was stunned. "What? Why not?"

The god sighed, then grabbed him by the shoulders and leaned in to whisper, "The Teachings are said to contain all knowledge—past, present, and future—and it is the Teachings on the future that could be dangerous to us all, man and god alike."

"The future? Are you saying everything is preordained, that our fate is already written here on the walls of this cave?"

"I fear it is so."

"But—"

She held a finger to her lips to silence him. "And if you are able to solve the riddle of these runes, you will have knowledge more powerful even than the gods."

Orthor gulped. "If the future is hidden within these runes, I will uncover it, but I would never knowingly do harm to our world."

"No, I'm sure you wouldn't." She looked over at the others, who continued their argument. "But there are others who might."

Orthor looked confused. "Who?"

"Never mind. All I ask of you is that if you are successful translating these runes, you tell me first."

Orthor shook his head. "But I am *obligated* to tell the queen first. That is my charge."

"If I am right, you would remove the queen from any danger by telling me first."

His eyes widened. "Danger? She's in danger?"

"Not yet, not now—other than the Mystrosians—but in the future."

"But I don't see how telling you first will help."

"It will. You'll have to trust me on that."

"But—"

"No buts. Now listen, when you solve the runes, summon me no matter what they say. Just shout these three words, and I'll appear instantly." She leaned down and whispered in his ear.

Orthor frowned. "But—"

But it was as she said. No buts, because with those three words, she turned away from him and vanished.

36

Calax wasn't convinced. "Do you really think she can do it?"

The Red Monk rolled his eyes yet again at Calax's misgivings. "Of course she'll make a difference. She's the Red God, after all. Powerful. Unstoppable."

Whelan chuckled. "Well, yes, or rather maybe. Have you forgotten about the White God?"

"I have not," said the Red Monk, thrusting a finger in the air for emphasis. "I am more powerful than the White Monk, so it stands to reason that my god is more powerful than his."

"Sounds like an Ichthian Standoff to me," said Calax.

The Red Monk snorted. "Well, if it is, all we have standing between us and death is the king's fool."

Whelan frowned. "You underestimate him, Pourcrey. He is no fool, that one. He may play one for food and shelter, but for my money, he's the smartest man in Enturia."

They fell silent.

Calax poked at the fire to rouse it to flame. They had all been sitting in front of the fire so long their faces were red and their backsides were cold as ice. "I think we should get some sleep," he said. "We've a long way to go in the morning."

The Red Monk nodded. "You're right, but I have one last question for our friend Whelan here."

"Oh?" said Whelan. "And what would that be? No, let me guess. You wonder why I deserted you and got here first."

"Indeed," said the Red Monk.

"The ceremony, of course. It had to be done at the—"

"Yes, yes," said the monk, interrupting. "At the exact place at the precise time. Yes, we know that. But leaving us without a word?"

Whelan nodded. "Okay, I'll give you that. I should have said something—it would have been the polite thing to do. But you all looked exhausted to me, so I decided to let you sleep. You weren't really needed for the ceremony, after all, and besides, my steed was fresher than yours and willing to ride fast."

"So you went," said Calax, "leaving us to worry and to force our horses harder than we should have. We thought Orthor had to perform the ceremony. And we didn't think we could make it on time."

Whelan looked over at Orthor, who had kept to himself once they'd arrived at Randall's Cave. He was consumed by the runes and even now ran his hands along the walls of the cave, tracing each rune with his fingers. "It's good that I performed it, though. He began with the wrong words, calling forth a beast only the Red God could deal with. If not for her, we would all be in that beast's stomach."

"Speaking of the Red God," said Calax. "I wonder what she's doing right now."

The Red Monk cocked his head. "Doing? Why, she's no doubt discussing stratagems with your so-called smartest man in Enturia. Thank the gods she's going to help us."

"Yes," said Whelan. "I wonder whether his latest gambit takes her and the White God into account. In my experience, gods don't like plans. They like action."

"And I'd like some of that," said Calax. "Come, we must to bed. Plan or no, Enturia is better off with us there rather than here."

The others nodded and began preparing their bedrolls for the night.

Calax glanced over at Orthor and shouted, "Time for sleep. Those runes can wait."

Orthor appeared startled by the sound of Calax's voice. "Um, yes, I mean no, I'm onto something here. At least, I think so."

"Sleep could only help," said Calax.

Orthor shook his head. "For you, yes. You need to get an early start. Not so for me. Go on then, get your sleep. I have work to do before I rest this night."

"Suit yourself," said Calax, turning away from Orthor and tending to his bedroll.

Orthor watched them bed down for the night. When the snoring began, which was almost immediately, he turned back to the runes. "Now, my friends, reveal yourselves."

Part III

"You mystify me. First you run away from my fire, just because you learned I was a god. Then you come sneaking back, curious to know the outcome of the battle. And now, after double portions of my mutton, you want me to jump to the end, declare a victor, and no doubt douse this fire, take my lute, and disappear into the night.

"I see your impatience, I do. The problem is, if I told you the victor, you'd be so startled, you'd pepper me with questions. Why did this happen? How could they have possibly thought that would work? And on and on. Believe me, I've told this story many, many times, and the way I'm telling it now is the best way; in fact, the only way to tell it and make it understandable to a person of your notable density.

"So sit back, have some more tea. My preamble nears its end and the battle even now begins. Good, I will take your silence as affirmation. So, the Red God and the White God are in position, or nearly so, each with instructions on how to proceed. Yes, from me. We shift back to Enturia now and the hand-wringing Bookins, who's not so sure about his plan."

37

Lord Braque watched his former fool, Bookins, pace back and forth in front of him. "Will you please sit down? You are making my neck hurt."

Bookins threw up his hands. "How can I? I keep thinking about the plan. Will it really work?"

Braque shook his head. "You know it will."

"No, no I don't."

"Then what is your concern? It seems a perfect plan to me, one that takes into account our strengths and weaknesses, and theirs. It is both bold and cautious, and I cannot see a single hole in your argument. This should play out exactly as you've foreseen."

"But what if it doesn't?"

"Again, you have provided for every contingency."

"Have I? It is my experience—and history's warning—that a battle is first lost on parchment."

Braque rolled his eyes. "And *won*, my good Bookins, and won."

Bookins stopped pacing. "Do you really think so?"

"I do, I do, so come, sit with me, enjoy the supper that arrived as you paced this damnably small room of yours. I doubt that I shall ever get used to sharing a room. I was king once, was I not?"

Bookins chuckled. "You were, and a good one."

Braque shrugged. "I tried, although the last few years things—and I— seemed to fall apart."

"Not so."

"Ha, you are too kind." He patted his hand on a nearby chair. "Come now, let's eat. A full stomach is always a wise stratagem."

Bookins looked down at the food. Despite his fall from king to lord, Braque still had great influence in the castle's kitchens. The meal laid out before them was worthy of a king, even a king among kings. "Well, it does look good."

Braque held up a chicken leg, which glowed red from pikney seasoning. "It is, it is. This chicken is a marvel. You must try it, and quickly, or I shall consume it myself."

Bookins took the chicken leg from Braque and ventured a curious bite. "Oh, my. It is all you said it was."

"Indeed." He patted the chair again. "Sit, dammit."

Bookins sat, then let out a heavy sigh.

Braque saw the look and handed him a cup of mead. "Don't sip at this. You need a guzzle to shake you from your misguided misgivings."

Bookins nodded. "Perhaps more than a guzzle. I just can't help feeling that I've missed something in the plan. So many things could go wrong."

"But so many things could also go right."

Bookins set down the cup. "Do you know what concerns me the most?"

Braque rolled his eyes. "Must we really continue this conversation? You are laying waste to my appetite."

"Of that I am sorry. But let me make one last comment before we engorge ourselves on this fine meal."

Braque wagged a finger at him. "One, only one."

"Yes, just one. It's the White God that concerns me. As our gambit unfolds, will he sense it? Will he have an answer for it?"

Braque huffed. "You worry too much about that god."

"Indeed you do," said the Red God, emerging as if from a vapor to stand before them. Her smile grew wide as their jaws dropped lower.

38

The Red God looked Queen Rhynt up and down, and then clucked. "You are a little one, aren't you?"

Queen Rhynt frowned. "My size is not the issue here."

The Red God shrugged and glanced down at Mela, Mila, and Spook, who were purring loudly at Rhynt's feet. "The hill tigers are a nice touch, though. Very, um, *regal.*"

"I'm glad you like them, but can we get back to the task at hand."

"My, my, impatience is not a good trait, my dear."

"Nor is delay."

The Red God chuckled, then turned to the others at the table: Baron Bookins and Lord Braque. They were sitting in the Council Chamber, at one end of the long table. The Red God, worried about security, had requested that only the four of them be present. Bookins had a plan, yes, but she wanted to be sure her contributions to that plan were kept as secret as possible. Before she even said a word, she had screened each of them to assure that no gelas were in the room. "There's delay and there's delay. Are you sure you don't want to wait until the return of Whelan, Calax, and my monk?"

Rhynt shook her head. "As much as I would like to wait—we could use each of them right about now—waiting is the last thing we should be doing. Am I right, Bookins?"

Bookins seemed startled. He had been thinking about his plan. Going over each point and stratagem in his head. Would it work? Had he left anything out? "Um, yes, yes you are, Majesty. The Mystrosians even now are proceeding inland from our eastern shores."

The Red God nodded. "To be expected. He is an impatient god." She turned to Rhynt. "In this case, *impatience* is a wonderful trait—for us. He's prone to making major mistakes at the worst possible moments. We can use this to our advantage, no matter Bookins' plan."

"What?" said Bookins, concerned. Was she really saying his plan didn't matter?

She chuckled. "Not to worry, Bookins. I see the worried look on your face. We will follow your plan so long as it holds true to its intent, to defeat the Mystrosians. I will help along the way, as needed. I know the White God well. His strengths, his weaknesses, his tendencies."

Lord Braque cleared his throat. "A word if I may, your godliness."

"*Godliness?* How quaint. Just call me Abo."

"All right, then, *Abo.* If you know him well, does he not know you well?"

The god smiled. "Oh, yes, and I'm counting on that. Where he will not vary from his nature, I will. If he knows I'll go right, I'll go left—against my tendencies."

Braque shook his head. "But won't that only work once? Surely he'll realize what you're doing."

The god raised her eyebrows. "The White God is a dolt. Logic and nuance are not part of his makeup. No, he will charge us in the only way he knows how to charge us." She turned to Bookins. "And victory will be ours."

"Shall we get on with it, then?" said Queen Rhynt. "Bookins, if you will, explain your plan in every detail to our new friend, *Abo.*"

The Red God turned to him as well. "Please."

39

The White Monk gave Porto, the White God, a questioning look. "We're going to do *what?*"

"Wait. We're going to *wait.* Is that so hard to understand?"

"But our six columns are already ashore and on the march. Delay can only risk our advantage. You even said this, just hours ago."

The White God shrugged. He knew this new ploy looked bad, but what was he to do? Randall said he must do it. To disobey would mean banishment, or worse. And besides, Randall had pulled him aside and told him in whispers that a Mystrosian victory was assured. He only had to follow the plan, even though every godly bone in his body shouted for him to disobey. "We must deal with the Red God now, and delay is just the thing, at least for now."

"The Red God? How do you know?"

The White God scoffed. "Come on, d'Porto. You know we gods sense everything. Nothing escapes me, and I see her even now discussing the Enturian's plan with their silly fool, Bookins. If she listens to him, victory will be ours. So, we wait."

"How long?"

The White God waggled his head. "A day or two, perhaps three."

"And how will you know when to move?"

"Oh, that's easy. We wait for them to make the first move."

"And what if they never move?"

The White God laughed. "That will not happen. The Red God loves war. The blood lust rises in her with every passing minute."

The monk frowned and shook his head.

"What is it, d'Porto? Why the grim look?"

"I have to explain this to the king. He will not be pleased."

The god laughed again. "You worry too much, d'Porto. Come, let us both speak to this king of yours. He will be more than happy, I assure you, when I explain the situation to him."

"I hope you're right. He is an impatient king. And he doesn't like Enturia at all. He's even suggested leaving."

"Leaving?"

"Yes, he finds it *uncomfortable.* The climate, this damnable mud, and these worse-than-damnable sucking flies." He slapped his neck and presented the squashed fly for the god's inspection.

"Hmm," said the White God. "The fly that sucks on you can also be made to suck on them." He put a hand to his chin. "Perhaps I could send a swarm of them west to their castle."

The monk laughed. "You can do that?"

"Oh, d'Porto, there is no end to what I can do. Every beast of the land, sea, and air."

The monk was encouraged. "And gelas?"

The god rolled his eyes. "Gelas? Yes, of course, and by the thousands if need be."

The monk smiled. "I feel a little bit better."

"Good, now show me to this king of yours."

40

The Red God tried to be attentive, to listen carefully to Bookins' plan, his so-called gambit, but two things made her thoughts drift away to other things and other times. First, she had a short attention span to begin with. She'd much rather be doing things than sitting at a table—*gods, there's not even wine!*—listening to an old fool drone on and on about the placement of resources and the timing of events. And second, and perhaps most important, Randall had already assured her that the Enturians would win no matter what she or the White God did. He just wanted her there for appearances' sake. It would be like a game, he said. Fun. Part of her—a large part of her—thought he was lying.

She was startled back to the meeting. Bookins was saying her name. Why, she had no idea. "What do you think, Abo? Abo?"

She attempted to gather herself. "What? Oh, oh, yes. How shall I put it? Your plan, dear Bookins, is worthy of awards."

Bookins blushed. "Do you really think so?"

"Indeed, I do. You have accounted for their strengths and weaknesses—and our own, including my humble contribution to the fray—and have laid out a sequence of events that, once played out, will no doubt be recorded in future scrolls and books. In a word, your plan is brilliant."

Bookins beamed and moved from the battle map back to the table and took his seat. He looked at the queen. "Perhaps we should have some wine."

Rhynt was about to reply, but the Red God cleared her throat with some force, reclaiming their attention. "There is just one little, tiny thing about your plan, Bookins."

Bookins gave her a confused look. What had he left out? Did he miss something? Was the plan incomplete? Worse, is it wrong in some way? "Um, what?"

"Don't worry, it's just a small thing. A trifling."

"What, then?"

She gave him a little grimace. "It's about the *timing.*"

"The timing? What, we strike at dawn."

She waggled her head. "That's just the thing. I think we should delay, wait for the return of Calax, Whelan, and my monk."

"But they're not needed in my plan until the third day. They will be here in time."

"Even so."

"But the Mystrosians march on us even now." He glanced over at the queen and then back at the Red God. "The queen's gelas have detected six columns moving against us. Waiting will just give them the advantage."

The Red God held up a hand. "Your information is incorrect." She turned to the queen. "Your gelas saw them marching, yes, but no longer. They have stopped in their tracks and set up camp."

"What?" said Rhynt. "Every column?"

"Indeed. And I have also witnessed a conversation between the White God and his monk. They are going to delay their advance by three days."

"What?" said Bookins. "Why on earth . . ."

"Yes," said the Red God. "It is a puzzlement. But isn't it true that your plan depends on their rapid movement toward us?"

Bookins nodded and let out a long sigh. "It does."

"Well, then," said the Red God, turning to Rhynt. "I heard a suggestion of wine, and I for one could use a glass or two."

"And me," said Bookins, puffing out his cheeks, a bit crestfallen by the need for a delay.

The queen stood, her hill tigers swirling around her. "I will have wine sent in. As for me, I want to get out of this armor, at least for a time. As wonderful as it is, it makes my leg itch."

The Red Monk watched her walk from the room, then turned back to Bookins. "While we're waiting, perhaps you can go over the plan again. There were a few places where I need further clarification."

Bookins was defensive. "What, is there something *wrong* with the plan?"

She tried to be reassuring. "No, no, not that. It is a fine plan, as I've said. There are just a few nuances I'd like to appreciate more." She pointed at the battle map on the wall. "For example, all this nasty sucking mud out there . . ."

"Yes?"

"Tell me more about it."

Bookins stood and shuffled over to the map. His legs and back were killing him and his throat was dry from too much speaking. He looked at the door, hoping to see a servant with a large tray filled with wine and glasses. Perhaps a nibble of cheese.

But the door remained shut.

He cleared his throat and pointed at a spot on the map. "There are six types of mud in Enturia, but . . ."

41

Whelan coaxed his horse up the gangplank, dismounted, and began rubbing his backside. Marthe took the reins and began moving the horse toward the storage bay, along with Calax's and the Red Monk's steeds. "Welcome aboard. Seems your travels were fast—and hard."

Whelan rolled his eyes. "Oh, you have no idea. Let me tell you, there is nothing more beautiful than a horse running across the plains, and nothing more satisfying than to be off it. By the gods, I am numb from the waist down."

Marthe laughed. "The others said much the same thing."

Whelan looked around. "Where are they, then?"

Marthe pointed toward the stern of the ship. "In my cabin. The cook has outdone himself. Laid out a fine meal for us."

Whelan laughed. "I hope it is not as sleep inducing as our meal before we last arrived in Enturia."

Marthe smiled. "Oh, no. Although if you eat your full, sleep will come quickly enough."

Whelan sighed. "I could use some sleep."

"Aye, you look more spent than your horse."

"Indeed. Even though I'm off that damned horse, my legs still feel him under me."

Marthe nodded. "That's why I much prefer a ship for my travels."

"You have chosen well."

Marthe waved him toward the stern. "Come, let's feast while my men take us out of this damned port."

Whelan shook his head. "You go ahead. I'd like to stretch my legs a bit, make them feel like they are part of me again."

Marthe chuckled. "The others had much the same troubles, although Calax seems to have adjusted quickly."

Whelan remembered watching Calax riding his warhorse, Gash. They rode as one, as if they were a single beast. "Well, he's more practiced than the rest of us. That is clear."

Marthe turned and gave him a little wave. "When you're ready, head to my cabin. Perhaps there will be food left when you arrive."

Whelan called after him. "There better be."

He watched him go, then turned his attention to the sailors scurrying about on the deck and climbing up to the sails. The anchor was being tugged up, lines were being loosed from the dock and pulled aboard, and the sails were dropping into place and catching the wind. It was like watching finely trained dancers.

Finally, the sails billowed and snapped full, propelling the ship away from the dock and out to sea. He moved to the rail and watched the docks of Port Ochno grow smaller and smaller.

He sighed. Two days at sea. He wondered whether the Red God and the White God were following his orders. They'd both balked at the idea of a delay, but he didn't want to miss a moment of the battle. Besides, the other gods needed to be in their places if his plan was to work. Yes, he could have just dematerialized and then shown up instantly in the Enturian council chamber, but he wanted to keep his identify secret for as long as possible. If that meant a numb rump and two days at sea, so be it.

His thoughts turned to Randall's Cave and that pesky young man, Orthor. Could the boy really translate the runes? He'd seemed so confident when they had spoken on the morning of Whelan's departure. Every objection and difficulty Whelan had raised seemed of no concern to the lad. Still, the chances of the boy's success were slim at best.

Even so, Whelan knew he'd have to keep an eye on the boy, a far-seeing eye.

42

Orthor knew that if he were to fail, the source of that failure would not be his knowledge and facility with runes, but his lack of knowledge of basic survival.

His first night in Randall's Cave he had struggled to start a fire and keep it going long enough to roast the single cave rat he was able to capture. The rat had proved bitter and stringy, just as Whelan had said it would.

Was Whelan also right about Orthor's abilities? Could he really solve this eons-long puzzle?

He glanced over at the flat-topped boulder he'd decided to use as a desk during his stay. The ten books he'd brought along were standing upright in alphabetical order between two rocks heavy enough to keep them from falling over. To their right, he'd stacked fourteen scrolls, which recorded the earliest knowledge of runes and Randall's Cave. To the left was the little cage and its two interred pigeons. Their cooing was soothing to his soul. That left the smooth middle of the boulder to lay out his quills and parchment. A small depression in the rock would serve as an inkwell.

He thought about the task at hand. Where to begin? Where to begin?

He threw another log on the fire, poked the coals back to life, and then walked over to his stony desk. He picked up the oldest scroll, which was made of weir deerskin. Despite its age, the scroll remained soft and flexible. He rolled it out and placed small stones at each corner to keep it open.

The writing startled him, as it always did, the work of Gregor Maxton, the first rune master, set down in Old Paudian in an ornate script in emerald green ink made from blaston berries.

Usually, he skipped Gregor's preliminary musings about runes, but not today. He wanted to start with the most basic considerations. In his experience, jumping to advanced techniques worked for many runes but not all runes. Difficult runes always forced him back to the beginning, to the basic techniques and considerations.

He glanced at the fire, which had already lost flame. He'd have to attend to it soon or begin all over again. For a moment, he thought to set down the scroll and deal with it, but Gregor's preamble was not that long.

He turned back to the manuscript. He imagined Gregor sitting across from him, reading the scroll to him, pausing at points for emphasis before moving on to the next salient point.

Harken to my words and give them heed, for they will be your savior if you read them or your undoing if you do not. The first thing you must know about runes is that they are meant to be difficult, and like any puzzle, they have but one solution. Looking for that one solution means considering all possible methods of puzzle construction. Knowing how the puzzle is constructed is key. Should the runes be read left to right, right to left? Top to bottom, bottom to top? Middle to ends? Is the first rune the last or the first? Is the puzzle maker using skip runes? Faux runes? Buried clues? Puzzles within puzzles?

All this you must consider, each in turn, to find the best—and only— path forward.

Orthor sighed and turned his attention back to the fire, which was barely smoking now. The scroll and the runes would have to wait.

He stood, brushed the dirt off his tunic, and walked back to the fire. Gregor was wrong. The first thing he needed was a good fire and a bad rat.

43

Queen Rhynt sat on a small chair beside the large bed that had once been Lord Braque's. Three handmaidens stood around her, one brushing her hair and the other two showing her gown after gown. They had already helped her out of her armor, leaving her in her undergarments. Rhynt tried to let them do their jobs, at least for a few minutes, but all this fussing over her was just too much. "Enough. Set the gowns down and leave me."

Pruscia, the youngest, tried to object, but Rhynt scowled at her and waved her away. "Shoo, shoo, all of you."

She watched them pile the gowns on a nearby chair and scurry across the room and out the door. As they left, she caught sight of two guards, who quickly looked away at the site of their partially clothed queen.

The door clicked shut and Rhynt let out a long sigh. Her hill tigers, who had found comfortable spots on her bed, took that as a sign to lift their heads and look around for danger. Seeing none, they yawned and went back to sleep.

Rhynt stood and stretched. All this talk about plans had made her tired. She walked over to the pile of gowns and picked up the one on top, quickly tossing it on the floor. She didn't even bother with the others. She didn't want to be that kind of queen. No, she wanted to be known as a warrior-queen.

She glanced over at the armor Zyrx had made for her, and gave it a reassuring nod. "We will be as one, proud armor. You and I, against all enemies."

Her voice awakened the tigers once more.

"Back to sleep," she said. "I'll be joining you momentarily."

She sat back down and began removing her artificial leg, also made by Zyrx. She wondered what he was doing now inside the floating tower. Something wonderful, no doubt. A new weapon. A new use for his invention, merilium.

The leg came off easily. She had to laugh at herself. The bed was at least ten steps away. She should have removed the leg while sitting on her bed. "Oh, bother."

She shrugged. Set the leg down and stood. Four hops later she was in bed, lying between Mela and Mila, with Spook at her feet.

She fell asleep quickly, her last thought Bookins' plan.

It had to work, but would the gods let it?

The Red God tried her best to pay attention to Bookins and his ongoing dissertation on the six kinds of mud. She had only asked the question about mud to help fill the time between Queen Rhynt's departure and the arrival of the wine. But the wine had come half an hour ago, and still Bookins droned on. Perhaps she should have taken the lead of Lord Braque, who had fallen asleep, his snore providing counterpoint to Bookins' drone.

She cleared her throat as loudly as she could. "Thank you, Bookins. You have already covered the mud I had in mind. Perhaps you can save your voice now and enjoy a glass or two of wine with us." She looked over at Lord Braque. "Or at least with me."

Bookins seemed taken aback by the interruption. "Oh, and which mud was that?"

"The sucking mud, the mud that can stop siege engines in their tracks."

"Ah, yes, but I still have one mud left, the slippery mud that plagues the hillsides, making climbs difficult and descents swift and unpredictable. You see, it's not really the mud; it's a kind of moss that lies just beneath and—"

"Wonderful to hear," she said, raising a glass. "Come, have some wine; we can discuss that mud another time."

Bookins focused on the wine for the first time. When had it arrived? *The Red God looks slightly drunk already. How many glasses has she had? Did she pay attention to my talk?* He shook all these questions off. Wine was at hand. "Yes, yes of course, I'd be delighted."

He shuffled back to the table and sat down. He'd been standing far too long, so the chair felt like a fine feather bed. "Ah, that's better."

The Red God smiled at him, poured him a glass of wine, and then cocked her head. "You are a curious man."

Bookins eagerly took the glass from her and near drained the glass in one gulp. He grabbed the nearby bottle and topped his glass off. "Curious? In what way?"

She looked up at the battle map. "This plan of yours—this gambit—appears to be the work of a master strategist, and yet you are only days removed from being the king's fool."

Bookins shrugged and took another sip of wine, which was already having a warming effect on him. "Oh, this Alamarian wine—the absolute best." He set his glass down and looked into the Red God's eyes. "There is an old saying, 'never judge a scroll by its curl,' and I think it applies here."

"Oh?"

"Yes, the thing about being a fool is that you have to know things."

"Wait," said the Red God, setting down her glass. "Don't fools just tell jokes and gambol about?"

Bookins chuckled. "I would only argue with your use of the word *just.* Yes, we tell jokes, we dance, we juggle, all with one goal in mind: to make the king happy. But we don't *just* do that."

She shook her head. "I'm afraid you've lost me. Please elucidate."

Bookins sighed and took a long sip of wine. He was beginning to have trouble focusing now. Wine in a tired man is a dangerous combination. But he attempted to press on. "You see, Red, to entertain a king—to entertain him year after year after year—requires both intelligence and knowledge."

She frowned at him. "Did you just call me Red?"

Bookins blinked. Had he? "Why, no, I don't think so."

"I'm sure you did, but go on. Knowledge and intelligence. Explain."

"Oh, oh yes, knowledge and intelligence. Let me make it simple for you. If I am to tell a joke to the king every few minutes, I must first know jokes. To know jokes, I must either hear them or read about them. To read about them, I must be able to read—let me tell you, many of the lords around here can't read a word. Anyway, to read jokes, I must have access to scrolls and that wonderful new invention, books."

"Yes, yes, more explanation, less rambling. So you read books? Please continue."

Bookins used her interruption to take another long sip of wine, which drained his glass. He reached for the bottle and continued. "Now, then," he said, pouring a glass, which overflowed a bit. "Oops, anyway, there's the library, you see. Tons of scrolls and a growing number of books on this and that, including warcraft."

"Ah," said the Red God. "So in your search for jokes, you took time out to read about war?"

"Indeed. Along with books on history, language, spells, and poultices—all manner of things—and you know what?"

"No, what?"

"Many jokes can be found in books that aren't about jokes."

"Really?"

"Yes, yesh, indeed that's true." Did he just slur his words? He'd have to slow down on the wine. Or not. It felt so good. He felt giddy and his bones had stopped aching.

"Give me an example."

He moved his hand to stroke his chin, but missed. Instead he waved it about, hoping to use his errant hand for emphasis. "Well, okay, take war for example. Sometimes armies and generals do hilarious things."

The Red God frowned. "What?"

He swept his hand in the direction of the battle map. It seemed to have more than five fingers. And they were so long. "Our plan will work, but not all plans do. And sometimes—well, you can find this in many a history scroll—sometimes plans can be foolish to the point of laughter."

He stared at her, waiting for a reply, but there seemed to be two of her now. He'd had too much wine, too fast.

She finally spoke. "Is this really true or is the wine making you say this?"

Bookins sighed heavily and slapped his hand on the table harder than he had intended. "Oh, Red, the first thing to know about war is that it is ridiculous. And so dangerous. Let me ask you one question."

The Red God knew it would do no good to correct him about how to address her. The man was drunk. "Yes, of course, but only one. I think we all could use some rest."

"Rest? Why yes, of coursh, but answer me this, Red. Why is it so easy to start a war and so hard to stop one?"

The Red God thought of a reply, but there was now no need. Bookins had dropped his head to the table and begun snoring.

She shook her head. "Mortals."

45

King Merek the Mighty blinked, then blinked again. "We're going to do *what?*"

The White Monk cringed. It was never good when King Merek asked you to repeat something. He always knew exactly what you said; he just wanted you to repeat it as a buildup to the unleashing of his considerable temper. "Delay, Majesty." He saw the king set his jaw. "But only a few days, Majesty."

King Merek looked down at the armor they had managed to stuff him in, which appeared to be two sizes too small for his ever-growing girth. Grapes and wine and every imaginable delicacy in the known world had a way of plumping up a man. "Do you know I just spent two hours getting into this armor?"

"Why no," said the White Monk, "but you *do* cut a fine figure in it, Majesty."

The king chuckled but not in a good way. "There's a word for people like you."

"Yes, there is," said the White God, walking into the tent with a flourish. "In fact, there are many ways to describe such a man, the kisser of arses being just one of a multitude of possibilities. For myself, I prefer sycophant to describe such a one, but that's just me."

King Merek looked back and forth between his monk and the glib intruder. "And who is this man, d'Porto? Do you know him?" He turned to the god, his voice rising with each word. "Is there any reason I should not have you beheaded on the spot for your unwelcome intrusion?"

"I don't think that would do you much good," said the god. "I'm a god, you see, the White God, Porto, to be specific. If you lop off my head, I'll just put it back on before lopping off yours."

King Merek's eyes had already gone wide. "Porto?" He turned to his monk. "Is this true? We have a god to help us?"

The monk bowed. "It is so, Majesty, and he will no doubt assure our victory."

King Merek smiled broadly at Porto. "Welcome, um, White God." He giggled and turned back to the monk. "How do you address a god, d'Porto."

The monk pointed a finger in the air and was about to reply when the god interceded. "Just call me Porto."

King Merek attempted to rise from the large pillow he was sitting on, but the armor made rising extremely difficult. "Um, could someone please help me up? This armor."

The White God waved his hand and King Merek floated to his feet. "How's that?"

The king waved his arms frantically as he rose higher in the tent. "No, no, not so high."

"As you wish," said the god. He waved his hand again, and the king gently descended to the ground.

"Oh, my," said the king. "This—having you—is just wonderful. We must attack at once!"

"No," said the monk. "Our god has pointed out the fallacy in that plan. We must delay."

The king turned to Porto. "Is that true? We must delay? Why?"

The White God had been dreading this question. His every instinct shouted attack, but his orders from Randall were to delay. "Yes, our success depends on a delay."

The king still couldn't grasp the concept. "But we're here, in vast numbers, overpowering numbers. Why should we not march at quick-step, surprise them in their castle, and win a glorious victory this very day?"

The god cocked his head. "A worthy scenario, King Merek, but the result would not be victory but defeat—horrible, horrible defeat."

The king shook his head. "You know this? Know this for a fact?"

The god nodded. "Of course. Why, even now, the Enturian queen sleeps in her bed. If she were about to attack, she would be in her armor and already advancing on us."

The king was incredulous, and jealous. He would have much rather been stretched out on his bed, entangled with his concubines. "Sleeping? You have actually seen this?"

"Not personally, but through a gela, yes."

"A gela?"

"Yes, a handmaiden to the queen."

"And you learned that they're delaying?"

"Indeed. It seems they plan to do nothing for several days."

The king sighed. "I still don't get it. Why should we delay? We could be at their gates, catch them unawares."

The god rolled his eyes. "We could be, yes, but you've forgotten one little detail."

The king squinted at the god. "And what would that be?"

"Why, their Red God, of course."

The king's eyes went wide. "They have a god, too?"

The White God shrugged. "They do, but not to worry, you have me, the superior god." He took a deep breath and thrust out his chest for emphasis.

The king tried to understand the situation, but couldn't. Whenever he was so puzzled, he always tried to see the good first, so rather than pressing the White God for a detailed comparison of the two gods, their strengths and weaknesses, and so on, he chose to see the good in the situation. "Well, then, if you say we should delay, we shall delay." He turned to his monk. "Find someone to get me out of this damned armor. If *she's* sleeping, I'll just have to out-sleep her."

The White Monk gave the White God a look that seemed to say, *See, I told you he was an idiot.*

46

Calax pushed back from the captain's table and patted his stomach. "Marthe, that was a boar worthy of the gods."

Marthe, who was still chewing greedily, his mouth full, gave Calax a meat-filled smile and an acknowledging nod.

The Red Monk had pushed back from the table long ago and was enjoying his second pipe of chumpsin weed, which had an acrid smell and produced a dense gray smoke that made his fellow diners' eyes water. "I'd have to agree, Marthe. And let us not forget the potatoes in cream sauce. Most excellent."

Marthe managed to swallow the large lump of meat in his mouth, and turned to them both. "All the credit goes to my new cook, a fine fellow who used to ply his trade in the now-closed brothel back at Port Ochno."

"Truly wonderful," said Calax. "Certainly far better than game and cave rats."

Marthe nodded and pushed back from the table. "Indeed. Now, gentlemen, if you'll excuse me, I have to see to the men and the sails. Like you, I want to get to Enturia as quickly as possible." He nodded at each of them and walked from the cabin.

The Red Monk lowered his pipe. "What do you make of Whelan? He's been acting strange, don't you think?"

Calax nodded. The Red Monk was right. The carefree minstrel he knew was now a distant, sulking man. "I honestly don't know what to make of it."

The Red Monk took a puff on his pipe and watched the smoke curl to the ceiling. "That whole business with the Calling Ceremony. Why did he not wait for us?"

Calax shrugged. "It is a mystery, true, but at least it worked. Your Red God is even now helping Bookins and Rhynt with the planning and preparations for war."

The monk shook his head. "I wish I'd been able to spend some time with her." He snorted. "Her. I wasn't expecting that. I thought he—*she*—would be a giant with a long beard and eyes that shot lightning bolts."

Calax chuckled. "It's not so bad to have a woman. I find them cleverer than men, and when the time comes, more ruthless."

"Really?"

"Yes, you've met my friend Phendour, have you not?"

"Yes, but only to say hello."

Calax smiled. "She's a warrior's warrior that woman. An archer without peer. Why, she can hit a rabbit's eye a mile away. I've seen it. And when the battle horn sounds, well, let me just say this. I would want no other warrior by my side, or to lead me into battle."

The monk nodded and started to take another puff from the pipe, but the pipe had grown cold. "This damned pipe. Won't hold a burn."

Calax pointed at the pipe. "You should get Zyrx to have a look at it. He's a genius when it comes to such things. Why, I bet he could make you a fine pipe out of that merilium of his."

The monk laughed. "Merilium, merilium, all this talk of merilium. Is it really that remarkable?"

Calax grunted. "Remarkable? It's more than that. It's a miracle is what it is."

The monk nodded and began stuffing more weed into the bowl of the pipe. "I will have to have a good talk with him."

"Yes," said Calax, "and perhaps we should have a good talk with Whelan as well. Find out what's going on with him."

The monk held a finger in the air. A flame erupted from its tip, which he lowered to the bowl of his pipe and began puffing and puffing."

Calax rolled his eyes. "You monks and your tricks."

The monk shrugged and blew out a cloud of smoke that rose to the ceiling and spread out in a circular wave.

47

Lord Braque watched Bookins pacing back and forth in the small bedroom they shared in the castle. The room was once for Bookins alone, but now that Braque had stepped down as king, it would have to do for two. A spare bed had been dragged in and placed along the wall opposite Bookins' bed, which left precious little space for pacing. Still, Bookins paced.

"I don't supposed you could stop that and sit down," Braque said.

Bookins ignored him. Something he would never have done while Braque was king.

"I said, would you please *stop that.*"

Raising his voice did nothing. Bookins turned and paced, turned and paced.

Now Braque screamed, "By the gods, sit down! I command you!"

Bookins stopped and looked down at Braque. "What? Did you say something?"

Braque started to scream again, but then thought better of it. He had the fool's attention now. "Just sit a moment. Let us talk."

"Talk? About what?"

Braque could not resist raising his voice. "About what? About what? Why, the reason you're pacing this damnably small room of ours."

Bookins nodded, then sat down on his bed opposite Braque.

"There," said Braque, "that's better. Now, what's going on with you?"

Bookins looked at the ceiling. There was so much going on in his head he didn't know quite where to start.

"Come on, Bookins, out with it."

Bookins took a deep breath and began. "It's that god."

"Which one, red or white?"

"Well, both, but the one I'm most concerned about is the red one, Abo."

"Really? I find her most intelligent—and astoundingly beautiful in the bargain. What's not to like?"

"Well, that's just it. I'm not quite sure. I can't put my finger on it, but there's something about the way she listened to my plan."

"Really? She seemed rapt by your every word."

Bookins snorted. "And how would you know? You were sound asleep and snoring the whole time."

Braque shrugged. "A king needs his rest."

"Aye, but you're no longer king."

"A lord then. A lord needs his rest, perhaps even more than a king."

"At any rate, she was not rapt, which is what I truly hoped for, some sign that she agreed with my various stratagems."

"And?"

"And nothing. She seemed bored and disinterested the whole time. Like she was putting up with the insane ramblings of a toddler."

Braque scoffed. "Oh, I doubt that, I really do. You have obviously read too much into her reactions. She is a god, after all, and not subject, I think, to normal human reactions."

Bookins shook his head. "That's ridiculous. No, she barely listened."

"And what if that's true? What harm?"

Bookins puffed out his cheeks. Braque just didn't get it. "If she is to help us with our plan, shouldn't she at least have the courtesy to *listen* to the plan?"

Braque waved his hand. "No, no, you think too much. You always have. Listen, all I know is that she's here to help us. Just think of it. We have a god behind us now. How can that not help our plan?"

Bookins threw up his hands in frustration. "I don't know, which is why I was pacing. Do you think she has her own plan? One that might not fit our own?"

Braque looked puzzled. "Her own plan? No, of course not. If she had her own plan, why would she even take the time to listen to yours?" His eyes went wide. "Oh!"

"Exactly. And I tell you, she *wasn't* listening. That whole thing about explaining the six kinds of mud to her—just a damned ruse to make me think she was all-in on the plan."

"Well, what now?"

Bookins pressed himself up from the bed and began pacing again. "That's just the thing. I don't know."

"By the gods, Bookins. Can you not think without pacing?"

Bookins didn't answer. He was distracted by a sound coming from the docks.

48

In the dream, Rhynt sat at the head of the conference table, trying to make sense of the strangers who sat facing her. She recognized the Red God right away, the only other woman at the table, but the others, all men, were unknown to her. Each wore different-colored shrouds: white, green, blue, black, red, and gray.

They just stared at her, saying nothing, their faces expressionless.

These must be the gods, she thought: Abo, Porto, Canto, Bedo, Indo, and Dado. Why are they all here? There should be but one god present, Abo, the god who would help them defeat the Mystrosians.

A sound made her turn to the right. Bookins and Lord Braque were at the battle map, Bookins speaking a language unknown to her as Braque shook his head and kept repeating, "No, no, no."

The door behind her slammed open, forcing Rhynt to turn around and leap to her feet. She grabbed for her sword, but had neither sword nor dagger nor any clothing at all. "What the—"

"My queen, my queen," shouted her three handmaidens in unison. "We bring clothing—and news."

They swirled around her, each holding a beautiful gown. She held out her hand, which seemed not to be her hand, but a hand of someone—something—other. She clenched her fist and the maidens froze in place.

"Well played," said a voice behind her.

She turned, and as she did, she noticed that she was in her fine green armor again, a sword held high, ready to strike. But she lowered the sword when she saw Orthor dancing in the center of the table, with Whelan at his side, playing the lute.

"What's past is future," Whelan sang. "What's future is past, till you come to the present, alas and at last. Turn to the left, turn to the right, the future has come to you this night." Whelan strummed his lute one last time and then dropped it to the table. "We are done here."

Orthor stopped his jig and walked quickly down the table to hover over Rhynt. "A rune and a tune; that is all you need know."

She started to say something, but the sound of a horn startled her.

She awoke with a start. Someone was blowing a battle horn. She pulled off her covers and raced as well as she could without her artificial leg to a window to see what the commotion was about. The docks were crowded with people. No, not people.

"Trolls!"

49

Bookins shuffled along toward the docks as quickly as he could, which was slow by any measure. Halfway there, Queen Rhynt raced by him with her hill tigers, who only stopped briefly to sniff at him before catching up with their queen.

Most of the trolls were in the water, swimming away, but he could see Bebo standing with his arms crossed, shouting something at the queen. A strong wind was carrying the words away.

By the time Bookins got there, Bebo was already a hundred yards at sea, swimming in the direction of Paudia.

"What happened?" he said to Rhynt.

"He's gone, they're gone."

"Did he say anything?"

She turned away from him, motioned her tigers to follow, and walked away, forcing Bookins to follow as best he could.

"What did he say?" he said, trying again.

Rhynt stopped and turned. "He said, 'No fight, no stay.'"

"Did you offer him a joke?"

She rolled her eyes. "Of course I did. He said, 'No jokes, not now.'"

Bookins stopped in his tracks as Rhynt began walking away. He turned back to the dock and watched Bebo and the other trolls swim away.

Rhynt took a few more strides, then stopped to watch the trolls as well. They had lost a valuable weapon in the trolls, all because of the decision to delay. She could see Bookins on the dock, waving goodbye to them. *Why was he smiling?*

She walked back to him, annoyed. "Why are you smiling? Is this funny to you?"

Bookins continued smiling. "No, you see, I was just thinking of the troll joke I was going to use to stop them, but . . ." He pointed at his legs. "These things weren't fast enough."

Rhynt stared at him, not sure whether to chastise him further. He couldn't help being old. Still, that smile angered her. They were losing an important weapon, one the Mystrosians didn't have.

She sighed. "All right, I'll let your smile go, but the loss is incalculable."

Bookins nodded. "I for one would not like to face them in battle."

They both looked out to sea. The trolls were no longer in sight.

"Or challenge them in swimming," said Rhynt. "How did they disappear so quickly?"

Bookins had nothing more to offer than, "They are strong swimmers."

Rhynt grabbed him by the arm. "Come, we must reconsider your plan—our plan—but first I would know how you came to know troll jokes."

Bookins smiled, then realizing what he had done, wiped it from his face. "I am a fool first and foremost, Majesty. Jokes of all kinds are part of my trade. I need only go to the fine library here and select among half a dozen scrolls and books on the subject."

"Really? You must show me this library. Is it not where Orthor worked before I sent him to Randall's Cave?"

"It is, indeed."

"Good, I would like to go soon, perhaps after we've discussed changes to the plan."

Bookins nodded and almost smiled. "I would like that very much, Majesty. The loss seems great, but there are always other options."

They grew silent as they walked back toward the castle. Then Rhynt broke the silence. "So tell me, what was the joke you were going to tell Bebo?"

Bookins felt safe enough now to smile, and did. "It is called *The Troll and the Seven Molfrumps*. Perhaps you've heard of it, Majesty."

Rhynt was about to answer, but she was distracted by a change in the light, as if a dark cloud had passed over all of Enturia. She looked up and her eyes grew wide. The sky was filled with arrows arcing across the sky and descending on them.

She grabbed Bookins by the arm and started dragging him toward the castle. "Run!"

Bookins' legs, long restricted to a slow shuffle, suddenly remembered the concept of running. He ran ahead, faster even than the tigers. "Faster, Majesty, faster!"

Part IV

"Oh, I see the look in your eyes. You have been waiting patiently for a pitched battle and now, when it finally arrives, I have stopped to sip my tea instead of pressing on with the death and dismemberment, the blood, the gore, the bold shouts of victory and the ever-present shrieks of pain and death.

"Abide, young man, the story will play out and you will have your fill of battle. I stop because the sky filled with arrows reminds me that a god disobeyed my instructions. I was still at sea, after all, disguised as a mere minstrel and still facing a full day's voyage to Enturia. I knew what was going on—I know everything most of the time—but I could do nothing about it without exposing myself as Randall, which I did not want to do just yet.

"So, to say that I was angry and frustrated would be an understatement. The question I struggled with was which god or gods betrayed me? The arrows were white, so it would have been easy to blame Porto, but Abo is crafty enough to unleash arrows on the people she is protecting. To get them to end the delay and get on with the war.

"And what about the others—Canto, Bedo, Dado, and Indo? Would they dare disobey? Perhaps, perhaps they would. So you see my problem. I was at sea, arrows were raining down on the Enturians, and my plan appeared to be unraveling even before it could begin. I was at the mercy of humans, you see, and that is always a problem. What would the Enturians do? What would the Mystrosians do? And how would I respond?

"Yes, yes, let's get back to the story and those raining arrows—but from a different perspective, one that will prove to be important in the scheme of things."

50

Zyrx moved away from the forge and wiped his brow. He had been within the Tower of Synt, the elves' realm, for five tower-years, which was the equivalent to just fifty hours in the world outside the tower. Still, fifty hours was a long time when a battle could break out any minute.

He had made the most of his tower-years, expanding the number of forges to a hundred. Thousands upon thousands of swords, daggers, lances, pikes, shields, and all manner of custom armor were being produced around the clock. Each tower-day at dawn, Zyrx and his workers would open the tower door and deliver the results of their labors. To the tower workers, their efforts had taken twenty-four hours, but to the stunned warriors outside only two Enturian minutes had passed.

And with the armor came more and more new recruits who had come of age every ten hours of Enturian time. The pace of production of both weapons and warriors was breathtaking, particularly to Blusk and Phendour, who had come within the tower just two Enturian days before to help train the young lads and lasses, an effort that had already stretched to nearly five tower-years.

Zyrx turned his attention to the fields surrounding the forges. He could see Blusk and Phendour conducting drills on weapons use and battle tactics to hundreds of new recruits. It was exhausting work for all of them, their only reward a few stolen tower-minutes for meals and a late-night gathering to review the tower-day and wonder what was happening on the outside. All had hopes that their efforts would make a difference, but all shared a common dread of what might be transpiring without them.

They had to remind themselves that time moved more slowly outside—a month's work inside was no more than an hour outside—but their anxiety was high nonetheless.

Zyrx wiped his brow once more and stood. He wondered whether he should wave Blusk and Phendour over for a short break in the shade. He kept a supply of mead handy for such occasions, which were rare but always welcome.

As he raised his arm to summon them, a rapping sound came from the sky above.

"What the—" he said, looking up. "What manner of magic is this?"

The sound continued, each rap seconds apart. He looked over at Blusk and Phendour. They and their recruits were also looking up, as were his blacksmiths, the pings of hammers on merilium falling silent as everyone looked at the sky.

Zyrx motioned Blusk and Phendour over and they were quickly at his side.

"What do you make of this?" he said.

"It doesn't sound natural," said Phendour.

"No," said Blusk.

Zyrx shook his head. "I do not like this."

"Aye," said Blusk. "Something is happening *outside.*"

Phendour's eyes went wide. "Listen to it, the interval between knocks," she said.

Zyrx and Blusk stared back at her, trying to understand.

"The time," she said, "the time. What we're hearing is happening much faster on the outside. It's almost like . . ."

"What?" said Zyrx.

"By the gods!" she said. "It's arrows, a volley of arrows. Thousands of them."

Zyrx and Blusk opened their mouths but said nothing.

Phendour had already turned and was running toward the tower door. She called back to them. "Come, come, we are needed—*now!*"

Blusk ran after her, but Zyrx ran back toward his forge. "Go," he shouted after them. "I will join you in a moment. There is something I must bring."

Blusk and Phendour did not reply, but continued running, the sound of the arrows growing louder, thunderous.

51

Bookins, Rhynt, and her hill tigers took cover in a portico near the front gate to the castle grounds, the arrows arriving a second later, covering the ground.

Rhynt peered back at the docks. The wave of arrows had stopped there, leaving the ground covered in arrows—and bodies. She tried to count the number of bodies, but stopped at twenty. There were just too many. "What do you think?" she said, turning to Bookins.

Bookins, hunched over, hands on knees, tried his best to answer, but his lungs were still having trouble taking in air. "Majesty, I think," he said. "I think . . ."

"Yes, what? How many do you think?"

He gathered himself and looked out at the carnage, shaking his head as he scanned the scene. "A hundred, maybe more. We'll have to wait until the arrows stop."

As if on signal, the last arrow fell just a few feet away from them. Then came the moans and screams of the wounded and dying.

Bookins stared at it. "White. The work of their god, or perhaps even their monk."

Rhynt shook her head in disbelief. "But there was to be a delay. What happened?"

Bookins shrugged. "Dunno. A mistake, perhaps. Or part of their plan all along. It's not important in any case."

"Not important?"

"In the scheme of things, I mean. We can go forward with our plan."

"But we need to wait for the others—Whelan, Calax, and the Red Monk."

"No," said Bookins, shaking his head. "The first part of the plan is a ruse, a feint, a distraction. We can handle that without them. And if I'm keeping track of time properly, the others will be here on the morning tide."

Rhynt nodded. "Very well, let us proceed."

Bookins looked out at the carnage. "But first we need to tend to the wounded."

"Aye," said Rhynt, turning to her tigers. "Mela, Mila, Spook, to me."

The tigers seemed hesitant at first, but with Rhynt's coaxing, stepped out of the portico and began moving among the wounded, roaring when they came upon each living person.

Rhynt and Bookins followed, shouting instructions to the warriors arriving to help.

Rhynt grabbed one of the warriors by the arm. "Go to the castle. Have them prepare every available space—halls, bedrooms—for the wounded." The man nodded and ran off.

Rhynt surveyed the scene. It was as Bookins had said. About a hundred dead and twice that wounded. The docks and all the fishing boats in the harbor had sprouted arrows, as had the Tower of Synt, which now looked like a white-flowered tree.

As she watched, the door to the tower opened and three small figures emerged, each increasing in size immediately.

Rhynt shouted over to Bookins, who was helping a young wounded boy stand. "Look, the tower."

Bookins turned, then shouted back at the queen. "It's Phendour and Blusk and Zyrx."

She was never happier to see them, but could only briefly wave in their direction before returning to the wounded. A fisherman was crawling in her direction, three arrows in his back.

"Spook," she cried. "Here, now."

The man stopped crawling and slumped to the ground.

52

The White Monk saw it happening, but didn't believe it was happening. There were no archers and no men, and yet thousands upon thousands of arrows were appearing out of nowhere and then streaking westward toward the Enturian castle, which was miles and miles away. He turned to the White God in disbelief. "You've started the war?"

The White God shrugged. "Well, somebody had to. It might as well have been me."

"But what about this important delay of yours?"

The White God tried not to look concerned. He knew that Randall would be upset with him. But he also knew that Randall was on a ship still almost a day's voyage from Enturia. Better to act now and apologize later. "A ruse. I sensed they'd follow our lead and stand down for a time. And it worked. The arrows even now are falling on warriors out in the open, many without shields or armor. In fact, if I had launched the arrows a second earlier, I would have caught the queen and that damned fool of hers out in the open as well."

The White Monk puffed out his cheeks and sighed. "So what now? Won't the Red God respond with a surprise of her own?"

The White God wasn't sure. Was his defiance enough to break her from her vow to Randall? Would she risk his wrath or would she continue to delay, knowing that Randall would focus his displeasure in full measure on him, the White God. "She could, but I don't think so. No, she will bide her time and wait for our next attack to unfold. She is more a reactive god than a proactive god."

"And our next step?"

The White God considered the question. Their forces were arrayed in six columns, each heading toward the Enturian castle from different directions. Should they all strike at once? Should they attack on the flanks in a pincer movement? Should the six columns now combine into one overwhelming force? Should they stick with the original plan, to lay siege to the castle and starve them out?

The White God looked over at the siege engines stuck in the mud. The longer they delayed, the stronger the Enturian position would be. And it would take weeks to move the siege engines through this infernal mud and into position. No, siege was not a good option. They must win, quickly and decisively if at all possible. "Our next step is to prepare for battle. And we must do that quickly. Send word to each column to march, and march now."

The White Monk shook his head. "But it will take weeks to get there with all this mud."

"Not if we leave the siege engines behind."

The White Monk was stunned. "But our plan was to—"

"Yes, I know, lay siege. But this mud has changed that plan. Leave them behind. If our new plan doesn't work—and I assure you *it will*—we can always come back for them."

The White Monk looked at the siege engines and nodded. "The men and the oxen will be relieved. Oh, what about them, the oxen?"

The White God shrugged. "Take them or leave them, I do not care which."

"No, I think we'll leave them. Taking them would slow us down, and besides, they aren't good eating."

"Then send your orders, monk."

The monk started to move away but quickly stopped. "What about the king?"

The god shrugged. "Inform him, if you wish, but *after* you set the columns in motion. We must not delay."

"Very well," said the monk, moving quickly away.

The god watched the monk spreading the word to his commanders and troops. The camp soon came alive. Some men doused fires. Others struck tents and saddled horses. All took up weapons and donned their armor.

The god could only smile. *Randall may be upset now*, he thought, *but wait till he sees what I can do. Yes, I've changed the plan, but the outcome will be the same. Enturia will be theirs, perhaps even before Randall sets foot in Enturia on tomorrow's tide.*

53

Marthe pushed back from the table. The meal had gone well as far as he was concerned. Good food, little talking, and fast. "Gentlemen," he said, tipping an imaginary hat. "There be plenty left in the pot, so take your time. I must see to the sails and the men. They are sore tired but need to keep at it if we're to make the shore by daybreak."

Whelan looked nervous. "Do you foresee any problems, captain?"

Marthe chuckled. "All you need worry about is being blinded by the rising sun in port, for we'll be there, perhaps even in the darkness. Now, unless there be other questions, I must see to my business."

He looked at them and all were shaking their heads. "No, then? Good." He turned to leave and then stopped. "Oh, while I was waiting for you to return from your business at Randall's Cave, I came into possession of a fine Paudian Port. I'll have the cook bring it in for all to enjoy." He nodded again and left the cabin, the door slamming shut behind him from a strong wind coming out of the west.

"By the gods," said Calax. "I have never seen or heard such winds. It is like a monster or some god is pushing us faster and faster toward Enturia."

The Red Monk chuckled. "I could do such things when I was younger, but not now. Yes, I can make wind—two ways—as you well know, but not like this wind."

"Aye," said Whelan. "Aging reminds us of what we once were—and will never be again."

The Red Monk shrugged. "Oh, I do not mind the aging or even the diminution of my powers, such as they are, such as they *were.* No, what I mind is these creaking bones of mine and the chills that come in the night. I awaken stiff as a plank."

Calax shook his head. "I begin to feel that as well. I am no longer the young warrior I once was. My strength remains, but my movements grow slower."

The Red Monk chuckled. "There seems to be no magic to fight the passage of time, Calax."

"Unless you're a god, of course," said Whelan. "I have heard and sung many a song that talked of such powers. Becoming young again, regaining strength. Such things are often granted by the gods."

"Yes," said the Red Monk, "but there's always a catch. Something the recipient must do in return."

"Oh, yes," said Whelan, "there's always a bargain involved, and the god always gets the best part of any deal. It's just the way they work."

Calax perked up when he saw the cook coming in with a tray of port and glasses. "Ah, welcome fine sir. We eagerly await this wine of yours."

The cook set the tray down, hard, in the center of the table, the bottle and the glasses jumping from the force. "Here it be, then. Have your fill." He turned and left.

Calax smiled, then let out a big laugh. "He seems a fine fellow, that one."

"He does," said Whelan, "but I much prefer his fine wine." He reached for the bottle and began pouring wine into each glass. "There is a song about Paudia. I think by the second glass I shall remember the tune and the words, but for now, a toast to this fine ship and its fine captain. Gentlemen, Enturia awaits our return."

They raised their glasses and clinked them together with each toast.

"To Marthe," said Whelan.

"And the good ship Marthe as well," said Calax.

"And to my creaking bones," said the Red Monk. "May the wine dull the pain."

"And to the wind in the sails," said Whelan. "Long may it gust, and with gusto."

Calax laughed. "And to our new friend, Orthor. May he solve the riddle of the runes."

"And learn to enjoy cave rats," said the Red Monk.

Whelan laughed along with them, but not with the same spirit. It was his turn to toast, but he set down his glass and motioned for Calax to continue.

Calax took the cue. "And to our arrival in Enturia. May we find it still there and our friends still fighting."

Whelan paused a moment, then raised his glass high. "And finally to the gods. May they protect us all."

"To the gods," they all said, with a toast and a clink and a final laugh.

The good ship Marthe sailed on, the wind howling.

54

The night had been long and sleepless for Queen Rhynt, but not for her hill tigers; they slept and snored as if nothing was going on. Finally, just before dawn, she gave up entirely on the idea of sleep and donned her leg and her armor. It had been built to be strong yet light, but it now felt like she was carrying another person on her back.

She peeked up at the high windows in her bedchamber. Still dark; she would no doubt be the first to arrive in the conference chamber.

"Mela, Mila, Spook, with me." The tigers continued to snore.

She clapped her hands with the call of each name. "Mila! Mela! Spook!"

The tigers slowly opened their eyes and looked around.

"Come on, you can go back to sleep when we reach the conference chamber. And I'll have food brought in for you."

The tigers knew the word food and were quickly on their feet and eagerly following her down the hall.

The walk to the chamber was sobering. The hallways were lined with temporary beds, each occupied by a wounded warrior.

Rhynt spotted a bone doctor and walked up to him. "How goes it?"

The doctor didn't recognize her at first, ignoring her entirely until she spoke again. "Sir, I would have an answer. How are the wounded? How many have we lost?"

When he finally recognized her, he startled at the sight of her and even more at the sight of the tigers. He bowed again and again. "Oh, Majesty. Sorry, your Majesty. I was distracted by the wounded, as you can see." He waved his arm to take in all the wounded in the long hallway. "Every hallway is much the same."

She sighed. "Do you know how many, sir?"

The doctor shook his head. "Many. Scores and scores."

She thanked the doctor and continued her walk to the conference chamber. At the end of the hallway, she descended the long flight of stairs Bookins always complained about. They seemed easy enough and despite the somber spectacle unfolding before her, she skipped down them, her tigers trying their best to keep up.

At the bottom of the stairs there was another long hallway, and it too was filled on either side with the beds of the wounded and dying. Here, however, the bone doctors recognized her immediately, all stopping their duties to bow as she passed. She nodded at each and encouraged them to return to their duties. "Pay no mind to me, gentlemen, attend your patients."

The hallway took a sharp turn to the right, the final turn she'd make to get to the chamber. As she made the turn, she could see two guards blocking the entrance, along with three of her handmaidens, each girl holding a tray of food. They startled at her approach.

"Oh, Majesty, you are early," said one of the handmaidens. "We have not yet set up."

"No matter," said Rhynt. "I have much to think about, so I will not get in your way." She looked at the trays. "There should be a tray of meat for the tigers."

The handmaiden looked flustered. "Oh, oh yes. We will get that right away." She set down her tray on the floor and scurried away.

Rhynt turned to the guards. "The door, if you please."

One of the guards nodded and quickly opened the door. "Yes, Majesty. And may I ask who I should admit and who bar?"

"Indeed," said Rhynt. "Admit Baron Bookins, Lord Braque, and the Red God. No others."

"Yes, Majesty."

"Oh," she said, "but when Calax Halfhand, Whelan the Wanderer, and the Red Monk arrive—*if* they arrive—please show them in immediately."

She looked at the trays and then at the two remaining handmaidens. "We will need more food, ladies, enough for seven and a little more than that. Bookins is a nibbler and eats more than the others."

The handmaidens looked at their trays and then back at the queen. "Yes, Majesty. These are but the first few trays. Others are being prepared even as we speak."

"Good, then," said Rhynt. She glanced at the trays again. "Will there be scones? With Dashan berries and molfrump butter?"

The handmaidens looked back and forth at one another, each wondering who would speak. Finally, one of them said, "I think the menu called for butter spins and acorn twists, Majesty."

Rhynt frowned. "Oh, I find them far too sweet."

The other handmaiden chimed in. "I will ask the chef to make the scones, Majesty."

Rhynt brightened. "Good, this will be a long meeting, I fear, so keep the scones and the other food coming."

The handmaidens curtsied as best they could while holding the large trays. "Yes, Majesty. We will just set our trays inside and then head back to the kitchens."

Rhynt nodded and followed them and the guards into the room, which was dark and cold. "Someone get the fire going, and see to the torches. We have a war to win, and heat and light can only help."

As the guards busied themselves with the torches and the fire, the handmaidens set their trays down on a side table and raced away. "We will be back with scones, Majesty."

She didn't answer, but turned instead to the battle map on the wall, which was barely visible in the darkness. "I hope you will shed some light on this plan, Bookins."

She pulled out her chair at the head of the long table, and sat down. Mela, Mila, and Spook were already curled up next to the fireplace, watching the guard fumbling with the kindling. He seemed nervous being so close to the tigers.

"Um," he said, "I'll have this roaring in just a moment, Majesty."

"Good," said Rhynt. "And keep it so. We will need all the roaring we can manage."

She looked back at the map and then at the door. "Where are you, Bookins?"

55

Bookins had seen his former king, King Braque, made speechless only once in his long life as king's fool. He was only twenty-three at the time and unsure of himself. The king, too, was only a few years older, and just as wet behind the ears. Bookins had recruited a band of itinerant players to entertain the king with juggling and acrobatics. He himself was an expert juggler, but the king wanted to see teams of jugglers.

To increase the excitement, Bookins had set up a makeshift stage, complete with draw-back curtains that would hide the players until the performance began. Unfortunately, when the curtains were drawn back to reveal the players, the players—men and women alike—were completely naked.

Bookins could still see the king sputtering, unable to form words, his face growing red from embarrassment and anger. And now he saw that same face again, though diminished in intensity by age and infirmness.

"You did *what?*" said Lord Braque, each word coming out separately and forced into being, the very last word coming out as a growl.

Bookins reflexively cowered. Braque may have just been a lord now, but he was still king to Bookins. "I know, I know, but I had to."

Braque rolled his eyes and roared, "Had too?"

Bookins sighed and threw up his hands in frustration. "I really had no choice. There are gelas everywhere, and I'm not sure the Red God is even on our side. All will be well, I'm sure, but for now, I have to keep my latest gambit secret."

Lord Braque let out an equally heavy sigh. "But you would hide this even from the queen?"

"In the meeting, yes, but I will pull her aside afterwards. She will see the wisdom in it, I'm sure."

"Wisdom? I'm not so sure about that. Keeping this secret will only undermine the trust you've established in that room. It will be gone once your so-called gambit begins—even if it works."

Bookins nodded. "I know that, but . . ."

"But you're going to do it anyway."

"Yes, yes I am."

Lord Braque looked up at the high windows of their shared room, where Bookins' pigeons were cooing. "Morning breaks. We must wend our way to the conference room and somehow pull off this dissembling you've forced on us."

Bookins glanced up at the windows as well. "Aye, the sky brightens."

"I wish my mood would."

Bookins nodded. "Don't worry, all will be well. This will work. It *must.*"

Braque stood slowly, pushing himself up from the bed. "By the gods, these knees of mine."

Bookins chuckled but then grunted as he stood. "And mine. We crumble, Majesty."

Braque growled at him. "Don't call me *Majesty.* I am *Lord* Braque now, lower even in stature and office than you, *Baron* Bookins."

Bookins winced at the word *Baron.* "I guess I deserve that. Come, we have many steps ahead of us—or at least I do. Where's that confounded rolling chair of yours?" He turned in a circle, finally spotting the chair. "Ah, there you are."

Braque whispered to himself. "By the gods."

56

Queen Rhynt sat in silence alone at the long conference table, waiting for the others to arrive. She laced her fingers together, then unlaced them, then laced them back. The sound of a young girl clearing her throat caught Rhynt's attention.

The girl, one of Rhynt's recently recruited handmaidens, stood near a side table laden with food. She looked away when the queen turned toward her, not wanting to disturb her queen.

"You seem to have a tickle in your throat," said Rhynt.

Rhynt could see the girl blush even from so far away. The conference room was huge. Its table seemed to be in another country, far removed from the food and the girl. Rhynt decided to take a different tack. "Have the scones arrived?"

The girl perked up. "Yes, Majesty." Her voice was high-pitched and came out almost like a whisper.

"Well, then . . ."

"Oh, oh," she said, reaching for the plate of scones. She scurried toward the queen, almost running. "Yes, Majesty, and they smell wonderful."

She stopped just short of the queen and laid the plate down with a clatter, the plate finally wobbling into place. "Oops," she said.

Rhynt laughed. "Thank you for that. I needed a good laugh right about now."

The girl nodded, not knowing what to do next. She started to retreat, then thought better of it, then thought better of thinking better of it.

"Stay," said Rhynt. "Please, sit down."

The girl shook her head. "Oh, no, Majesty, I mustn't."

Rhynt sighed. "Just days ago I was a servant just like you. You are a peer in my eyes. Come, I would talk to you—and share my scones."

The girl's eyes went wide. She looked at the queen as if Rhynt had lost her mind, and at the scones as if they were poison. "Oh, Majesty," she said, shaking her head and slowly backing away.

Rhynt had had enough. She slapped her hand down hard on the table, bouncing the plate of scones. "Sit!"

The girl quickly complied, pulling out a chair next to the queen and sitting down, her eyes fixed on the surface of the table.

"Look at me," said Rhynt.

The girl slowly raised her head, her large violet eyes darting around the room, as if she had never seen it from this perspective, in a chair beside the queen. She was about the same age as Rhynt, but frail and thin, with long black hair that made her already pale skin looked paler. Her face was round as the moon and her features flat. Her nose was barely a nose. More a little two-nostril bump. "Yes, Majesty." Her nose twitched to the left when she spoke, and she ended each sentence with a little puff of a sigh, as if the sentence had exhausted her.

Rhynt huffed out a breath of her own. "Please, stop with this *majesty* business. Henceforth, you and I will speak as friends."

"But—"

Rhynt held up a finger, silencing her. "Enough. We are friends now. My name is Rhynt, a former pisspot for the Red Monk. I know you are a handmaiden, but what's your name?"

The girl blinked. "Um, I too was a pisspot, but not for a royal. Just my aging father. When you became queen, there was a call for young handmaidens, so . . . here I am."

"And you are?"

"Pricilla."

"A nice name. Should I call you that, then?"

The girl nodded, then shook her head. "I'm known around the castle as Pricilla, but my friends call me Priss."

Rhynt smiled. "Priss it is, then."

Priss nodded. "Yes, um . . ."

Rhynt laughed. "Not *majesty*. When we're alone, we're Rhynt and Priss."

"Very well."

"So, Priss, tell me about your typical day. When do you arise, who gives you orders, what do you like and dislike about your job, and so on?"

Priss started to answer, but the sound of loud laughter coming from just outside the conference room door made her leap to her feet and return to her position by the side table.

Rhynt was about to motion her back, but the door swung open and the laughter, now even louder, burst into the room along with the laughers: The Red God, Bookins, Lord Braque, and the biggest surprise: Whelan, the Red Monk, Calax, Zyrx, Phendour, and Blusk.

Rhynt leaped to her feet and raced into the arms of Calax, who was taken aback by her hug. "Majesty?"

She gave him another quick hug, then turned and hugged Zyrx, Phendour, and Blusk in turn. "I am so happy to see you all. Come, have some food, find a place at the table. We have so much to discuss this day."

57

King Merek the Mighty crossed his arms for the third time and set his face in a scowl. "The answer remains no, and will stay no. So go, go, all of you."

The White Monk and the White God had tried every trick and ploy to coax the king to follow them into battle against the Enturians, but he was determined to remain behind with the siege engines and his concubines.

The White God had already given up. "If you do not wish to go, so be it. We will report back as soon as we have victory in our grasp."

But the White Monk had not; he was seething—and determined enough to try one last time. "Majesty," he said, trying his best to control his anger, "the men will want you there, to lead them, to challenge them, to lead them to victory." He glanced over at the concubines, who lay on soft pillows at the rear of the tent. "Why, even your concubines wish this, Majesty."

Merek seemed taken aback. "What?"

"Your concubines, Majesty. Imagine their ardor when they see you return from battle victorious."

Merek glanced at his concubines, then turned back to the White Monk. "Do you think?"

"Oh, I do, Majesty. Their passion will be unparalleled."

The king smiled, then shook his head. "No, I see what you are doing, d'Porto, and it won't work. I'd much rather be spending the next days here with them than traveling these sucking-mud roads—if you can even call them roads."

"But Majesty—"

"No, I have made my decision. You can go. Lead the army with your god and leave me be. If you win, fine. If you don't, fine. Frankly, I don't even know why we're here. The only thing they have to capture is mud. No fine wines like Alamaria. No gold, no gems—nothing but muck and mud."

The monk puffed out his cheeks, turned to the White God, and shook his head. "We will go, then. I will leave a small contingent of warriors to protect you in our absence."

The king shrugged. "Go, and take them all. I have a sea of mud to protect me. All I require is a few of my Royal Guards and a retinue of servants to tend me and my harem."

The monk nodded and bowed as he backed his way out of the tent with the White God, who bowed to no one.

"This is good," said the White God. "He would have just slowed us down."

The monk nodded agreement. "You are right, but still, I meant what I said about his presence. Having your king at your side means something."

The god chuckled. "You make too much of this—and him. He is a fool, and each and every one of your warriors knows this."

"We shall see." He looked around the camp. Everyone was on the move and seemed happy about it. But d'Porto still had his doubts. "We shall see." He took a step forward and was suddenly knee-deep in mud.

The White God chuckled. "Of course, the king *does* have a point."

58

Priss stood quietly by the sideboard as each of the attendees walked by picking up pastries and scones and fruit and tea before moving to the conference table and sitting down. She tried not to watch their faces, but it was difficult. Every emotion seemed to be on display.

The Red God, who was beautiful beyond Priss's understanding, seemed bored and dismissive of the others; she passed by the pastries and scones, sneering at them, and picked up only a cup of warm tea. Priss wondered whether a god had to watch her figure.

Bookins came next and gave her a nod and a smile as he loaded a plate with pastries; he seemed nervous but ready. Lord Braque, on the other hand, looked sad, as if he had suffered some form of defeat; he waved off everything, including the tea.

Whelan was just the opposite; he wore a broad smile on his face and hummed to himself as he picked up the largest scone on the tray and took a big bite, crumbs falling to the floor.

Next came the Red Monk, who looked tired and weary from his recent journey; he barely looked at the food, but kept his eyes on his god, fascinated by her every move and trying his best to parse her out.

Calax had a hand in the middle of the monk's back, coaxing him forward so he could fill his plate with everything; save for his armor, he looked like an ordinary man and certainly not the image she had created in her mind about the hero of the Battle of Whent Hill.

Then came Zyrx, the dwarf, a man said to work magic with metal; his face was red and sweat beaded on his forehead. He seemed happy enough, at least to Priss. She tried her best not to smile when he passed by. She had heard tales of his anger and wasn't about to have that anger directed at her.

Blusk and Phendour moved down the table as one, each whispering to the other, both ignoring all but the cups of tea. Blusk was the very image of a warrior, thick and strong, and Priss thought Phendour even more beautiful than the Red God. Her skills with a bow were the stuff of legend. If Priss had had her druthers, she would have gladly picked up a bow to serve beside Phendour.

Priss watched Blusk and Phendour join the others at the table. As soon as they sat down, the queen nodded in her direction, indicating that she should now leave. These discussions were not for her.

Priss nodded back and walked slowly toward the door. She didn't want to leave. There was talk around the castle of a new plan by Baron Bookins. She would have given anything to hear it. But perhaps that was the point of Rhynt's insistence that she leave immediately upon the serving and seating of her advisors.

She turned back to look at the table. Everyone was watching her go, eager to begin. She picked up her pace, opened the door, and stepped outside the room. She could hear the queen begin, her voice firm and strong.

"Thank you for coming. We have much to discuss." There was a pause and then, "Bookins, you have the floor and our rapt attention."

She wanted to stay there with an ear pressed up against the door, but the guards had other ideas. "Move along now, miss. This meeting be not for you."

She gave the guard a weak smile and moved away. Rhynt had told her to meet her in the queen's chambers at midday. Perhaps she would share the plan.

At any rate, it felt good to have a new friend, and a queen at that. She smiled to herself and scurried down the hallway.

59

Queen Rhynt watched Priss walk from the room and wondered what her new friend was thinking. She seemed reluctant to leave, but staying was out of the question. She had no need to know.

As the door clicked shut behind Priss, Rhynt turned back to face the others. "Thank you for coming. We have much to discuss." She paused and looked at Bookins, who seemed distracted and nervous. "Bookins, you have the floor and our rapt attention."

Bookins nodded and pushed himself up from his chair. "Thank you, majesty." He turned to the others at the table. "Our queen is right; we have much to discuss."

He walked over to the battle map and pointed to the eastern shore of Enturia. "Yesterday, they were here, just landing and disembarking with their men and siege engines." He pointed farther inland, a few miles closer to the castle. "And now they are here and here and here and here and here and here, six columns, each over a thousand strong, moving through the lands we so aptly call *The Muds*, at forced march in our direction."

The statement made some at the table gasp and others to turn to the person next to them and whisper: *I told you so; we are lost; this plan better be good; this scone isn't half bad.*

Bookins cleared his throat loudly to get their attention. "It is as I foresaw and as I have accordingly planned." He suddenly stopped and walked back to the map, pointing once again at the eastern shore. "I almost forgot. There is a seventh column here, just yards off the shore, and going nowhere. It comprises their siege engines, about twenty members of the Royal Guard, and King Merek the Mighty himself."

Rhynt could not contain herself. "The king? Their siege engines? How do you know this, and more to the point, does your plan account for this new development?"

Bookins smiled and nodded at Abo. "Our new friend, the Red God, provided the gelas."

The Red God rose from her chair. "Not just gelas, Bookins, but gelas that even now go undetected by the White Monk and his impulsive god." She sat back down, waving a hand for Bookins to continue.

"As for the new development," said Bookins, "yes, my plan has always taken this as a possibility. The fact is, the king is irrelevant wherever he is. Having said that, we must still consider his role in the battle. If he had led his troops, their arrival would take many, many days. He has no martial skills, and he is like an anchor on the progress of his warriors. He has demands. He must rest. He must satisfy his concubines. He must bring along all the comforts of home. And so on. The effect on our plan is that we now know that the Mystrosians come in force unhampered by their king, and they come fast."

Rhynt looked worried. "How long before they reach us?"

Bookins waggled his head and looked at the ceiling as if trying to solve a problem in mathematics. "Um, your question has an imprecise answer, which is *it depends*. They move in six columns, each facing different terrain and objects to overcome, the six kinds of mud just being the start of the complexities."

The Red God stood again. "And each column has its own gela to report back its position and progress to the White Monk and that godly imbecile, Porto."

Rhynt nodded. "And what is our response?"

Bookins walked back to the map. His knees were killing him; all this back and forth was taking its toll. He laid his finger on the center of the map, a point almost midway between the eastern shore and the western shore. "My plan, my gambit begins when all six columns reach this point."

Rhynt seemed puzzled. "Why would they arrive at one point? If that were their goal all along, why would they split into six columns in the first place?"

Calax jumped in. "That does seem odd."

Now Phendour was on her feet. "Shouldn't we attack them before they join forces?"

Blusk was quickly at her side. "Aye, we must attack now."

Bookins chuckled and motioned them all to sit back down. "Come now, sit down and I'll explain."

They sat back down, looks of concern on each face. *Does this Bookins really know what he's doing?*

Bookins took a deep breath. "Majesty, Calax, Phendour, Whelan, Zyrx, Blusk, d'Abo, your godliness." He paused to nod at each of them, and then turned back to the map. "You are new to Enturia. Here on the map you see its shape, but very little of its terrain and the challenges it presents to any invading army."

"I can see that," said Rhynt, "but would not their gelas see the terrain and make adjustments accordingly. Surely, they split into six columns for a reason."

Bookins smiled. "They did, Majesty. They hoped to hit us at six angles. Unfortunately, whereas their gelas can see the terrain and what lies ahead for each of their columns, they do not *understand* that terrain and the unique challenges that face them every step of the way."

Calax spoke up. "I don't get it. If they see a clear path before them, why would they be forced back upon one another to form a single force?"

Bookins nodded. "A fair point. Let me give you an example." He walked to the map and pointed toward the north of Enturia. "A column approaches from the north. Their map and their gelas show a clear, unmistakable path to the north walls of this castle. If all goes well, they will be upon us in but a day. Or so they think. But that will not happen. They face natural pits covered in creeping gorse, which not only hides the pits, but serves to trip anyone who walks upon it. And that is just the beginning for the farthest north column." He stopped and looked at Abo, who was smiling and nodding. "Abo, do you remember my discourse on the six types of mud in Enturia?"

She did not. She was barely paying attention. "Yes, of course."

"Their northernmost column faces the third type, which I'm sure you remember is the sticky type. After just a few strides, once you have this mud on you, your ankles will soon stick to each other, making movement of any kind difficult at best."

"Sounds like the perfect time to attack them," said Blusk.

Bookins laughed. "Only if you want to be *glued* to them."

Blusk raised his eyebrows. "Oh, right."

"So," said Bookins. "Each column faces problems with their terrain—pits, mud, tripping gorse, cliffs, mountains, chasms—but wait, for there is certainly more."

"More?" said Rhynt. "And what would that be?"

"Ah, Majesty, Majesty, that would be *beasts.*"

Zyrx suddenly stood up on his chair, so that everyone could see him and hear him. "Bookins, before you talk about these beasts and the challenges faced by the Mystrosians, I think we need to talk about a significant challenge of our own. I had hoped you would begin the meeting with it, but you haven't, so . . ."

"What is it?" said Rhynt.

"The trolls, Majesty, the trolls. They are gone, and we are weaker for it. And majesty, do you know how many hours—nay, months—within the tower it took to fit them with armor and weapons? And do you appreciate what the trolls and those weapons could have done for us in battle?" He rolled his eyes. "It is incalculable."

Rhynt began to respond, but Bookins interrupted her. "Majesty, if I may. You are right, Zyrx. They would have made an imposing force. No question. No question." He paused for a moment. "But the fact is, trolls are unpredictable. And as we've seen, *impatient.* There sudden departure is a mixed blessing. On the one hand, we have lost a powerful force, one that could have given us the edge in the coming battle. But on the other hand, they posed a real threat to the rolling out of the plan. I don't think we could have counted on them except on the first charge. After that, in my opinion, they would have been unpredictable, the last thing you'd ever want in a battle."

Zyrx nodded. "I see your point, and it is a fair one. But still . . ."

"Yes," said Bookins. "And I see yours."

Rhynt looked back and forth between the two. "Thank you for bringing up the trolls, Zyrx. I, too, had wondered about their loss." She turned to Bookins. "Now, then, about those beasts."

60

The beast came every night, forcing Orthor away from the fire and deeper into the cave, where dark shadows hid him. He watched as it walked into the cave, its neck yards long, ending in a snake-like head with a maw of sharp teeth. And yet it wasn't really a snake. Where its neck joined its body, it looked like a wild boar. But unlike the boar, it had flippers for hooves and a tail equally as long as its neck, which ended with a grouping of five long spikes.

It sniffed around the fire every night, sure that there was something to eat, but it never ventured deep into the cave where Orthor hid, along with his pigeons. It was curious. There was nothing to stop the beast but a natural arch covered in runes, and yet, for whatever reason, it never dared walk under it. And Orthor could tell by the way the beast sniffed and sniffed that the beast knew he was there in the shadows.

Orthor had spent hours and hours going through his books and scrolls, searching for the name of the beast and any advice about dealing with it, but his search had been fruitless. There was no mention of any such beast. Some were similar, but all were beasts known only in Enturia.

There was the Mud Spilt, from northern Enturia, which also had a snakelike head, but unlike the beast he was dealing with, the Mud Spilt had seven heads, each connected to a mud-gray neck that emerged from a flat, wide body that had neither legs nor tail. The Mud Spilt burrowed into the mud up to its seven pairs of eyes, waiting for anyone or anything that dared cross its path.

He had found the reference to the Mud Spilt in *Hawkeye's Compendium of Dastardly Beasts*, page 345, with an accompanying woodcut print of the beast, said to have been based on a drawing by

Plastius the Elder more than a thousand years ago. Orthor wondered whether time had improved the beast's demeanor, but he thought not.

He had then turned his attention to the next section in the book, "Beasts of Central Enturia," the most fearsome of which was the Tree Shrike, a winged beast about the size of a wild turkey, black as night and with a long beak filled with row after row of sharp teeth. It was said that three or more shrikes could pick a man clean in a matter of seconds. The population estimate was an astounding 300,000. The only good news about the shrike was that it only hunted at night. Travelers were advised to build their fires high and keep them ablaze throughout the night. The whole idea of the shrike made Orthor shudder.

He had then turned to the next section, "Beasts of the Southern Plains," which was filled with scores upon scores of predators, some as small as molfrumps but all mean and ravenous. There seemed to be no safe place to take a step in the plains of southern Enturia. The smaller beasts didn't interest Orthor all that much. Yes, in numbers, they could strip the flesh from a man equally as fast as the shrike, but such attacks were rare. A single man walking alone through the plains would go unnoticed by these small, subterranean beasts. It would take an army to attract their attention.

He had flipped through these smaller beasts, settling finally on the largest beast in all of Enturia: the Plains Bear, a beast taller than three men standing on each other's shoulders and near as massive as a siege engine. Hawkeye's book documented a plains bear attack on a caravan of pilgrims some four hundred years ago. Of the ninety pilgrims, only one survived—a small boy who had hid himself under one of the bodies. Orthor looked at the bear population figures, did a little math, and estimated that the southern plains of Enturia probably contained more than six thousand such bears, which commonly hunted in family units of five or six, although it was reported that attacks sometimes involved hundreds of bears working in teams. Hawkeye discounted these reports as pure fantasy, however. "When you're under attack, it's hard to count bears," he had said. "More running, less counting."

He had thought to turn to the next section, "Beasts of the Coastal Regions," but had been distracted once more by his work on the runes. He had left the book open near the fire, so he could quickly get back to it when he had finished his studies for the day.

He could see the book now, just behind the nameless beast, who was sniffing in his direction. The beast came closer and closer, but after some minutes, it let loose with one final snort, raised a leg, and pissed on the rune wall. From Orthor's investigations of the runes, it appeared that the beast had a favorite spot to do its nightly business. The runes along that section of the wall were being eroded away by the beast's nightly stream. In just a few more years, Orthor knew those runes would be unreadable, so once he had discovered the beast's terrible habit, he had focused his efforts on that section of the wall. A bit of honeywort applied to his upper lip kept the stench bearable.

As for the runes themselves, they were much like the others, all slashes and dots and curlicues whose combined meanings continued to escape Orthor's grasp. Of note, however, was the way the sun shone on them each morning. The shadows it created transformed each rune with the passing of each second, making each appear to be more than one rune, or a series of runes, if you will, as if each rune formed a sentence on its own.

Orthor had already filled seven scrolls, just on this sunlight phenomenon. It added so much complexity to his task that he wondered whether one lifetime would be enough to solve the riddle.

A sound from a dark corner of the cave caught his attention. His rat trap had done its job once more. He would have a fine rat stew this day composed of six rats, a chopped wazeele root, and a handful of green tree lichens. On some days he would add a few spring-up mushrooms, which only appeared after a hard rain. They greatly improved the taste and made him feel giddy for hours afterwards.

The thought of stew made his stomach rumble. He set his parchment aside, threw another log on the fire, and began searching for his stew pot. After a few seconds, he spotted it along the rune wall. The beast had apparently kicked it there in his latest sniff-about.

He picked it up, rubbed off the dirt with the sleeve of his tunic, and began walking toward the rat trap. He remembered Whelan telling him how to build it. He wondered how Whelan was doing now. And the others. Had they made it safely back to Enturia?

61

Bookins paused to let his words sink in. Blusk was the first to react. "By the gods!" he said, turning his head this way and that, looking for the reactions of the others, who seemed drop-jawed stunned.

Except for the Red God, who was smiling in a way that baffled Blusk. "Why do you smile?"

She shrugged. "Why, we all should be smiling. Fearsome monsters attacking our adversaries? What is there not to like about that?"

Blusk blinked. "I see your point, oh godly one, but another point is that we too must face those monsters to get to the Mystrosians."

Bookins raised a finger in the air. "Not necessarily."

"What do you mean?" said Queen Rhynt, who had been sitting in stunned silence at the thought of those beasts. "If beasts are in the north, the south, the middle, and the coasts, surely we must deal with them as well."

"I thought the same thing, Majesty, until our young friend Orthor set me straight."

"Oh?" said the queen, leaning toward him, as did the others.

"Indeed, Majesty. The young man pointed me to an ancient scroll, *The Ramblings and Wanderings of Flacius Turmadala*, which sets forth a safe, beast-free corridor between us and the Mystrosians, or at least those who survive the beasts." He walked over to the map. "From the castle, we proceed due east to this spot here. I know it well, as does the king. It is now my baronial estate and almost in the direct center of Enturia." He moved his fingers on the map. "As you can see, it sits on a bluff, perhaps a hundred feet high, looking out at a vast plain. And I assure you—*Flacius Turmadala assures you*—the path is free of all beasts. It is called the Plain of Sorrows."

"Excellent," said Rhynt. "And where exactly do you think we'll encounter the Mystrosians?"

Bookins moved his finger once more, finally tapping on a spot on the map. "Any Mystrosians who survive—and believe me, there numbers will be greatly diminished—will join forces here, on the eastern end of the plain. The terrain, the mud, and the beasts guarantee it. As water flows to the lowest level, so too shall those warriors seek the path of least resistance." He tapped hard on the map. "And that is here and here alone."

Bookins looked around. Everyone at the table was smiling except for Whelan. "What is it, Whelan? What troubles you?"

"Are you seriously going to base our battle plan on the ramblings in an ancient scroll?"

Bookins nodded vigorously. "It is *true*. I have confirmed it with Orthor, who has confirmed it as well."

"What kind of confirmation?"

Bookins looked puzzled. "What kind? Why, other more recent scrolls and books by many a trusted Enturian scholar. It's all there in our library, in the written record."

Whelan rolled his eyes. "I have traveled the known world and have never—*never*—heard tell of such monsters. If they existed, which I assure you, they don't, then I would have certainly heard a song or two by my fellow minstrels."

Lord Braque, who had been struggling to stay awake, finally found a topic that interested him. "Pish and posh," he said, pushing himself to his feet. "What is known of Enturia in the outside world is little and none." He turned to Bookins. "What Bookins says is true. Even as a child, I was told such stories of the Enturian beasts. And the route he would have you travel is exactly the path my parents took me on our many visits to the new baron's estate, which was once mine. I remember my father cautioning me to stay on the path, 'or the beasties will get you,' he would say."

Whelan scoffed. "Stories a parent tells a child to get them to comply. That is all it is."

Bookins raised his hhands, palms up. "What can I say to convince you? A truth is a truth, and I can do nothing about that but follow the direction to which it points."

Whelan sighed and looked around the table. "I see you all want to go along with this, but leave me out of this fantasy of yours."

"It is no fantasy," said Bookins, walking away from the map and back to the table.

Whelan pushed back his chair and began walking to the door. "I will leave you to it, then." When he reached the door, he stopped and looked back at them. "I will only say you have forgotten something important, something that will be your ruin."

Rhynt was on her feet. "And what might that be, minstrel?"

He sneered at her. "You have forgotten the gods."

Rhynt pointed at the Red God. "We have a god, one who seems not to object to our plan."

Whelan laughed. "You have *one* god, yes, but there are others." He jabbed a finger in the direction of the Red God. "And *she* is not our savior!"

He opened the door and slammed it behind him, the sound echoing around the room for some seconds.

Bookins sighed and sat down. "Well, then, that is my plan."

They sat in silence, the only sound the deep purring of Mela, Mila, and Spook, sound asleep by the hearth.

Part V

"Well, of course I was upset. Wouldn't you be? The White God had defied me, and I could tell by the way she looked at me that the Red God had something similar in mind. I had to get out of there. Regroup. Find out where in hell the other gods were. Canto, Bedo, Dido, and Indo had gone missing—despite my orders. I had to find them, set them straight. Remind them who was in charge, which was me and only me.

"Okay, okay, forgive my anger, and yes, I know you have a question, and yes, I know what it is, and yes, I will describe the battle that ensued.

"That Bookins was craftier than I gave him credit for, and him but a fool. I tell you, when you leave this fire, never estimate a man's worth by his job or his position. Kings can be fools, and fools can be kings.

"Now, where was I? Ah, yes. Beasts. Monsters."

62

Whelan and Canto, the Blue God, stood atop a bluff, the highest point in the landscape, looking down at the rolling hills of northern Enturia. The godly skill that had transported him here had taken its toll on Whelan, who had not transported himself for years. It felt like he had been in the jaws of a Cave Bear and been shaken violently.

He tried to shrug it off. "Why are you here? You were to stay with the siege engines, protect them."

The Blue God drew back his cowl and let it drop on his shoulders. He was handsome, as were all the gods, with curly black hair, sea-blue eyes, and a face that seemed worthy of marble. "They left the siege engines at the shore, along with their king. I saw no point in wasting my time there."

"But why are you here, in the north?"

The Blue God shrugged. "There were only four of us to watch six columns. I just chose the first to leave the camp."

"What of the others?"

"You would know better than I. I didn't think to ask who was watching whom."

Whelan puffed out his cheeks and let out a big sigh. "Do I have to do everything myself?"

The Blue God knew better than to answer.

"All right," said Whelan, turning back to look once more on the rolling hills, which were covered by strange gray trees swaying in the wind, each branch tipped by a large blossom of some sort. "Where is this column of yours?"

The Blue God pointed out at the rolling hills and the swaying trees. "There."

Whelan held a hand to his brow and squinted. There was no column to be seen. "Where? I see only hills and trees."

The Blue God laughed sardonically. "You see hills, yes, but those are not trees."

Whelan looked harder, his jaw dropping as he finally realized what he was seeing. Hundreds and hundreds of Mud Spilts, each of their seven jaws filled with Mystrosian warriors, or pieces of them.

"They came suddenly," said the Blue God. "There was nothing I could do."

Whelan was having trouble forming words. "But . . . but surely some survived."

The Blue God nodded. "Yes, they formed up on the other side of this bluff and headed southwest, hoping to reach the next column."

Whelan looked at the Mud Spilts again, and only then realized that there was no wind. He was seeing only the writhing of the beasts' necks. "How many survived?"

The Blue God sighed. "We started with well over a thousand warriors, and now—now—I would guess more than half are dead."

Whelan shook his head. "And the wounded?"

The Blue God frowned. "Are you serious? The Mud Spilts leave no wounded."

63

The Red God rolled her eyes. "That man, how can he call himself a minstrel? He seems to sing an angry song all day."

Rhynt nodded. "Something is bothering him; he is not usually like this."

"Well, he hates my plan, that is certain," said Bookins.

"No," said Rhynt, "it seems to be more than that." She looked at the closed door. "I will have a talk with him, find out what's going on." She turned back to the others. "But let us continue. Bookins, what next?"

"I have sent a small contingent of observers to my estate. From there, they can spot the Mystrosians—when they come."

"And I have sent gelas—or at least I'm *trying* to send gelas—there as well. They will move among the various columns of Mystrosians and report back."

"Trying?" said Rhynt.

The Red God nodded. "Not to worry. I am meeting some resistance, but their god is no match for me. Eventually, and unbeknownst to them, my gelas slip through. What I can tell you so far is that Bookins' beasts are indeed falling upon each of the columns. Death and dismemberment seem to be the order of the day."

Rhynt shuddered. "I know they are no friend to me, these Mystrosians, but I cannot think of a worse death."

"Indeed," said Bookins. "Now, as I said, we have observers in the field. The Mystrosian are diminished, true, but they will still be a formidable force when we face them."

"Can you tell us where, Bookins?" said Rhynt. "On the map I mean."

Bookins had already told her, told them all, but she was queen, so he just nodded and walked to the map. "My baronial estate is here, and my best guess now is that the battle will take place here, along this vast plain, the Plain of Sorrows."

"I can't say I like that name," said Rhynt.

"Indeed, Majesty," said Bookins. "It was named following a battle that is now known as the Battle of Sorrows, a horrific battle between the Enturians and the Mercadians thousands of years ago. Although we won the day, our losses were astronomical. Or so it is said. It was a long time ago, and historians have a way of magnifying things."

"So much history," said Rhynt. "When this is over, I must spend some time in our library. It seems there is much to know. For example, I have never heard of Mercadians."

Bookins smiled. "Few have, Majesty. But a reading of a scroll or two will tell you that they were a warrior nation, from the island of Mercadia, of course."

"And what happened to them?"

Lord Braque woke from another of his little naps. "Did someone say Mercadia?"

"Yes," said Bookins. "I was just telling the queen that—"

"That they are no more. Their island, much like Dido, was volcanic. It was only a matter of time before the volcano exploded and the island sank into the sea, along with the last of the Mercadians."

"Well, maybe the last," said Bookins. "There is a story that a single ship escaped the fate of the others and that—"

"Yes, yes," said Braque. "That they found another island as yet undiscovered by the rest of us. I think that tale is one based on fear. Fear that they might return to battle us once more."

Rhynt waved a hand in front of her face. "Okay, I seem to have taken us off the track." She turned to Bookins. "So we will fight on the Plain of Sorrows?"

"I do believe so, yes."

She turned to the Red God. "Do you agree?"

"I do," said the Red God. "Everything seems to be unfolding as your fine strategist Bookins has foretold."

She turned back to Bookins. "So, master strategist, when do we march?"

Bookins looked around the table, then turned back to Rhynt. "We march now, Majesty. We march *now.*"

Some smiled, some frowned, some chuckled and looked around nervously, but it was Calax Halfhand who captured the spirit of the moment, slapping his hand on the table and roaring, *"Yes!"*

64

The White God, now a crow, flew from column to column, trying his best to help the Mystrosians below, who were under attack by unknown beasts.

The warriors in the northernmost column had been set upon by ravenous, seven-headed beasts, their strength reduced by half. He spotted Canto, the Blue God, almost immediately, his blue-jay sigil standing out from the rest of the warriors. Working together, they tried every spell and charm they knew, but to no effect. These seven-headed beasts seemed immune from godly intervention. He could only wish the Blue God well and fly to the next column to offer whatever assistance he could, which was proving to be little or none.

The next two columns were thankfully free from attack, but the terrain—cliffs, chasms, and sucking mud—was not only slowing them down, but forcing them farther south. Bedo, the Green Monk, was doing his all to speed up his men—he wanted revenge for the killing of his monk, and battle could not come too soon for him—but the more his men struggled, the deeper they sank into the mud. He had ordered "slow and steady," which was working, but he was very frustrated by their progress.

The White god flew on, hoping to see an intact center column, the column that contained the Mystrosians best warriors, but he barely escaped himself. The column was under attack by razor-toothed birds as big as wild turkeys. The Green Monk had told him that Dado, the Gray Monk, was leading this column, but there was no sign of his gray cape with the lightning bolt sigil. The god had either fled or been consumed like his warriors. The White God could only linger for a few seconds before flying on. The center column was no more, picked clean to the bone and now just a pile of bones that stretched for miles.

Thankfully, the next column was intact, but just like the other "safe" columns, the warriors were making slow progress through a slurry of knee-deep mud. The White God squawked words of encouragement to Indo, the Black God, and flew on, hoping against hope that the southernmost column would only be dealing with mud.

His hopes were dashed at the sight of them. Some were under attack by small beasts in the mud. Some men, though still alive, were stripped to the bone up to the thigh. Others were fighting off small jumping beasts that emerged from the mud and went for the warriors' faces.

But that was just the beginning of the gore. Warriors were being tossed through the air, lifeless, by what must have been several hundred enormous bears. Only a few warriors remained, and they were fighting to move northward toward the other columns.

The White God had seen enough. He would have to find the White Monk, if he still lived, and report the devastation of their ranks. Seven thousand of the best warriors in the known world had set out, but only four thousand would be able to face the Enturians.

Their plan to strike from six different directions was shattered. What warriors remained were being forced toward the center columns and a large plain a few miles to the east. It would be the perfect place for the Enturians to strike, but the White God knew that if they did, his men would not be up to the task. They would arrive at the plain greatly diminished and fully exhausted.

He would have to buy them time, if necessary. His men would need time to rest before proceeding across the plain to the Enturian castle. But if the Enturians were on the march, heading toward the plain, he would have to figure out a way to slow them down.

He took one last look at the struggling columns, then turned west and flew toward the Enturian castle. He had to find out where they were and what they were up to. And then he'd have to slow or stop them.

But how?

65

Queen Rhynt looked around the conference table once more. She could tell they were ready. "Bookins has given us a fine plan. Now we must execute it." She turned to Calax. "How long before you can assemble your warriors?"

Calax hesitated. "An hour, perhaps two."

She turned to Phendour. "And your archers?"

"I would say two hours. I'd like to collect the last batch of arrows from the floating tower."

"Well then," said Rhynt, "two hours it is." She turned to the others. "Make ready, say your goodbyes. We march to the Plain of Sorrows this day."

Everyone rose from the table as one and started moving toward the door, some faster than others. Calax reached the door first and as he opened it, a stream of servants pushed in, eager to clear away the food and straighten the room.

Among them was Priss, who made certain to give Rhynt a friendly nod when she came into the room. Rhynt returned the nod, then had a thought. "Priss, over here." She waved her toward the conference table, then caught the arm of Phendour, who was on her way out. "Stay a moment, Phendour."

"Very well, Majesty. What is it?"

Rhynt waited for Priss to arrive, then grabbed her by the arm as well and pulled her close. "Phendour, this is Priss, one of my handmaidens. I have a sneaking suspicion that she'd rather be a warrior."

Priss beamed. "Yes, how did you know?"

Rhynt smiled at her. "I sense things—about people. You are no handmaiden. There is something fierce inside you." She turned to Phendour. "How long to turn her into a competent archer?"

Phendour gave Priss the onceover, squeezing her arms, turning her in a circle to assess her shoulders, and finally giving a nod to Rhynt. "She has the makings of one, but I would need a couple of months with her to make her useful in a battle."

Priss seemed crestfallen.

"The good news, though, as the time moves at a different pace within the floating tower. Two months in there is but two hours out here."

Priss's eyes went wide. "You mean I can? I can be an archer?"

Phendour smiled. "If the queen says so, yes."

Rhynt chuckled. "And I do say yes."

Priss began jumping up and down. "Yes, yes." She started to give Rhynt a hug, then thought better of it, turning instead to give Phendour a big smile. "I am ready when you are."

Phendour grabbed her by the arm. "Then come. I have more to do than just teach you the ins and outs of notch, draw, loose."

Priss turned her head to Rhynt for one last word before being dragged out of the room. "Thank you, Majesty, thank you. I shall make you proud."

Rhynt smiled at her, but then laughed out loud as soon as Phendour and Priss disappeared out the door.

"Laughter is good in such times," said Bookins, who startled her. He was slowly pushing Lord Braque out of the room in his rolling chair.

Rhynt's smile disappeared. "I fear there will be little time for such laughter once we set out for your estate and the Plain of Sorrows."

"Oh, no," said Bookins, "we must keep our humor at all times. Otherwise, we will be undone."

Rhynt gave him an appraising look. "Such wisdom from a fool."

Bookins laughed. "Yes, Majesty, even from a fool such as I."

"I meant no offense."

"Oh, none taken, Majesty. If there is one thing a fool learns early, it is that his words will often be dismissed."

"I do not think that way," she said, her voice softening as she attempted to mollify him.

"I can see that, and if I may say so, I am sore amazed."

"Amazed? Truly? And why?"

"You are so young. I did not expect such wisdom in our new queen. In fact, truth be told, I thought Calax the better choice to succeed King Braque."

Lord Braque turned his head up to them. "It's Lord Braque now, so let's just get on with it, shall we? Push, man, push."

Rhynt looked at Bookins. Bookins looked at Rhynt. They both tried not to laugh.

"Yes," said Bookins, finally. "We must to our quarters to prepare for our journey—and war."

They walked on in silence, save for the squeaky wheel on Braque's rolling chair.

"Majesty," a voice called out from behind them.

Rhynt new the voice well, and turned to meet it. "Yes, Zyrx, what is it?"

Zyrx held out a small crown to her. "A crown that will fit is all."

Rhynt took the crown in her hands and turned it in all directions, letting the light play on it. "What wonder is this?"

Zyrx beamed. "Took me months to get it just right. You'll find it lighter than Braque's, and I have made it both strong and flexible. It will not fall off unless you yourself take it off."

Rhynt ran her fingers around its rim. "It is clearly some form of your merilium, but these stones, I have never seen the like."

Zyrx leaned in and whispered. "Elven stones, mined within the tower. They come in all colors, as you can see, but that's just the showy part. What's important about them is that they possess some charm. They can protect you, guide you, even speak to you."

"Speak to me?"

"Not in a voice, mind. But you will hear them in your thoughts."

"Them?"

Zyrx shrugged. "Each stone is like a separate person, each with his own powers."

Intrigued, Rhynt slipped the crown on her head and waited expectantly. "I hear no voices."

"No, Majesty, you will only hear them when you need them. I have tried a similar crown—more a helmet, really—for my work at the forge, stones specifically selected for doing such work."

"And the stones talk to you?"

"Yes, in my thoughts. Once they stopped me from striking in the wrong spot, saving me from ruining a fine sword."

"I thank you for this, Zyrx. I shall wear it always."

"Particularly in battle, Majesty. It will protect you." He turned to Bookins and Braque. "Perhaps all of us."

"Yes, yes," said Braque. "Can we move this show along, then? I have necessities to deal with."

Bookins rolled his eyes. Zyrx and Rhynt tried their best once more not to laugh. But failed.

66

Lord Braque's mood did not change when Bookins loaded him into the royal wagon; he was eager to get on with the business of war, and the relative comfort of the wagon was something he didn't care for.

"I should be a'horse," he said.

"Well, you look like a horse," said Bookins, slipping briefly back into his role as Fool.

"No, seriously, I should be at the front, marshaling my troops."

Bookins chuckled. "They are not your troops anymore."

Braque growled. "Well, it's not fair."

"Fair? You're the one who gave up your kingship. Do you wish to take it back?"

"No, of course not, but if fate decides to strike her down . . ."

"Ha! In that event, your last remaining child, Calax Halfhand, would become king. You are out of the picture now. When it comes to royal succession, you are as good as dead."

Braque sighed. It was true, and it seemed a wise decision at the time, when he assumed his death was but moments away. He would just have to accept his fate and move on, for what little time remained to him. "Promise me one thing."

Bookins frowned. His former king looked deadly serious about something, and whenever that happened, Bookins knew to listen and listen carefully. "Lord?"

"When we get to the Plain of Sorrows, find me a horse. I would fight in this battle, and die if needs be."

"But lord . . ."

"No, don't try to dissuade me. Think about it. Would you rather end your life in a fight to the death or end it trying to make it to the pisspot before you wet yourself?"

"Um, are those my only choices?"

Braque couldn't help laughing. "Come now, Bookins, you know what I mean. My kingship was long and peaceful, but little was accomplished."

"Little? Little? Why, you helped create our vast library."

"Yes, I did." He remembered the number of journeys his librarian had had to take to collect all the scrolls and books, the combined wisdom of the ages.

"You kept us out of war."

"Yes, I did, though it was only through hiding." Until now, Enturia was thought to be a myth, a tale Paudians and others would tell their children, of a land filled with beasts. As it turns out, that was mostly true, at least on the western half of the country.

"Hiding is good betimes."

"It is. Still, a library and peace would have happened anyway. All I did was sow my seed wildly."

Bookins didn't answer.

"Ah, I see we agree at last. So make it your business to find me a horse."

Bookins nodded. "I will. Now, I must take leave of you to speak to the queen. She has many questions about the journey to the estate, as well as the Plain of Sorrows." He looked around the wagon. "Over there you'll find food and wine, enough to distract you."

Braque looked at the food and wine and nodded. "Very well, but when you come back, bring that horse."

Bookins waved goodbye and climbed down from the wagon. Warriors were everywhere, making their final preparations for the journey. Many had already formed up and were marching west.

With the help of a passing warrior, Bookins was lifted into the saddle of the smallest horse he'd ever seen. It was no larger than a pony, yet he could tell by its mane that it was a fully grown, even old, horse.

He managed to coax the little horse forward and was soon by the side of Queen Rhynt, whose horse was much taller. He had to strain his neck to speak to her. "Hail and well met, Majesty."

Rhynt looked down and laughed. "Why, Bookins, could they not find you a horse?"

Bookins rolled his eyes. "I should expect such jibes, but this actually is a horse, Majesty. Just small."

"I have questions for you," she said.

"Anything, Majesty."

"What is our current strength?"

Bookins looked back at the column of warriors. "With the help of the elves and the floating tower, we have grown from an army of 700 poorly trained warriors into a force of over 7,000 fully trained, fully armed fighters, most elves. And if Phendour and Blusk are to be believed, our warriors are superior to the Mystrosians in every way."

Rhynt smiled down at him. "Oh, I hope so. I'm beginning to like this queen thing. It would be a shame to lose it so quickly."

"Don't worry, my plan should work."

"I don't like the sound of *should*. We *must* win this fight."

"And we shall."

"So, then, I know we have discussed this before, but have you made any further changes to the plan I need to know about?"

Bookins hesitated. Should he tell her? For now, he thought not. "No, Majesty, nothing since the business with the trolls. We will make it to my new estate, which I am eager for you to see. It was King Braque's hunting lodge." He thought to tell her that the king's hunting usually involved young women, not wild game, but thought better of it. "We should be there by late afternoon, enough time to get you settled in one of its fine rooms, set up camp for the army, and rest before the battle."

"And that happens tomorrow morning?"

"The battle? Yes, I should think so. The Red Monk and the Red God will keep watch, through gelas and such and whatever gods do to keep track of things. Their latest guess is that the Mystrosians will arrive just before dawn. The good news for us is that they will have spent the night marching, while our warriors will be fully rested."

"Good," she said, then sighed.

"A heavy sigh, Majesty. What concerns you?"

"Nothing really. I worry what will become of Orthor if we lose."

Bookins shook his head. "First, Majesty, we will *not* lose. The battle is unfolding as I have foreseen, and I see no reason to back away from my confidence in the outcome. There will be losses, make no mistake, but we will come through it."

"Yes, I believe that, and I believe in you. Still, I have heard that a battle can turn on the flight of a single arrow."

"That is true, Majesty, but I am confident that it will be our arrow and not theirs that wins the day. Oh, and two, Orthor's allegiance is to knowledge and its pursuit. Countries, kingdoms, *battles* do not interest him except from an historical perspective. I imagine him working in someone's library, but I doubt he cares whose."

"Well, I hope he is *our* librarian, for years to come."

"Indeed," said Bookins, turning at a sound behind him. It was Zyrx riding up on a horse even smaller than Bookins'. "Hail, Zyrx."

"Yes, yes," said Zyrx, ignoring Bookins and turning to the Queen. "I've had a special request I need to talk to you about."

"Oh?"

"Yes, the king—I mean the Lord—Braque has asked me to make him a suit of armor."

Rhynt looked taken aback. "Armor? What, he expects to fight in his roller chair?"

Bookins interrupted. "He is set on fighting, Majesty. An act of courage and honor to round out his life."

Rhynt nodded and turned to Zyrx. "Is such a thing possible? I mean to make armor in the time that remains before battle."

Zyrx puffed out his cheeks. "I don't know. I suppose I could try if—"

"Majesty," interrupted Bookins. "You can't be thinking to let him do this."

Rhynt sighed. "He will be fine. He can stand—or rather sit—with me at the rear. I will make sure he stays far from the action."

"But Majesty, he has also requested a horse. He fully intends to charge headlong into the battle, come what may."

"He can have a horse, but I will make sure that there will be no one to help him on it."

"Majesty . . ."

Rhynt shook her head. "No, Bookins, he shall have his armor and his horse. I will ask him to stand by me so that I might have the benefit of his counsel."

Bookins looked down. "As you wish, Majesty." *This will not turn out well,* he thought.

67

King Merek the Mighty was terrified. He could hear the screams of his guards as they were taken one by one by some unseen beast. He thought to look outside, see what manner of beast it was, but his knees were shaking too hard for him to move without tumbling over.

Instead, he dropped to the ground and curled himself into a ball. Considering his girth, a very large ball. He could hear his concubines whimpering behind him. All but one.

"Do something," she said.

King Merek wondered whether she was talking to him. He decided she wasn't; such insolence would only get her whipped. And yet now, here she was at his side, poking him in the back with a finger as sharp as a dagger. "Get up, Majesty. There is no safety here."

He said nothing, but tightened himself into an even tighter ball. The sound of many heavy footsteps could be heard outside. The beast must be huge!

"Majesty, if you move now, we can make it to one of the landing boats and row our way to a ship."

The King considered this. He would have to unloosen his grip on himself, stand, move to the opening flap of the tent, and then run— actually run—a hundred yards or more to the shoreline. He was not sure he could be anything other than a ball of overly-fed flesh. "No," he heard himself saying, "we will be safe here. The monsters will pass by. They can't see us."

Even King Merek had to agree with what she said next. "You, Majesty, are a fool." She turned to the other concubines. "You are all fools. Come, save yourself before it is too late."

The concubines cowered in the darkest corner of the tent, all shaking their heads at her words.

Another shriek came from outside. Whatever it was was closer to the tent now. "It is too late," said King Merek.

And then suddenly it was all quiet outside. The concubine and King Merek listened intently. Seconds passed, then a minute without a single scream of pain and horror.

"It must be gone," said King Merek in a whisper.

"Yes," said the concubine. "So come, stand, we need to get to the ship."

"But it's gone."

The concubine tried not to raise her voice, but it was difficult. She had to control every word that came out of her mouth, keep it to as much of a whisper as she could manage. Whisper or not, her words came out angry. "To your feet!"

King Merek, to his surprise, responded instantly, uncoiling himself from himself and standing. "Yes, you are right." He hesitated. "Still."

"Still what? Come on, we have to get out of here."

Fear had taken hold of the king once more. "But we're safe now."

The concubine screamed at him. "Fine, you stay here and die." She turned to the concubines in the corner. "All of you, just stay. See how long you live."

With that, she turned away from them, ran to the tent flap, and was gone.

King Merek sighed. He was happy to have her gone.

But his happiness was short-lived. A scream, her scream, came just seconds later. And her scream set off the other concubines, who began screaming and running around inside the tent, each looking for a safer place.

King Merek lost control of himself and shouted. "Quiet!"

He had to yell it again and again before the concubines returned to the darkest corner of the tent, where they resumed their fearful whimpering.

All was quiet outside. As the minutes passed, King Merek began to breathe easier. *Whatever was out there must be gone now,* he thought. He tried to remember the number of screams, but he had lost count between ten and fifteen. Perhaps some of his guards were still alive. *Yes, that must be true,* he thought. *They're hiding, as we are, or maybe they made it to the one of the ships.*

He thought to think more about it, but his thoughts were interrupted by the sound of heavy footsteps—far too many to count—approaching the tent. He imagined an enormous, many-legged monster, its fangs dripping with blood.

He dropped to the ground and curled himself into a ball, but it was for naught. The tent around them disappeared and all he could hear was his own scream.

His last thought was of his mother. And then all was darkness.

68

The march had taken longer than Bookins expected, but they still arrived at Bookins' new baronial estate, the king's former hunting lodge, well before sundown, time enough for the men and elves to set up camp nearby on a bluff overlooking the Plain of Sorrows.

The hunting lodge itself was set back twenty yards from the edge of the bluff, far enough to prevent night-time strollers from plummeting to their deaths, but close enough to view the Plain of Sorrows in its entirety. Unlike most hunting lodges, which provide for the short-term needs of but a few hunters and are spare in their furnishings, the king's former lodge was really more a small castle, with more than a dozen bedrooms and all the fortifications and battlements of the castle they had just left. If need be, the well-stocked lodge could be defended for a year or more, even fight off the most sophisticated siege engines.

Bookins did not take the strength of the lodge into account in his plan, but it did put him at ease that he could sleep in comfort and safety just a night before the battle.

As promised, the former king had provided the lodge with a retinue of servants to handle any task that Bookins might imagine: cooks, manservants, gardeners, housemaids, kitchen maids, livery men—even his own blacksmith. He had greeted them briefly at the gate, and then they had all scurried off to attend to their duties, including completing preparations for the evening's dinner.

Bookins personal manservant, a young man named Cresh, escorted Bookins to his room, which Bookins knew had been the former bedroom of the king. Younger than Bookins by at least two decades, the young Cresh strode quickly and with ease, unlike Bookins, who struggled to keep up.

He was taller than Bookins by a head, but walked hunched over, as if he had been teased by his height as a boy and sought only to be as tall as his playmates. His hair was flaxen and pulled back into a ponytail that Bookins could see was tied off with a strand of dried rabbit gut. With his hair pulled back tight against his head, his face itself looked larger than a normal face, every feature heavy and pronounced, from his beetle brows to his long, sharp nose to his whiskerless, dimpled chin. His eyes, a strange creamy blue, seemed to bug out of their sockets.

Cresh stopped two or three times on their way to the room so that Bookins might catch up.

"I'm coming, I'm coming," said Bookins, shaking his head. "These old bones of mine."

Cresh bowed slightly. "Come at your own pace, baron. A hot bath awaits. Perhaps just the thing to shake off the stiffness that comes from a long ride."

Bookins couldn't help letting out a long sigh. "Oh, my, that would be wonderful."

Cresh motioned him down the corridor with a long sweep of his arm. "It is but a few more steps, baron."

And it was.

As soon as Cresh opened the door, Bookins relaxed. Unlike the rest of the lodge, which had still not responded fully from the fires started in its many hearths, this room was warm and, to Bookins, blessedly humid. Cresh gave him a quick bow, turned, and left, closing the door behind him.

Bookins looked around the room. It was much as it has been when King Braque last used it: a bed large enough to accommodate six people sat against the far wall, windows opposite to catch the morning light; large tables on either side of the bed for serving food and drink, each with several finely carved chairs around them; a door that led to a private commode, where a man might do his business without facing the outside cold; large wardrobes across the other walls, each emblazoned with the Braque crest and filled with the king's "hunting clothes," which typically involved a hunt for wild women rather than wild game.

And finally, the item of furniture that Bookins desired most: a large wooden tub in the center of the room, carved from a single Mas Blossom Tree, a tree whose wood gave off a scent that cast off all your worldly cares.

Not even an approaching battle could prevent Bookins from doffing his clothes and easing into the steamy waters, breathing deeply of its restorative vapors.

He looked down at the clothes he had just cast off and for the first time realized that he had never switched from his brightly colored fool's clothes to something, well, more baronial.

Crest must have thought me a fool, he thought, and then laughed at himself. *Well, of course he would.*

The water seemed to revive him almost at once. Pain subsided, his joints grew limber, and an overall feeling of satisfaction and calm overwhelmed him. Time itself seemed to pause. The only sound was his breath and the motion of the water as it rippled around him, restoring him.

Bookins thought about his life to come, after the battle. He would spend it here, surely, in this very tub, soaking until his hands turned plump and white.

But as the water cooled, his thoughts strayed to the battle and his plan. *It had to work. It must.* He looked out the windows at the Plain of Sorrows. It was empty now, but tomorrow morning would be a different story entirely.

He knew how he would array his forces and when to set its elements in motion. The beginning moves would be textbook, what any Mystrosian general would expect. But then, then, if his forces could hold, his gambit would come into play.

There is nothing like a surprise, he thought.

69

It came as a complete surprise, and a painful one as well. As he walked back into the cave after collecting some more pop-up mushrooms, he stubbed his toe on something and tripped, falling flat on his face.

After some moments and a string of words the Librarian had told him to avoid, he rolled over on his back and sighed. His knees were throbbing from the fall, and his hands were scraped and stinging with pain.

He shook his head and pushed himself up to a sitting position, looking back at the cave entrance to see if he could find what had tripped him up. A small bump, no bigger than a mushroom cap, protruded through the ground.

Curious, he thought. Had that been there the whole time? He had gone in and out of the cave hundreds of times since his arrival and had never had a problem before.

He scrambled to his feet and walked over to the bump, bending over to get a good look at it. At first he thought it was a rock, but then as he moved his head back and forth, he saw a sparkle, as if from a jewel or brushed metal. When he rubbed his finger across it, it gleamed even more in the sunlight.

"Well," he said. "Look at you. All bright and shiny this morning. Let's have a closer look at you."

He stood up and walked over to the boulder he had been using as a desk and workbench, and picked up a small knife and a brush he sometimes used on his hair after a swim in the river. He plucked a few hairs off the brush and returned to the mysterious object.

At first he used the little knife, trying to pry the object out of the ground, but it was far too big, so he turned to his brush. It was slower than a knife, but he knew it would cause less damage.

He brushed at the object again and again. Minutes passed. Hours passed. The object slowly began to reveal itself. The shiny part was a ring, about the same size as the ring he could make with his thumb and middle finger. It was clearly metal of some kind, and it surrounded a piece of glass. He had seen a man wear such a thing once to improve his vision.

The ring came away from the rest of the object easily, and when it did, he could see there were two short pegs on either side, also metal. He looked at what remained in the ground. It appeared to be a tripod, though smaller than any he had ever seen. It was barely taller than his knees.

"What in the world," he said. "Are you some kind of tool used by very short people?" He shook his head. "No, I think not. Something else, then."

He renewed his brushing until he could get the blade of his knife under one leg of the tripod. It lifted easily, and once up, he was able to tug on it and pull the rest out of the ground.

"Well, then, you are indeed a tripod, are you not?" He tried to set it up on the ground, but one of the legs was stuck to another. "Perhaps some more cleaning, though."

He picked up the ring and the tripod and walked down to the river, washing off both in a pool of water near the banks and far from the strong currents.

"Well, now," he said. "You are a delight for the eye."

He held up the ring to his eye, and the whole world distorted and grew blurry. "Interesting."

He finished washing the tripod, and then walked back to the cave's entrance.

"You're not here by accident, I think. Someone was using you for something. But what?"

He went back to the spot where he had tripped and set the tripod on the ground, opening its legs wide to create a stable base for the ring and its glass.

"Let me see now. The ring has to rest on the top somehow."

He turned the ring this way and that and finally noticed two notches that would be the natural home for the ring. And it was.

"Okay, you're together. Now what?"

He considered the possibilities. One, its owner dropped it and it became buried over time; its location is meaningless. Two, the device was meant to be here, exactly here, and its owner was using it to see something or do something. Three, he had no idea what it was and thinking about it was useless.

He rejected one and three and focused on two. It was meant to be here and it had a specific use, perhaps a very important use.

And then it seemed to happen all at once. The sun rose higher in the sky and a beam of light raced through the glass to the rune wall within the cave. Orthor jumped back. Something was twinkling on the wall just to the left of the beam coming through the ring.

He raced over to the wall, and when he saw it, his jaw dropped. How could he have missed this? It was a small stone, much like a diamond, but flat and as big as a thumbnail. It seemed to be the same kind of metal as the ring.

He looked back at it. "Oh, my, you were looking for this spot on the wall, weren't you?"

He moved back to the tripod and started moving it this way and that until the beam of light hit the center of the shiny metal on the rune wall. The beam immediately changed direction, hitting a spot on the opposite wall of the cave.

But there was nothing but cave wall to see at that spot.

"Ah," he said. "I don't have the angle right."

He went back and adjusted the angle of the beam slightly, and suddenly the beam hit another piece of metal, reflecting the light back once more to the rune wall, where the beam spread across a series of runes at the base of the wall.

Orthor raced over to his boulder, grabbed a quill, the ink pot, and a parchment, and began writing down the runes.

"This must be a clue," he said. And then he changed his mind. "No, this must be the *key,* the key to it all."

He looked at the strange runes and laughed. "Ha, I've got you!"

70

Whelan and the White God stood alone just inside the tree line of the eastern edge of the Plain of Sorrows. Neither was happy.

"I flew over them earlier. They are a strong force, stronger than I imagined," said the White God.

"And our force has been greatly reduced. Still, two things encourage me about our situation."

"And what could that possibly be. Our dead and wounded outnumber the living, and they are exhausted to a man."

"They'll have half the night to recover."

"Is that the first of your encouragements?"

"No, that was an attempt to get you to shut up and listen."

The White God smiled, but Whelan could tell he was seething.

"So," said Whelan, continuing, "First, I think our Mystrosians are better warriors, better trained. The Enturians are new to war, and so are these strange elves that seek to help them. I would not be surprised if they turn and run."

"And second?"

Whelan turned and looked back into the trees, where the Mystrosian warriors were setting up camp. "Knowing now what's behind them, our men will never retreat."

"The beasts?"

"Yes, the beasts. I am sorry I did not anticipate that. I should have known."

"And I," said the White God.

Whelan turned again and looked through the trees. "Any word on Dado?"

"No, the Gray God is gone."

Whelan shook his head mournfully. "Beasts that can take down gods? What strange magic beats at the heart of this land?"

"Whatever that magic is, it does not like us."

"Aye, but we're through it now. All we have to do is march across that plain and Enturia will be ours."

"Our prize a land of god-eating beasts."

Whelan laughed. "I will have to write a song about it." He turned and started walking deeper into the woods. "Come, I would have a word with Canto and the others about the coming battle."

The White God paused and looked across the plain. He could see lights coming from a structure of some sort high on a bluff on the western end of the plain. "Enjoy your evening," he said to himself. "We come for you with the sun."

He turned and followed Whelan in the direction of their camp. Fires had sprung up, and the smell of roasting rabbits filled the air.

71

The banquet was rich in food and sparse in conversation. Unlike many banquets attended by Bookins over the years, the guests straggled in rather than arriving in a near parade. *Not surprising*, thought Bookins. *They all have duties to perform to ready the army for tomorrow morning's battle.*

Even knowing this, however, he was saddened that the very first banquet he had ever hosted was such a somber occasion. He wondered whether he should rush back to his room, change into the clothing of a jester, and perform one of his best routines. But after looking around the room, he knew it would take more than an old fool to rouse the people around the table.

Not that people weren't trying. Lord Braque remarked on Bookins' fine new clothes, even though he didn't seem aware that the clothes were from his own closet.

"Your new clothes are wonderful, Bookins," he said. "I couldn't have done a better job picking them out."

Bookins forced a smile. "Yes, thank you. I must say it's a big change from my usual garish garbs."

Braque gave him an appraising look. "Mauve becomes you. A fine choice, I think, for old men such as us. As I recall, I had an outfit very similar to this, though the sleeves were puffier and the buttons fine shells and not these, these—what would you call those?"

Bookins looked down at his chest. "I think those are coral, from the northern reefs."

Braque leaned closer to Bookins. "Yes, that's exactly what they are. How wonderful."

Braque grew silent, then nodded to himself and returned to his plate, picking up a greenbird leg and separating the thigh from the drumstick with a quick, firm twist.

Bookins looked to his right. Calax was attacking another greenbird with much the same technique used by Braque, but more forceful and quicker. Calax caught Bookins looking at him and nodded. "A fine bird. My compliments to the cook."

Bookins smiled back. "I am glad you are enjoying it."

Calax said nothing and looked away.

Bookins tried to sigh without actually sighing. Things were not going well. He surveyed the table again, looking for some person or topic to get the conversation going.

"The greenbird is wonderful, don't you think?" he said to the table in general, hoping someone would respond. But all he received back were nods and satisfied grunts.

He tried again. "Has anyone seen Whelan?"

Some shrugged, not caring. Some shrugged, not knowing. Others looked briefly around the room, then shrugged in a way that only acknowledged what Bookins had suspected: Whelan was nowhere to be seen.

Bookins offered a solution. "I know he was upset with the plan, but I would not have expected him to miss a banquet. The man loves food and never misses a chance to entertain."

Zyrx, at least, was paying attention. He gulped down the food in his mouth, took a sip of wine, and then turned to Bookins. "Baron, I do believe I saw him talking to Marthe at the docks in the hours before our departure."

"And since?" said Bookins.

Zyrx shrugged. "No, not really. Perhaps he was angry enough to sail away, back to Paudia."

Bookins shook his head. "Perhaps, but everything I know of him suggests a battle would be just the thing he'd want to watch—to help him write new songs."

Zyrx nodded absently, then turned back to his greenbird. "This really is wonderful, Bookins. If I am not mistaken, the cook has marinated it in Alamarian wine. That fine port they make."

"You may be right."

"And the spices. Superb!"

"Indeed."

Zyrx took a bite and smacked his lips. "I seem to detect grapnut and just a little smidge of smudge oil."

Bookins didn't know. "A smidge of smudge? I have no idea."

Zyrx frowned and went back to eating, leaving Bookins on a conversational island again.

He looked toward the opposite end of the table, where Queen Rhynt sat with her new protégé, Priss, who was all fitted out in new armor, with a quiver of arrows peeking out from behind her shoulder. She had changed much in her two months of training within the floating tower. The once thin and frail girl was now more muscular and lithe, no doubt the work of Phendour. Her black hair, once long and flowing, was now cropped short, all the better to keep it out of her eyes when she took arrow to bow. The girl looked nervous, out of her element. The queen was patting her on the hand, trying to calm her. Bookins thought it would be wrong to interrupt.

He turned back to his own greenbird, which was largely untouched. He wasn't hungry, his appetite defeated by the approaching battle. There were so many details to remember.

He started to pick up the bird, but then there was a loud strum from a lute. *Whelan!*

Everyone perked up as Whelan entered the room, humming the beginning of a well-known ballad about unrequited love. Everyone except Queen Rhynt, who glowered at him.

He saw the look, stopped his strumming, and offered her a deep bow. "Majesty, I beg your pardon for storming out of that meeting." He turned to Bookins and gave him a friendly nod. "I know the error of my ways now, and only seek to entertain while I can and to help whenever and wherever I am needed."

"Thank you, Whelan," she said. "We have missed you. More, we were upset at your departure and happy that you have joined us here."

Whelan bowed deeply. "Thank you, Majesty."

"I only ask one thing of you," she said.

Whelan blinked. "Oh, what?"

"That you not sing us songs of love, of loss, of victory, or of defeat."

Whelan blinked again, hard. "But Majesty, what then is there left to sing?"

"Nothing, I hope. Now, now, take that look off your face. We love your voice and your songs—well, most of them, anyway—but had you arrived earlier, you would know that we are all lost in our own thoughts."

"Thinking of tomorrow, no doubt."

"Indeed."

"But wouldn't a song help you forget?"

"That is just my point. I do not want to forget, and I don't want anyone at this table to forget, that we must stay focused on what comes tomorrow. Steel ourselves, not wallow in the emotions brought to us in the songs of a minstrel."

"Why, Majesty, you hurt me to the core."

"Ha! If it is a hurt, you hide it well. No, we will not have such merriment this night. Tonight is for reflection and resolve. Save your songs for the end, when Bookins' gambit plays out and we can rejoice in victory."

Whelan turned to Bookins and frowned. "But what if your so-called gambit fails, my dear Bookins? What then?"

Bookins could hear the pops and creaks when he straightened his back and rose to the challenge. "The plan will work." He turned to the others at the table. "If we all do our part and do it well."

Whelan smiled and bowed to Bookins. "May it be so, baron." He turned back to the queen. "May I at least join you at table? I can see by the way some eat that the bird must be wonderful."

"It is," said Zyrx, waving a drumstick in Whelan's direction.

Rhynt laughed. "Yes, indeed it is. Come, Whelan, there's a place here next to our newest warrior, Priss."

Whelan at first seemed to take offense at being placed anywhere but next to the queen, but then he shook it off with a smile and sat down next to Priss with a curious look on his face. "Have we met? You look familiar, and yet not."

"Yes, I was once handmaiden to the queen. You and I bumped into each other back at the castle."

Whelan suddenly remembered. "The girl with the tray."

"Which you knocked out of my hands."

"I didn't see you coming."

"Nor I you." She giggled.

"But look at you now. I would have never known. You are so, so . . ."

"Warrior-like, I think you want to say," said Rhynt. She pointed to Phendour, who was at the opposite end of the table talking in hushed tones to Blusk. "Her training works miracles."

"Indeed," said Whelan. He wondered how many warriors such as this she had trained. They might be a more powerful force than he ever imagined. He turned to Priss. "Good luck on the morrow."

"Thank you."

"And tell me, how many are there of you? I mean archers."

Priss started to answer—they numbered just over a thousand—but Rhynt put a hand on her arm. "Enough, Whelan, we have enough."

Whelan tried to make light of his question. "Goodness, I was only wondering . . ."

Rhynt held up a hand. "I have been reading a scroll, a very old scroll on the art of war."

"Yes? By whom?"

Rhynt frowned. "The name escapes me, but that's not important. What's important are the words. The author—my word, I should remember his name—had a list of things you should never do before a battle, and one of them was never to reveal your strength to anyone, friend or foe."

Whelan cocked his head. "Well, I can certainly understand not wanting your enemy to know, but look at me, I am your minstrel, a true friend to one and all here."

Rhynt shook her head. "Wheedling will not help you. The author was quite specific about that. Friends sometimes get captured by foes, and thus the information is passed along by reward or torture."

"I do not like this author of yours, whatever his name."

"*Her* name, actually, and oh, I remember now. It's Gwendolyn of Ichthia."

Whelan brightened. "The warrior queen. Oh, yes, I have heard of her. In fact, I have a song that—"

Rhynt cut him off quickly. "No songs," she said, glaring.

Whelan sighed. "As you wish." He looked around the table, his eyes settling on Bookins, who was midway through a bite of greenbird. "I say, Bookins, how goes the battle?"

Bookins startled, then tried his best to speak with a full mouth. "Um, erm, it goes."

"Are you still confident in your plan?"

Bookins gulped. He wasn't really sure. He'd played out the battle in his mind so many times, and come up with so many new variables—what if they do this, what if they do that—that almost any outcome seemed feasible. "Yes," he said, his voice soft and falling away before returning more forcefully. "Yes, absolutely."

Whelan looked down the table. The Red Monk was talking on and on at the Red God, who was doing her best to ignore him and glare down the table at Whelan. He glared back, then continued his questioning of Bookins. "So, is there no role I can play in this affair?"

Bookins shook his head vigorously. "For a minstrel? No, you'd best stand on the bluff with me, Lord Braque, and the queen. There will be no better view of it."

"You will not participate in the battle?"

Bookins chuckled. "If I were a young man, I would be there at the point of the spear. But as you can see, I am far from a young man. Besides, from the bluff, the queen and I will be able to view the battle and make any adjustments."

"Wait a second," said Lord Braque, who had been almost asleep in his chair beside Bookins. "The bluff? I will not be on the bluff. I will be down there, sword held high, lopping off heads and whatever comes my way." He paused to look around the table to see how everyone had reacted to his bold plan. Everyone else was eating or involved in their own whispered conversations. "Well, anyway, that is *my* plan."

Bookins glanced at the queen. She needed to say something to the old fool. And she did.

"And a *wonderful* plan it is, Lord Braque, but I would have your counsel, at least in the early stages of the battle. You will join us on the bluff. There you can watch the battle unfold and choose the exact spot where your courage will be needed most."

Braque beamed when she said courage. "I knew you would be the wisest of leaders, Majesty. Of course I will join you and bide my time, as you say, before charging into the fray."

"Thank you, Lord Braque. Knowing you will be by my side heartens me, as I'm sure it does Bookins and the entire army."

Braque beamed again and looked around the room for affirmation. No one was paying attention. He started to say something to the entire table, but the queen was now on her feet, raising her wine glass.

"To victory," she shouted, startling everyone else at the table, who quickly grabbed their glasses and scrambled to their feet. "To victory," they roared.

Rhynt smiled. "And now, gentlemen, to your beds. We have a long, fateful day ahead of us."

Everyone set down their glasses and began moving to the door. Whelan moved quickly away from the queen's side and caught the Red God just before she reached the door.

"I would have a word," he whispered, grabbing her by the arm and attempting to move her away from the door. She let him move her out of earshot of the others, but then twisted away from him.

"And I would have you unhand me."

He sneered at her. "What are you up to?"

She caught the look and sneered back. "I am up to what I have been told *by you* to do: watch, listen, learn."

"Ha! As if. You have ignored me at every turn."

"There has been nothing to report. *Nothing.*"

He squinted at her and moved closer. "And why is that?"

She snorted and pushed him away. "Because our dear Bookins has bared his soul to us, has he not? What part of his plan do you not already know? No, don't look away. Hear me. There is nothing else to learn. We have every detail, every single one, and now all you have to do is counter them. When he thrusts to the center, you must be there. At every turn, you must be there."

Whelan seemed to relax, his suspicions somewhat allayed. "Aye, and I have done that, will do that. All the gods save the Gray God are in position."

"What? Has he turned tail?"

Whelan wasn't sure how to answer. Would she even believe that a god could be taken down by beasts, however strong? He didn't, and wondered whether the god, who had never liked Whelan's plan, had in fact turned tail. "I'm not sure. He went missing during the march from the ships."

The Red God looked concerned. "So there's now a hole in your plan."

Whelan leaned in again and whispered, "Which is why I need to speak with you—*now*."

72

"Oh, master," whispered Orthor to himself. "If I could speak to you now, what advice would you give?"

He held up the parchment and stared at the runes once more. "I am baffled, befuddled. If these runes are the key, I must have the wrong lock."

He blinked. It might just be the other way around. Perhaps he had the wrong key. He had spent hours walking down the wall of runes, torch held high, held close, to find a match of some sort, some keyhole for his key, and found nothing.

He looked back at the tripod at the entrance to the cave. Perhaps it had been in the wrong position when the sunlight hit it. Or maybe he had used the tripod and its strange glass too soon or too late. Perhaps there was a different key or multiple keys to unraveling the secrets hidden in the runes.

He thought some more and could almost hear the voice of the Librarian. *Context,* the Librarian would say. *What do we know about the runes and who placed them here?*

Orthor would have answered that the runes were said to be the Teachings of a god called Randall.

And what do we know about gods?

Orthor would have asked for clarification.

I mean, would a god really have more than one key?

Orthor would have answered no, they are all said to be lazy above all. So it must be a single key, then?

Yes, I think so.

But what about the timing? Would I get a different result if I used the tripod at a different time of day?

Orthor knew the Librarian would heave a heavy sigh at this point, exasperated by Orthor's dull brain. *Think about it, Orthor. The sun only shines into the cave for a few minutes each day. Now, if the beam of light had only found one of the reflecting pieces of metal, that would be one thing. But that's not what happened, is it?*

No, it reflected off two pieces before shining on the runes.

Exactly. Now, what's the mathematical probability of a single beam reflecting off two pieces? No, don't answer. The answer is, of course, astronomical. *You have found the correct runes. Now the question is* what do they mean?

Orthor chuckled ruefully. That was the question and the major source of his befuddlement. He had looked to see if the five-rune sequence repeated itself somewhere else on the cave wall, but it did not. The sequence was unique. And he could not find any of the five runes anywhere else on the wall.

The Librarian came forward once again. *That is wonderful news!*

Wonderful? In what way?

It means these runes are unrelated to the other runes.

You confound me further, master. He could picture the Librarian's eyes rolling.

It's not a key, Orthor. It is something else.

Orthor shook his head.

Come now, Orthor. Think of your training, specifically your readings on the subject of runes. Remember Gorscius's *Rune Paths and How to Follow Them?*

Orthor shrugged, then nodded. Yes, he had spent hours studying that seminal text.

Come now, Orthor, there are only three possibilities.

Orthor thought a moment, then brightened. It had to be a key, a direction, or a misdirection.

But we're dealing with a god, are we not? A lazy god who wouldn't waste his time on misdirection.

A direction, then. A direction!

He imagined the Librarian patting him on the back and saying, "Good boy!"

His delight was short-lived, though. He looked at the runes again, and the runes stared back at him once more.

"By the gods! What direction?"

73

Rhynt's conception of a battle always involved the headlong rush of one army against another. Two sides, each in different colors, under different banners, would charge each other, steadily closing the gap until the sides met in a blur of swords and sprays of blood.

She'd never thought about what was unfolding before her just below the bluff where she stood with Bookins, Lord Braque, the Red Monk, a signalman, and half a dozen royal guards. Mela, Mila, and Spook paced back and forth along the edge of the bluff, growling. Rhynt wasn't sure how they'd behave when the battle began.

She could see Calax and Blusk, both on horseback, riding back and forth down the lines, encouraging their warriors to form up in the groups and patterns set forth by Bookins in his plan.

She looked back and forth and finally found Phendour and her archers. There were nearly a thousand of them, so despite her best efforts, she could not find Priss among them. She hoped she had done the right thing converting her from handmaiden to archer.

"That was quite a sigh, Majesty," said Bookins.

She managed a smile. "I had never imagined all of this."

"Nor I. A plan on paper is nothing like the real thing."

Rhynt shook her head. "No, it is even more wondrous—and terrifying."

"Indeed it is, but don't worry. All will be well. The weather is perfect and the warriors are as ready as they will ever be." He pointed to the eastern end of the Plain of Sorrows, where the Mystrosians were forming their lines for battle. "And from what I can see, our enemy is greatly reduced in number."

Rhynt closed her eyes, said the words, and began far-seeing the Mystrosian lines. "You are correct. I would put their strength at half of ours, and many among them seem wounded."

"The beasts have taken their toll, then. That is good."

"I also see, um, something odd."

"Oh, what?"

"I thought the Mystrosians wore black, with white crow sigils."

"That is true, Majesty."

"Well, how do you explain men moving among them in different colors?"

"What? What colors?"

"Let me see. Two in white—the monk and his god, I would suspect."

"Yes, I have taken them into account."

"But there's more. All are robust men, tall and muscular, and clearly commanding parts of their army. One is dressed all in blue and the other in green."

Bookins stammered. "Blue and green? Are you sure?"

"Yes."

"Do they have sigils? Can you see them?"

Rhynt strained to see them more closely. "Um, the blue man has a jay, the green a diamond."

"By the gods!"

Bookins' shout pulled her out of her trance. "What is it?"

"They have recruited the Blue God and the Green God, something I had not thought possible. Tell me, are there others as well? One in gray with a lightning bolt sigil, and one in black with a moon sigil?"

Rhynt dropped back in her trance and scanned the Mystrosian lines. After several minutes, she shook her head and dropped out of the trance. "No, I saw no one else."

Bookins sighed. "Still, I must assume that they are there as well."

Rhynt looked more than concerned "We are facing five gods, with only one on our side?"

"So it appears," said Bookins.

"Here," said the Red Monk, interrupting them. "Did I hear you correctly? They have five gods?"

Rhynt nodded. "And we have but the Red God."

The Red Monk sighed and looked around the bluff.

"What is it?" said Bookins. "You seem nervous."

"Aye, at *least* nervous. And a little more terrified."

"What are you saying?" said Rhynt.

"The Red God, Majesty. I have not seen her since our dinner last night. I've looked in her quarters and everywhere between here and the lodge. She is nowhere."

Rhynt looked once more at the Mystrosian lines. "Well, I don't see her with them." She turned to one of her royal guards. "Take two men and search the lodge and the grounds. See if anyone has seen her."

The guard bowed and started walking away.

"Wait," said Rhynt, looking around. "Where is Whelan? I thought he'd certainly be here."

Everyone else looked around with the same result: No Whelan.

Rhynt turned back to the guard. "And see if you can find Whelan as well."

"Yes, Majesty." He bowed again and quickly moved away, motioning for two other guards to follow him.

Rhynt sighed. "What now, Bookins?"

The very words that were screaming in his head.

74

The White God flapped his wings and glided along the Mystrosian lines. They were fewer now, but a few hours rest seemed to have revived them. There was no sign of lethargy as they quickly formed the lines and formations that would take them into battle.

Canto, Bedo, and Indo waved as he passed over them, but there was still no sign of the Gray God, Dado. The White God knew any slack would have to be taken up by him personally. He would have to forgo merely watching the action to being in the action, a full fourth of the force under his command.

He dipped a wing and turned left, flying over the Plain of Sorrows to assess the terrain, which was as he expected: flat and bare of all vegetation. When the battle began, he knew they would have to deal with the dust kicked up by both armies. He had a thought about that and tucked it away.

By midway across the plain he could see the Enturian lines clearly. They were forming up in a classic formation. The sight of it made him caw loudly. It would have to do for the laugh that would have erupted from him in human form. The formation was known more for its faults than for its advantages. Maintaining it was difficult and would slow their advance.

He flew on, straight for their lines, swooping down to view the formations close up, then lifting higher to fly up and over the bluff above their lines. He nearly flew into a hill tiger as he cleared the bluff's edge, but he was too fast for the claws that attempted to pull him from the sky.

He climbed higher, circling the bluff. He had a clear view now of everything going on below. Their new queen was easy to spot. Her crown twinkled in the light of the rising sun, which made him caw again. They would have the sun in their eyes when the battle began, another advantage for the Mystrosians.

He looked closer. Aside from the hill tigers, which would be formidable obstacles, the queen was protected only by a handful of guards. A small force skirting the lines could easily make its way around the Enturians and capture the queen.

This battle could be over in less than an hour, he thought as he wheeled around and flapped his way back toward the Mystrosian lines. All this talk from Whelan about a fool's so-called gambit was ludicrous. Victory would be theirs, and easily.

The crow cawed just that as he flew back over the Mystrosian lines, the other gods shaking their fists with delight.

75

Calax coaxed Gash along the lines of men and elves forming up on the western edge of the Plain of Sorrows. He kept one eye on the warriors and one eye on the bluff, waiting for the signal to move forward. But what he saw on the bluff was an animated exchange between Bookins and Rhynt. *What are they shouting about? Something must be wrong.* He wondered whether he should break away and find out what was happening, but he just as quickly realized that breaking away now would send the wrong signal. He was out in front of the army and he had to keep them ready and confident. An army with doubts rarely won.

He picked up the pace, urging Gash into a gallop, raising his sword above his head to hearten the men. The roar he was hoping for came quickly. They were ready. *We just need the signal*, he thought. Or signals. The first signal would be for Phendour and her archers. They would launch a volley of arrows across the plain, but well short of the Mystrosians, a ruse designed to make the Mystrosians think they could advance at least as far as the arrows. And when they did that, a second volley would come, and a third, taking out many of the Mystrosian warriors.

Then signals would come for Calax and Blusk, who each led half of the warriors on foot. They would move slowly at first, then break into predetermined groups, each going in different directions, for different reasons. If Bookins' gambit worked, the Mystrosians would be in complete disarray, and the Enturians would win the day.

If not.

If not, it would be a long bloody day, with the outcome in the hands of the gods.

Calax thought about the Red God. Bookins had never mentioned her role in the battle, if any. What would he have her do, and was she up to facing the White God?

He slowed Gash to a walk, then turned him around and galloped back down the lines, cheers erupting as he passed by. He looked up at the bluff again. Rhynt and Bookins had calmed down and a signalman was walking toward the edge of the bluff, his flags at the ready.

Calax took a deep breath Let us begin!

· · ·

Zyrx could see that something was amiss the moment the queen and the fool came into view. Both seemed beyond worried. Rhynt was shaking her head and Bookins looked absolutely ashen.

"Here," said Zyrx, striding up to them. "What's wrong?"

The queen simply said, "Gods!"

Bookins was more expansive. "They have five gods against our one, and the one we have has gone missing." He shrugged. "Other than that, everything is going according to plan."

Zyrx looked at the enemy lines. They were so far away, all he could see was a blur at the edge of the plain. "Are you sure? I mean about the five?"

Rhynt nodded. "I can far-see, remember? They are there."

Zyrx squinted in the direction of their lines. "If you say so, but in any event, gods are not all that."

Rhynt laughed ruefully. "Not all that? They are gods."

Zyrx shook his head. "Did the gods foresee the beasts that tore into them?"

"Well, no, but—"

"So why do we think they know Bookins' plan?" He turned to him. "Have you lost confidence in your plan?"

Bookins shook his head. "No, no I have not. It will work. It must."

Rhynt raised her eyes to the sky. "But. They. Are. Gods."

"You keep saying that," said Zyrx.

"They have powers, do they not? Plan or no, they have powers."

Zyrx frowned. She had a point. Then again. "Look," he said, "I will put our new weapons and armor up against any god, any day."

Rhynt nodded. He had a point. Then again. "But they have never been tested in battle, let alone a battle with gods."

Zyrx took offense and began stammering, struggling on how best to counter her argument.

Bookins jumped in. "You are both right, but for the moment, let's set aside whatever advantage the gods give them. We have superior numbers, superior armor, superior weapons, and a plan that is already unfolding in exactly the way we have planned. They sought to come at us from six directions, and now they are down to one. They sought to overwhelm us with their numbers, but walked right into the land of the beasts." He stopped and pointed toward the enemy lines. "And now, when we let our arrows fly, I am sure they will take the bait. Let us at least take my plan that far. Loose the arrows and let's see how they react. If I am right, a hundred gods will make no difference."

Rhynt sighed and looked at both of them. Yes, she would take the chance. She turned to the signalman. "Let loose the arrows!"

• • •

The White God landed at the center of the Mystrosian lines and transformed into human form. He couldn't find a single other god at first, but then he spotted Whelan and the others—all save the gray god, who was somehow killed by beasts—standing in a tight group and peering at the Enturian lines.

"There you are," he said. "I have news."

"And so do I," said Whelan, putting his hand on the shoulder of the Red God.

The White God could not believe his eyes. "Red? But I thought you were—"

"Yes," said Whelan, "that is what I wanted all of you to think. She's on our side, has been since the beginning."

The White God bowed to her. "Welcome, it will be good to hear what you have learned of the fool's latest plans." He turned to Whelan. "I, too, have news—and a way to beat them, now."

Whelan raised a brow. "Now? What do you mean?"

"The queen is lightly guarded, and there is an easy, concealed path to reach her. When the battle begins, we need only skirt their forces and claim their queen. It will be over in minutes."

Whelan smiled at him. "Excellent, you have done well." He turned to the Red God. "Are there any last-minute changes that we should know about?"

She shook her head. "No, he still plans to begin with a volley of a thousand arrows."

Whelan laughed. "Ridiculous!"

"I know," said the White God. "They will fall far short of our lines, and we shall then have their measure."

"Indeed," said the Red God. "As I understand it, they have untested weapons. He wants to see how far the arrows will go before committing their forces to the field."

The Blue God chuckled. "He is indeed a fool. He has given us the perfect opportunity to advance with impunity."

"Aye to that," said Whelan. "Now, let's go over our assignments once more. And Porto, you know the terrain best, so I think you should lead the group that will capture the queen. Take what men you need and go, now."

The White God nodded once and was gone, racing up the lines, grabbing men as he went.

"Now," said Whelan. "We need to give Porto and his men cover. Here's what we need to do."

A low whistling sound made them turn toward the Enturian lines. A cloud of green arrows glistened in the early morning sun.

"Here we go," said Whelan. "Here we go."

$$\cdot \ \cdot \ \cdot$$

Priss loosed her arrow and tried to follow its path, but a thousand more joined hers, arcing above the plain and falling in a perfect line, just as Phendour had taught them. Priss was delighted and looked around for Phendour, hoping to give her a nod and a smile. Spotting her was easy; she was moving down the line of archers now, urging them to break from their reverie and notch a second arrow.

"Notch!" Phendour screamed and moved down the line, leaving Priss standing there among the others.

Priss notched her arrow and waited for the next command, *draw*. She didn't know when that command would come, so she turned to the archer next to her and smiled. "We did it."

The other archer, a young girl no older than Priss, nodded nervously, fumbling to notch her arrow. Her hands were shaking.

"Here," said Priss. "Let me help."

The girl pulled away. "No, I can get this." She fumbled some more and finally got the arrow to notch. She tried to calm herself and make ready for the next command, but her whole body was shaking.

"What is it?" said Priss, glancing at the girl, then peering up the line to see if Phendour was returning.

"Their arrows," said the girl.

Priss scoffed. "Will fall well short, I'm sure."

"How can you be so sure? Their arrows had no trouble reaching even to our castle the other day. What makes you think they can't reach us now, when we're so close?"

Priss hadn't thought about that. She was certain those arrows at the castle must have been charmed by some god. *So why not here?* she thought. And the thought gave her pause.

She looked at the Mystrosian lines. A blur was rising from it, a blur she soon realized was arrows arcing toward them. She dropped her bow and raced out in front of their ranks, shouting as she went. "Shields!"

• • •

Whelan watched the White God race away and wondered whether the god was up to the task. He had never much liked him; he tended not to follow instructions and was arrogant beyond his talents. But perhaps capturing the queen would redeem him. Whelan hoped so. And to help, he decided on a set of stratagems to distract the Enturians, particularly Bookins, who was proving more capable than expected.

He turned to the Red God. "Here, make yourself useful. On my signal, send a volley of arrows into their lines."

The Red God blinked. "Arrows? Real arrows? I can't do that."

Whelan rolled his eyes. "And you call yourself a god."

"I am what I am, or rather, what you made me. I have skills, yes, but they are more in the subtle arts: persuasion, deceit, and dissembling. But arrows, no, I can't do that."

"You misunderstand me. I know full well your limits. No, not real arrows. The illusion of real arrows. Perhaps two thousand of them, of any color you desire."

The Red God sighed. She could do that. "Illusions of arrows? To what point?"

"Deceit and distraction—your specialty."

The Red God smiled. "Oh, oh, I see."

"Fine, but on my signal, not before."

The Red God shrugged. "Whenever."

Whelan turned away from her to the Blue God. "And I will need another distraction as well, Canto."

Canto cocked his head. "In addition to the arrows? Why?"

Whelan almost reached out and grabbed the god by the throat. *How stupid can he be?* "As you well know, nothing sells a distraction like another distraction. What usually follows a volley of arrows?"

Canto looked puzzled.

Whelan shook his head. *Apparently very stupid.* "Think, Canto, what did we do at the Battle of Whent Hill?"

Canto's puzzled look continued some seconds before his face lit up. "Oh, we advanced."

"Yes, but first smoke, then the advance."

"So you want me to—"

"Yes, a horde of gela warriors, charging headlong toward the Enturian lines."

"To draw fire," said Canto, brightening.

"Yes, yes, exactly. But only on my signal."

Canto nodded. "Of course, of course."

Whelan turned next to the Black God, Indo. "Remember that smoke screen you created at Rock's Reach?"

Indo nodded. "Of course, but it was more like a fog. Is that what you want?"

"Mostly, yes, but it should emanate across our entire line of warriors and roll toward the Enturian lines, obscuring everything as it goes."

"Very well, just tell me when."

"On my signal."

Indo nodded.

Whelan motioned the three gods closer to him. "Each of you will have a different signal, first to you, Abo, then to Indo, then finally to you, Canto. Arrows, smoke, charge, in that order. Do you understand?"

They all nodded.

Whelan smiled back. This would be wonderful. He could only imagine the consternation it would cause in Bookins' mind.

"Now, Abo, launch your arrows."

The Red God walked a few paces away from them and raised her arms.

• • •

Calax Halfhand saw the arrows coming and held tighter to Gash's reins, steadying him. "Easy boy, I have seen this before."

And he had, on the battlefield at Whent Hill. A ruse perpetrated by a god, to lure his forces into a trap. If he was right, a rolling fog, almost like smoke, would come next, followed by an army of gelas. You couldn't kill them; you could only die, either from them or the real army that would flow in from all sides.

He turned to his men and elves. Terror was already beginning to set in. "Hold! Hold your positions! Shields up!"

He knew the shields were pointless—the arrows would disappear as they neared the ground—but he also knew the appearance of safety under a shield was important.

He watched the arrows reach their peak and begin to fall. *If I am wrong, this day will not go well,* he thought.

But he was right. The arrows plummeted and disappeared just above their upraised shields. Warriors began emerging from under them, a look of both surprise and relief on their faces.

Calax put Gash into a trot and moved up and down the lines. "Hold now. Do nothing until my signal. This was a trick of a god, and there will be more tricks. Hold until I signal."

He didn't know how any of them would react when they saw the fog or the false army. He could only follow his instincts.

He looked up at the bluff, where he could see Bookins and the queen. Her tigers were roaring.

• • •

The queen lowered her shield and peered out at the battlefield. "What was that?"

Bookins smiled. "A ruse, to scare us."

"But why not real arrows?"

Bookins shrugged. "They could have been real; the gods can do such things, but if I am right, their intention at the moment is to scare and confuse us, make us think too much about what may come next."

"And what will come next?"

"If I am right, we will need more men here, on this bluff."

"What? Why?"

"I am not a particularly well-read man, but there is one thing I have read over and over: Tildear's *History of the Battle of Whent Hill*."

"A book? What are you talking about?"

"A particular ruse used by a particular god during the battle. It had a singular purpose: to capture the queen of Ichthia."

Rhynt spun around, looking for intruders. "Mela, Mila, Spook—to me!"

• • •

Despite Calax's warnings, Priss stood frozen in place as she saw a dense fog rolling toward their lines. It was coming fast, unnaturally fast and a roar as if from a thousand thousand warriors was erupting from it. Will they really be fake warriors, as Calax had said, or would this be a ruse on top of a ruse, fake arrows leading to real warriors?

She managed to look away from the fog long enough to assess how her fellow archers were handling what was charging at them. Some were frozen in place, as she had been just seconds ago, and some were fumbling with their bows, trying to notch arrows, their hands shaking.

She looked back at the fog, which had reached the row of arrows they had launched just minutes before. This was to be their ruse, to trick the Mystrosians into underestimating the reach of their arrows. That seemed of little importance now.

The fog grew closer, as did the roar of whatever hid within it. Priss realized she no longer had her bow; she had dropped it to give the shields order, and had forgotten it in her terror. Her eyes darted frantically in all directions, searching for the bow. "My bow! Has anyone seen my bow?"

No one answered; they were too busy notching arrows.

She started to shout again, but stopped. She could see her bow on the ground, far off to the left.

And something else.

A glint of shining armor, moving swiftly along the northern tree line. She blinked and looked again. More glints, more movement.

Then she turned back to look at the fog. It was nearly upon them, and their lines were not holding. Archers and warriors alike were backing up, some scattering. She looked for Phendour but couldn't see her.

She grabbed her bow and began running.

•   •   •

If Whelan had had his lute handy, he would have strummed a happy tune and danced a jig. Everything was going according to plan. A small force was even now approaching the queen. Arrows had scared their main force, and the fog had shaken them to their very core. Fog was nothing to a god, so he could see clearly the movement in their lines. *They are breaking*, he thought. *And so quickly. The Fool was a fool to think he could take on a god, let alone me, Randall, the god of gods.*

He resisted the temptation to let out a loud hoot, and turned as calmly as he could to Canto. "Now."

Canto nodded and moved to the center of their lines, lifting his arms up to the sky. Moments later, ghostlike figures began to emerge by the hundreds in front of their real line of warriors. It only took a minute for them all to appear like real flesh and bone. Each one was different in their way, but all were fierce in aspect. The Enturians would be terrified.

Satisfied with his work, Canto turned back to Whelan, who nodded his approval. "Release them!"

Canto threw a fist in the air. "Charge!"

The gela warriors began screaming and running, their combined war cries deafening as they disappeared into the fog and launched themselves toward the Enturian lines.

Whelan, looking through the fog, could see their effect on the Enturian lines. He could see Calax, Blusk, and Phendour riding up and down the lines, trying their best to control the men and elves, who wanted nothing more than to run.

He turned to Canto. "Make them run faster, scream louder."

Canto threw both arms into the air and shouted one word: "More!"

The effect was immediate.

•   •   •

Phendour slammed her heels into the horse's haunches and galloped up and down the line of archers, urging calm, but she could see the looks of terror in their eyes. Her lines, once a model of discipline, were crumbling. She knew that she was on the cusp between control and chaos, and chaos seemed to have the advantage.

Several of her most talented archers had already thrown down their bows and bolted. Most disheartening was the sudden disappearance of Priss. Phendour had had high hopes for her. She had toned her body, followed every instruction, and by the end of training, was hitting targets with a consistency and accuracy that challenged even her teacher.

She turned her attention to the Mystrosians. A vast army, real or not, screaming at the top of their lungs, was closing the distance. They were well within range now, but there was no way to get control of her archers fast enough to do any damage.

She glanced up the line, where she could see Calax and Blusk having similar problems controlling their units, and then looked up at the bluff, where she could see Rhynt and her hill tigers in what looked like a frantic exchange with d'Abo and Bookins.

She turned back to the Mystrosians. They were coming impossibly fast.

Bookins did his best to think as the Red Monk and Rhynt peppered him with questions, some general, others specific. What's happening? What should we do? Shall we launch arrows? Charge? Bookins, are you even listening?

He was. "Stop!" Perhaps he had been too sharp. Rhynt and d'Abo both jumped back.

"Here now," said Rhynt. "We only—"

"Seek answers," said Bookins as calmly as he could manage. "Yes, and I assure you, I have them."

"Well, then, said Rhynt, glancing down at the plain and the charging, screaming Mystrosians. "Out with it!"

He nodded quickly and turned to the Red Monk. "Those are gelas, something you should be able to deal with. I knew this would happen, or at least thought it might, but I did not expect the reaction of our warriors. I thought they'd stand their ground."

"Less talk, more answers," said Rhynt. "They are nearly upon us."

"Stop them," said Bookins to the Red Monk. "Can't you stop them?"

The Red Monk looked down at the battlefield. "There are so many. I don't think I can do this by myself."

"Then let me help," said Rhynt. "I am a demigod, am I not? I should be able to help."

The Red Monk blinked as if he had just been presented with an unimaginably delicious slice of nander pie. "Yes, of course—um, maybe."

He took her by the hand. "Follow my every action and word, and repeat them. It is like far-seeing. You must concentrate, and if this works, you will not just be far-seeing, you will be far-doing."

He tugged her toward the edge of the bluff. "Now," he said. "Raise both arms and repeat after me."

The Mystrosians kept coming.

•   •   •

Calax put Gash into a full gallop and headed down the line to get Blusk and Phendour. Their lines were crumbling and words didn't seem to be working on restoring order.

He reached Blusk first and told him his plan, which Blusk quickly agreed to and joined him on his ride to Phendour.

"Phendour, we need to show them," said Calax, "just like the Battle of Whent Hill. These are just gelas."

Phendour nodded. "I was wondering when you'd reach that conclusion. My archers are about ready to scatter."

"Let's do this," said Blusk. "They're almost upon us."

Calax turned to look at the approaching horde. "All right, let's go!"

They turned their horses in the direction of the Mystrosian gelas and raced toward them. The gelas paid no attention and continued their headlong charge. In seconds, the three were upon them, charging down the enemy line, the gelas disappearing as the three rode through them. And then, suddenly, all the gelas disappeared.

The three of them pulled up and looked back at the bluff. The Red Monk and Rhynt were on its edge, arms raised, shouting words in a language Calax did not recognize.

"Looks like we're not the only ones who figured it out," he said.

"Aye," said Blusk. "Spoiled our fun, they did."

Phendour laughed. "I don't call that fun, but come, let's get back to our men and elves. We need to regroup before the real army of theirs comes charging."

They split up, each heading for their place in the lines, fists raised in victory to the cheers of their men and elves, who seemed more relieved than victorious.

The gelas were gone now, but the smoke and fog remained, making them wonder what would come through it next.

The woman's voice was clear and lilting and seemed to come out of nowhere. "Well done, Rhynt. Now, take care to your north. Evil comes betimes."

Rhynt let go of the Red Monk's hand and whirled around to find the woman behind the voice, but there was nothing and no one.

"What is it?" said the Red Monk. "You look as if you've seen some ghostly apparition."

Rhynt calmed herself. "No, it's nothing. Just a little jumpy is all." *But it had to be something, someone,* she thought. And then she noticed the tingling around her head where her new crown sat. *The crown! The elven jewels! It is as Zyrx said. Some wonderful magic.*

"Well, you look positively ashen, my dear—I mean, Majesty."

"The excitement, I guess." She gave the Red Monk a big smile. "We did it, did we not?"

"Indeed, we did."

Bookins was quick to join in. "It was wonderful, wonderful. I think you've saved my plan." He frowned. "At least I hope so."

Rhynt tried to focus on his words, but the words of the woman in the crown—*take care to your north*—made her turn away from him and stare at the tree line at the northern end of the bluff.

"What is it?" said Bookins, following her eyes. "Is there something there?"

She turned back to him. "No, no—at least I don't think so."

"Good," said Bookins, turning back to look down on the Plain of Sorrows. "Now, we must do something about this smoke or fog or whatever it is." He turned to the Red Monk. "Can you do anything?"

The Red Monk shook his head. "I have tried many charms and incantations over the years, but this damnable fog is god-borne. I can do nothing."

"Can you far-see through it at least?"

The monk shrugged, then looked at Rhynt. "Maybe. Perhaps. Majesty, shall we try this together. Perhaps our combined strength will see us through." He chuckled. "Or through us see."

Rhynt nodded. "Yes, let's try."

She walked with him back to the edge of the bluff, where they joined hands once more.

"I will count down from three, Majesty."

"I'm ready."

He lifted her hand into the air and began counting down. When he got to one, the woman in the crown spoke once more. "Evil comes. Run!"

• • •

Rhynt broke away from the Red Monk, heeding the words of the crown, and looked in all directions. Nothing had changed. *Where is this evil, this danger?* she thought.

"To the north," whispered the crown. "Run!"

"I will do no such thing; I am needed here."

Her words startled the Red Monk, who was still trying to figure out why she had broken away from him. "What are you talking about?"

"Nothing, sorry, but I've seen all I need to see of the Mystrosian lines. They have moved to our line of arrows."

"Yes, so we should—"

"Signal the archers, yes, I know." She turned to Bookins and the signalman. "Your ploy worked. They are poised at the arrow line."

Bookins nodded and motioned the signalman to the edge of the bluff. The man began waving the signal flags, ordering the archers to loose arrows, but he was only able to signal "loose" before six arrows suddenly appeared in his side and he toppled off the bluff.

• • •

Rhynt's scream startled Lord Braque, who had been asleep in his rolling chair, waiting for the battle to begin. He looked around for her, but the first thing he saw was a volley of arrows arcing up away from the Enturian lines toward what looked like fog rolling along the ground midway across the plain. *By the gods*, he thought. *What magic is that?*

He tried to force himself to his feet, but the new armor Zyrx had made for him, though light to any other man, made it difficult for him to stand. It felt like a horse was sitting on him.

But an arrow pinging off his armored forearm was all he needed to launch himself to his feet. He looked for the queen and spotted her a few yards away, standing with Bookins, Zyrx, the Red God, and her tigers, hidden behind the shield wall of her guards, each shield flowering with arrows.

He turned to the north to find the source of the arrows, but all he could see was arrows streaking from the cover of the tree line. *There must be a score of them*, he thought.

Arrows began pinging off his chest, forcing him back. He looked around for his shield and found it leaning against his roller chair. He raised it up and immediately heard the thud of half a dozen arrows.

And then the arrow song stopped, replaced by screams of pain coming from the tree line. *What's this?* he thought. He lowered his shield. The arrows had indeed stopped.

But then a man burst from the trees, charging with his sword held high toward the queen. He was dressed all in white, with a black crow sigil. Guard after guard rushed the man, but were quickly cut down.

And on he came, quickly, furiously.

Braque blinked. *This is no man,* he thought.

He turned toward Rhynt and her last remaining guards and shouted, "God!"

Then he launched himself toward the god. He did not know how he could stop a god, but he suddenly felt young and alive and invincible. "To me, god!"

• • • •

The woman in the crown was screaming in Rhynt's head, but Rhynt could not make out the words. There was a ringing in her ears like the sound a bell makes, but drawn out, never ending and drowning out all other sounds. She thought she heard the word *hand* but it could just as well have been *sand* or *land*, and none of those words made sense.

She could see Lord Braque attempting to rush at the oncoming god, but he was so weighed down by his new armor, he could only take a single step before the god rushed by him, knocking him to the ground. And now the god was rushing at her as the ringing in her ears grew louder and the voice of the woman in the crown disappeared entirely.

As he rushed up to her, she jumped to the side, away from her hill tigers, who had surrounded her, roaring at the god, and rolled away into the grass, then leaped up and launched three daggers in the god's direction. The daggers struck home, one in the neck, one in the shoulder, and one in the heart. Any ordinary man would have dropped dead on the spot, but the god just laughed, plucked the daggers out, and threw them aside.

She retreated to the safety provided by her hill tigers, who quickly surrounded her and the others once more as the god cocked his head back and forth, stretching his neck. "And now for you, Queen Rhynt, and your pitiful kittens, and you Bookins, and you Zyrx, and even you, Monk. You can fall here or surrender. The choice is yours."

The ringing in her ears suddenly stopped, replaced by the voice of the woman in the crown. "His hand, his right hand."

Rhynt blinked. She had no idea what that meant. The left-handed god's right hand was empty. "What do you mean?"

The god rolled his eyes. "I thought I was clear. Surrender or die."

She started to reply—*Never!*—but now a new sound drew her attention away from the god and the woman in the crown. A half-dozen archers burst from the tree line behind the god and began firing arrows, which the god took in his back with a shrug and a laugh.

The god glanced back at them. "They never learn." Then he turned back to Rhynt. "So, what is it to be? A long life or one lost on the end of my sword?"

The voice in her head was frantic, insistent. "You must strike the right hand of the god!"

Rhynt looked down at the god's hand. He caught the look and seemed to understand, pulling it back and moving it behind his back. "That will not work, little one."

And then his eyes went wide and he shouted out in pain, pulling his right hand from behind him and looking at the arrow that had pierced it. He took one final look at Rhynt, a mixture of pain and rage, and then transformed into a crow, flapping his wings to loosen the arrow, which dropped away.

Rhynt watched the crow rise into the air and begin climbing higher and higher. A voice suddenly startled her. It wasn't the woman in the crown—the voice was too high and shrill, a young girl's voice. Priss's voice. "Die!"

Rhynt turned to see Priss launch an arrow into the air, then followed the arrow's path as it climbed to meet and penetrate the crow, which let out a single squawk and plummeted to the plain, dead.

Rhynt spun back around with a smile. "How did you know to do that?"

Priss shrugged. "Um, did you not hear the voice?"

• • •

Bookins wasn't sure what had just happened. One moment he was standing there, waiting to be killed, and the next he was swiveling his head to see a young archer launching an arrow at a crow. He turned toward Lord Braque, who was grumbling to himself, trying to push himself up with arms long withered away to mere flesh and bone. Whatever muscle he had once had was only to be seen in old portraits of the young king.

"Here," said Bookins, shuffling up to him. "Let me give you a hand." But even lending both hands, Bookins was unable to lift Braque up. He let go of him and motioned for help to the group of archers who had burst through the trees just moments before. The archers lifted up Lord Braque easily and backed him into his roller chair.

Lord Braque nodded his thanks, then turned to Bookins. "Did you see it—that archer? By the gods, she's killed a very god!"

Bookins blinked. "You mean the crow?"

Lord Braque rolled his eyes. "Of course I mean the crow, the animal form of the White God."

"Yes, yes, of course," he stammered.

"We have them, Bookins! Launch your attack, man!"

The plan? thought Bookins. *Yes, the plan.* "Indeed," he said, turning away from Braque and shuffling as fast as he could to where the signalman had once stood. He grabbed the signal flags from the ground and began waving them. "Loose arrows! Charge!"

Whelan watched the crow spiral down to the ground, an arrow through its breast. Fortunately, only he and the other gods could see through the fog. If his archers and warriors had seen the crow's descent, their lines would surely have broken and all would have been chaos and headlong flight.

He had to act now, decisively.

He had poised his forces at the edge of the line of arrows laid down by the Enturians, a foolish move on the Enturian's part, giving away the range of their arrows, which was remarkably short. His archers could best that easily.

He leaped into the saddle of his horse, raised his sword high, and shouted, "Loose arrows!"

He watched the archers fumbling with their bows. And then he heard an impossible sound, the sound of arrows, hundreds and hundreds of arrows headed their way.

His archers began to fall and those not hit hesitated, not sure whether to fire or run. Whelan had to act quickly. If he stayed where he was, the army would be cut down. If they retreated, they'd lose the advantage. He turned to the entire mass of his army.

"Charge!"

Calax watched the arrows rise into the air and disappear into the fog. The screams that followed heartened him and made him ever more eager to charge into the fog, whatever it may conceal.

And the signal came quickly.

He looked up the line to make sure Blusk had seen the signal, and saw Blusk already rallying his warriors, their war cries beginning to build into near deafening crescendo.

Calax turned to his men, who had already been caught up in the sound of the war cries rolling down the line, and shouted the word they had all been waiting for. "Charge!"

Calax urged Gash forward, coaxing him from a trot to a gallop to a full-out charge in seconds, their speed making the two of them, who flew along the ground as one, war horse and warrior alike, meld into a fluid blur that seemed to make the scudding clouds stop in their course across the sky to admire them and their gleaming armor, green as emeralds, which challenged even the sun in brightness, only the puffs of their breaths in the chill morning air bearing witness that what bolted across the plain was horse and man and not some by-god miracle neither dreamed nor imagined forming a spear to breach the Mystrosian lines, which seemed to waver and gasp at the very sight of them.

Just behind Calax, the men and elves in his command rushed forward as one, charging toward the Mystrosians, who were just emerging from the fog, their cries matching the Enturians now, the ground itself rumbling with the sound of their feet pounding toward each other.

A hundred yards into the charge, the armies met, and it was like a clap of thunder as man met man, sword met sword, and shield bashed shield.

And then the fog rolled over all of them, and they were lost from view, the battle's progress marked only by screams of pain, the ping of swords, and the thump of shields.

Bookins and the others stood motionless on the bluff, straining to see anything, whether friend or foe. And the battle raged, the fog persisting despite the heat provided by the sun, which seemed to be speeding through its arc across the plain, hours passing like minutes as the battle raged without surcease, the sounds of pain now just another sound, just the marking of another fallen warrior.

On and on it went till the sun began to fade, each army finally backing away, no longer able to clearly see the opponent in front of them.

And then all was silence.

Bookins looked out into the darkness and then bent over and took a deep breath. They had survived day one, and the plan had not yet unraveled.

He looked over at Rhynt, who also seemed to be breathing for the first time in hours. "Majesty."

She nodded, then managed a smile. "Baron."

"We live to fight another day."

"Aye, you've made history this day. Statues should be built to you for this day alone, come what may."

Bookins chuckled, then shook his head. "A bit premature, Majesty. There is an old saying: History does not make for good sculpture—its clay never sets."

Rhynt gave him a quick smile. "Then we will have to set it in stone tomorrow." She looked around her. "Come, we must see to the wounded and get reports from Calax, Blusk, and Phendour."

She spotted Priss standing apart with the other archers. "Priss, to me."

76

When King Braque built his hunting lodge fifty years ago, he had insisted on a counsel room, so that he might carry on business when he wasn't carrying on with the half dozen maidens he always brought along.

It was a big room, though not nearly as large as the counsel room in the castle. Here wood replaced stone, and stuffed animals—on walls, hanging from the ceiling, or propped up in corners—replaced tapestries and ancient armor. The only thing bigger about the lodge counsel room was its hearth, which occupied nearly the entire length of one wall. The hill tigers sat there, of course, curled up in front of a fire tended by two servants.

Bookins had insisted that they use that room to discuss the events of the day and plan the next day's stratagems, and Queen Rhynt had agreed. As everyone filed into the room, it was easy to tell who had fought on the plain and who had spent the battle high up on the bluff, away from the blood and dust. The armor of the bluff people was bright and shiny and gleamed like the finest jewels. The armor of the plains people was coated in orange dust that had been kicked up as the armies had rushed one another, making them look like beetles that had emerged from a long sleep in the soil.

Sleep itself was a worthy topic for the plains people. They were beyond exhausted and only wanted to end the meeting before it began, so they might return to their men and elves and see to their needs, including tending the wounded, before catching what sleep they might before sunrise.

Calax Halfhand was the first to sit, slumping into a hard wooden chair and wincing from a gash on his thigh. He didn't know what he could contribute to this meeting. He remembered his headlong gallop into the fog and the Mystrosian lines, but then everything was a blur until the sun set and no man stood before him. He was a berserker, after all, a killing machine whose only thoughts were blood and gore and the mechanics of swordplay. His armor, more than any of the others, was more red than green, swirls and splashes of blood, mixed with the orange dust, giving it the look of an intricate tapestry, a tapestry woven with the blood of hundreds.

Queen Rhynt sat down at the head of the table, gave Calax a nod and a smile—she was so happy he had survived—and waited patiently as the others took their places, most trying to position themselves the same way they had done back at the castle, as if they were not sitting in just another chair, but *their* chair.

Finally, everyone was seated and the table grew silent.

Rhynt cleared her throat and began. "Thank you for coming. I know you have other things to attend to, not the least of which is a good night's sleep, but I think it's important for us to assess what happened today and what we might expect on the morrow. Those of you who led the various units of our army, please report on your actions. Then we'll hear from Baron Bookins. Did the plan work? Are changes needed? And so on." She nodded at Calax. "Calax, as supreme commander, please give us your overall assessment of today's battle."

Calax startled. He had been looking away, watching the flames of the fire, his eyes heavy-lidded from exhaustion. "Um, yes, of course."

He stood to make himself better heard. His wound thanked him and made him wince. "Ah, ah." He shook it off. "Sorry, I bring back a wound that may need tending before I rest this night."

"Shall we stop so you might tend it?" said Rhynt, concerned.

"No, Majesty, it is nothing compared to the wounds I have seen this day. Our army accounted itself well for the most part. The training provided by Blusk and Phendour saved us. Though the Mystrosians are better warriors—I say this with all due respect to our own warriors—we matched them blow for blow and pushed them back across the arrow line." He turned to Zyrx. "And our armor is far superior to theirs, thanks to Zyrx and his blacksmiths."

Zyrx beamed. "We do our best. Thank you."

"There is, however, a flaw in our armor."

Zyrx blinked. "Flaw? What flaw?" There was more than an edge to his voice.

"Take no offense, Zyrx. It is not a flaw in your armor, but a flaw in the coverage of your armor. Strike a sword against your armor and the sword will bounce off, leaving hardly any dent at all. But where the armor is missing, around the neck, the sword has no problem. We left a lot of headless warriors on that plain today."

Zyrx put his head in his hands. "Oh, no."

"Do not fret. The armor is still superior."

Zyrx said nothing. He was too upset to speak.

"Majesty," said Calax. "That is my report. I can only add that if the sun had cooperated, I think we could have overwhelmed them, if not by overall skill, then by courage and determination."

"That is good to hear," said Rhynt, "but what of casualties?"

Calax looked down at the table. "My group lost a third, about seven hundred, with another two hundred wounded." He turned to Blusk. "What about you, Blusk?"

Blusk stayed seated and was slow in answering. "We were hit hard, about eight hundred dead and, like Calax's group, about two hundred wounded, though most of those wounds were minor. They'll be able to join us for tomorrow's battle."

Rhynt turned to Phendour. "And you?"

Phendour looked up and down the table. "We fared much better, being at the rear. Only a handful killed or wounded. We'll be able to press harder tomorrow."

Rhynt nodded. "Good." She turned back to Calax. "And what of the Mystrosians? Can you estimate their losses?"

Calax shook his head. "Majesty, as you know, I tend to lose myself in a battle. I remember the charge and little else till the setting of the sun. Blusk, what do you think?"

Blusk chuckled. "Majesty, as you can see from Calax's armor, he had a busy day. At one point, though I was busy as well, I saw him surrounded by Mystrosians and then, in a nonce, all of them were on the ground, screaming and bleeding out." He turned to the question at hand. "But as for their losses, I would estimate that they have lost fewer than we have, perhaps no more than five hundred men. They are skilled, and it shows in the numbers."

Rhynt frowned. "What do you think of our chances on the morrow? We are greatly reduced in strength."

Blusk nodded. "Yes, we are, but as Calax said, we not only stood our ground, but pushed them back. Yes, there will be fewer of us tomorrow, but I would match our determination against their skills any day."

"I agree," said Calax. "Come what may, we will be ready."

Rhynt looked around the table and was about to turn to Bookins, but she noticed Whelan sitting apart by the fire. "Whelan, what are you doing over there? And where have you been?"

Whelan smiled, stood, and strummed his lute. "Here, there, and everywhere, Majesty. Collecting stories, working on new songs to hearten the victors and anger the losers."

"And who would those victors be, minstrel?"

"From what I saw, I'd have to agree with Calax and the others. The Mystrosians are spent." He looked over at Bookins, who was frowning at him. "I'm no strategist, of course, not like our Baron Bookins, but I think if we commit our entire force at once, we can overwhelm them. I dare say, we'll have a short day tomorrow."

"I hope you are right," said Rhynt. "Come, join us at the table—there is a seat next to Phendour—and we'll hear what Bookins has in mind for us tomorrow, whether an all-out charge or something more clever."

Whelan strummed his lute once more, made a deep bow, and then moved to the seat next to Phendour.

Rhynt waited until he was seated. "Go on, Bookins. You've heard of today's actions and results. We around this table survived, but how about your plan, this gambit of yours. Is it still in play or do we have to reassess and try something else?"

"Good questions all," said Bookins, standing. He looked around the table, nodding at each person. "Majesty, though our losses have been considerable, the plan survives. As hard as it is to accept, this day's losses make tomorrow all the better. Yes, we will have to make minor adjustments—that was always to be expected—but the overall plan hasn't changed in any major way since I first discussed it with you, Majesty."

He turned to Whelan. "A headlong charge? I think not. Remember, now that the Red God has gone over to them, they not only have five, or rather four, gods supporting them, they have a god who knows the plan—if she was listening. I was never sure of that."

"So we need to make adjustments? Is that what you're saying?"

"Yes, and one of them involves the gods." He paused to look over at Priss, who was sitting on the other side of Phendour. "By chance or some magic, we now know that a god may be killed."

"And how was that done?" said Whelan, leaning forward.

Priss spoke up. "It just came into my head."

"What came into your head?" said Whelan.

"To strike at the god's hand. It must be a weak point because my second arrow took him down when he attempted to fly away."

Whelan slumped back into his chair. "Interesting. I will have to craft a song about that."

"In any event," said Bookins, "we need to inform our army what to do when they face these gods in battle."

Everyone around the table nodded, and the news of weakened gods seemed to cheer them.

"Now then," said Bookins. "This is what we must do."

77

When the meeting ended, Whelan took care not to rush out of the room. He lingered a while, making small talk with Calax and the queen before strolling out the door, walking down the hall, and disappearing.

"It was magnificent!" he said to the other gods. "Bookins laid out his plan for the morrow, Calax revealed a weakness in their armor, and a young archer—I think her name was Briss or some such—somehow figured out how to kill a god."

The last words startled the gods, which prompted a laugh from Whelan. "Fools, you need only wear an armored glove on your non-sword hands. All will be well. We will strike first—I know exactly when—and we will strike at their necks. Heads will fly, and we will be victorious."

The other gods seemed heartened by his words, but Whelan let them celebrate for only a moment. "Now, where's the food? My host the queen was less than accommodating. She offered no food, no drink, just words and words and words." He paused a moment, then laughed. "Of course, that might make a fine song."

78

Calax, Phendour, and Blusk sat as close to the fire as they could without burning their feet. A cold mist had settled over their camp on the edge of the Plain of Sorrows, promising a foggy morning and a possible delay in the battle.

"I hate fighting in fog," said Blusk. "It's just not fair to friend or foe. Give me sunlight and let the best man win is what I say."

"Tell me about it," said Phendour. No archer likes to launch an arrow and not know where it hits."

"Aye," said Calax. "But it could be worse. Rain would turn this plain into an orange puddle, sucking us down in its mud."

Blusk laughed. "You're right about that, Calax. A warrior, however good, always looks for a better day—and more advantage."

They grew silent for a moment, each staring at the fire, lost in their own thoughts.

But then they heard heavy footsteps, though oddly spaced, approaching them from the darkness. Calax started to draw his sword, but a booming voice stopped him.

"Hold, Calax. It's just me."

Zyrx walked up to the fire and dropped a piece of armor at his side. "Here, try this on for size."

Calax pulled the armor over and twirled it around in the firelight. "What's this?"

"The answer," said Zyrx. "I hope." He took the armor away from Calax and turned it so everyone could see the top. "Here, you see, I've added a collar that swoops up from the shoulder and curls away from the head, but high enough to protect the neck. Any sword strike at the neck will be deflected away."

Blusk beamed. "That will save hundreds, if not thousands."

"It is a fine piece of work, Zyrx," said Phendour.

"Aye," said Calax, less enthusiastically. "But what good is one piece of armor. We need thousands."

Zyrx chuckled. "And you shall have them."

"What? How? We fight in just hours."

Zyrx shook his head and smiled. "You forget the tower. An hour here on the plain is thirty-six days in the tower. My blacksmiths will have months to make the armor, and you can expect it well before dawn."

Calax gave him a puzzled look. "The tower is here? I thought we left it back at the castle?"

"We did, at least initially, but I had it moved here just in case we might need it."

Calax laughed and slapped Zyrx on the back, nearly toppling him over. "Ha! That is wonderful! Why, if Whelan were here, I'm sure he'd come up with a song."

79

Bookins paced back and forth along the edge of the bluff, alternately looking down at his army and across the plain at the mist that was slowly burning off in the early morning light. He had spent a sleepless night, every thought on what might go wrong. One false move, one move made at the wrong time, in the wrong way, would unravel the gambit. In the end, he had decided that the only course was to trust in his army and his plan.

Still.

Still, the day had begun with an unexpected mist, a natural mist and no concoction of the gods along the Mystrosian lines. Only the sun could burn it off, and the sun was taking its precious time, time needed for his plan to work.

A voice from behind startled him. "Will you please stop pacing?"

It was the queen. "Yes, no, I don't know. I worry, Majesty."

"About the new armor?"

"No, that is good. We will certainly lose fewer men and elves—if all goes well."

"Bookins, look at me."

He stopped pacing and turned to face the queen. "Yes?"

"It will work, mist or no mist."

Bookins gave her a wry smile. "I see you have noticed it."

"Yes, but it will burn off."

"Will it? I wonder. It is thick and slow to change. We may have to abandon the plan."

Rhynt scoffed. "Nonsense. The plan you explained to me cannot fail."

"But what if—"

"Stop, I will hear no more!"

"But Majesty . . ."

Rhynt started to reply, but a change in the mist took her words away. "What's that?"

Bookins turned and looked back over the plain. Hundreds of warriors appeared to be emerging from the mist.

.   .   .

Calax spun his arms around in a circle and then across his chest, testing the new armor. It was flexible and fit him like a skin, and it was as Zyrx had said: the new neckpiece did not interfere with his movements.

He looked down the line of men and elves. He had never seen so many smiles before a battle. The new armor had lifted their spirits. They were feeling confident, perhaps invincible.

A nearby warrior, an elf who towered over him, tapped him on the shoulder. "Supreme Commander, the flags are moving again."

Calax looked up at the bluff. A signalman was waving flags at him. "What the—"

All the message said was *look*. Look? Look *where*?

He turned back to the bluff. Everyone was pointing out toward the Plain of Sorrows. He turned to see if he could see whatever they were seeing, but all he saw was the mist, which had grown thinner but still obscured the Mystrosian lines.

He was about to call for his own signalman—*what are they talking about?*—when he saw what looked like balls floating in the mist and spread out before him in a straight line, perhaps a hundred yards away.

Curious.

He squinted to get a better look, and what he saw made him gasp, a gasp that was quickly joined by the gasps of others. There was no mistaking what they were seeing: the heads of hundreds of fallen warriors, staring back at them atop pikes thrust into the ground.

Rage began to grow in him, a rage he knew all too well, a rage that unchecked would turn him from leader to berserker. He tried to calm himself, but he could not control the roar coming from him.

He gripped his sword and began to draw it from its scabbard.

Bookins could see the effect that the heads were having on the warriors below him. He had hoped that the new armor would harden them against such provocations. Yes, the Mystrosians had lopped off hundreds of heads, and the heads on the pikes were their way of saying, "Come then, and we'll lop off your head as well."

Bookins wanted their reaction to be, "Look, they have wasted hundreds of pikes that could have been used to kill us. They are fools."

But the reaction below him was a mix of fear and rage. Calax's bellow was unmistakable. He was rising to the Mystrosian bait, and that is the last thing Bookins wanted.

"Signalman," he shouted. "A new message, please. Tell them to hold firm."

The signalman waved his flags, and their message seemed to have an immediate effect. He could hear the message shouted up and down the lines below: *hold firm! Hold firm!*

Bookins looked out at the plain again. The mist was burning off more quickly now. He could see the line of pikes and beyond them the lines of the Mystrosians, ready for battle.

He turned to Rhynt, who had been standing beside him with her hill tigers. She seemed untroubled, almost serene. "Majesty, it is almost time. Are you sure about this?"

Rhynt cocked her head and smiled. "We shall see." She looked up at the sun, then down at the mist. "The sun says yes and the mist agrees."

Whelan almost danced with delight when he saw the Enturian's reaction and heard Calax's unmistakable roar. "Ready yourselves," he said to the other gods. "If I know Calax, that berserker will have them all in a full charge soon enough."

He looked down the line of Mystrosians and gave the order. "Advance!"

He marched them a hundred yards and then stopped them just short of the line of heads, where they would await the Enturian's charge well out of the reach of Enturian arrows. And when the Enturians charged, they would be met by a hail of his own arrows. Any Enturian who made it to the line of heads would have to fight their way through that fence to even begin to engage his army.

He looked out across the plain. He could see Calax astride his massive warhorse, trotting up and down the line of warriors. "Come on, Calax, what are you waiting for?"

Minutes passed and nothing happened. All the Enturians now stood silent, barely moving.

"What's this game you play, Bookins?"

He looked back at his men, who seemed as confused as he was. Then a sound from the Enturian lines drew his attention. They were shouting something, but he couldn't make out the words. And then his eyes grew wide as he saw a lone warrior on the smallest horse he'd ever seen moving slowly toward the line of heads. "What's this?"

• • •

Rhynt was the first to see him, and screamed. "Braque! It's Braque!"

A chill ran through Bookins. His former king was trotting toward the Mystrosian lines. "No, he'll ruin everything!"

He turned to the new signalman. "Retrieve that fool."

The signalman began waving his flags, but Rhynt could see that no one was looking back at the bluff. Their eyes were fixed on Lord Braque and his little pony.

She screamed at the signalman. "Too late!" Then she called for her hill tigers. "Mela, Mila, Spook, to me."

The tigers were there in an instant, curling their bodies around her legs and purring. She pointed out across the plain. "Bring that man back!"

The tigers continued curling around her legs.

"By the gods," she screamed, then bolted for the path that led down from the bluff, her hill tigers in pursuit.

Bookins couldn't believe his eyes. "Majesty, no!"

But she was gone, racing to the bottom of the path and out onto the plain, her hill tigers running beside her as if they thought they were playing a fine game.

• • •

Whelan had barely recovered from the ridiculous sight of Lord Braque charging at them when he spotted the tigers and Queen Rhynt. "By my gods, we will have them!"

He started to give the order to charge, but then hesitated. Bookins had said he would wait for the Mystrosians to charge before engaging. Was this some ruse to draw them forward, within the range of the Enturian archers?

In the seconds it took for him to consider the question, curious became curiouser. A warrior had separated himself from the line of Enturians and was now galloping toward Braque and the Queen. "It's Calax! This is no ruse. It's an old fool on a tiny horse trying to die with dignity. And the other fools are trying to save him. Ha!"

He turned to his army and raised his arm, but before he could shout a command, he heard a new sound, a sound like arrows in flight, but much deeper, as if from arrows ten times the size of a normal arrow. He looked at the sky and gasped.

• • •

Bookins had dropped to his knees, certain that his plan had failed. Nowhere in it had he made room for the deranged charge of Lord Braque. The queen was out there now, vulnerable to attack and capture. His gambit was unraveling even before it began.

But then a shadow came across the plain, forcing Bookins to look up at the sky, and what he saw thrilled him. "Yes, yes, at last!"

He stood up and tried his best to do a jig worthy of a fool, but his knees wouldn't cooperate. He stopped and looked out across the plain again. Arrows—huge arrows!—were falling in a thick line around the Mystrosian army, forming an impenetrable fence.

And then the ground shook.

The trolls—his trolls!—had arrived, and just in time. Bridge trolls, mountain trolls, and impossibly tall forest trolls began emerging from the tree lines on either side and surrounding the fenced-in Mystrosians.

Bookins spotted Bebo at the front of the Mystrosian lines, holding the squealing King Merek the Mighty high above his head.

Bookins shook his fists with joy. "By the gods! By the gods!"

• • •

As the trolls approached, Whelan heard a new sound, the sound of swords and shields dropping to the ground, followed by screams for mercy. And then came the loud voice of a troll, shouting "Surrender!"

The sight of King Merek wriggling in the troll's raised hand was the final blow. Whelan sighed and turned to the other gods. "We're done here. Meet me at the cave in three days."

And with that, they all disappeared.

• • •

The warriors along the Enturian lines were stunned, but none more than Calax, Blusk, and Phendour, who had spent hours discussing the battle plan with Bookins and the others. The sudden appearance of trolls had never been part of the plan they discussed. Why hadn't Bookins trusted them with the *real* plan? Was he afraid of infiltration by Mystrosian gelas? Did he think they might have a traitor in their midst?

And then Calax remembered the Red God, who had indeed betrayed them, and his anger subsided. Bookins must have suspected her from the very start. Calax looked up at the bluff. Bookins was on his knees, weeping with relief and joy. They would have to have a long talk, but for now, Calax turned back to his men, raised his sword to the sky, and shouted "Victory!"

• • •

Queen Rhynt heard the shouts erupting from the Enturian lines and turned briefly to join them, raising her sword and pumping it into the air. Then she dropped the sword to the ground and ran with her tigers over to Bebo, who was lowering King Merek to the ground.

"Bebo," she shouted. "You did it!"

She ignored Merek and hugged Bebo's leg. "You've done it, you've done it."

Bebo reached down and patted her on the head. "Nice queen, nice queen, now joke."

"What?"

"We win, give joke."

She laughed and motioned for Bebo to bend over so she could whisper in his ear.

His eyes grew wide as a grin became a smile and then a chuckle and then a booming guffaw only a troll could manage.

Epilogue

Orthor unsaddled his horse and dropped the saddle at the entrance to the cave. He wasn't sure whether his reading of the five runes was correct, but it seemed to at least point to the next step. When all was said and done, he decided to look at the runes the way anyone unfamiliar with runes might look at them. He would think of them as just pictures.

The first rune appeared to be a poorly drawn man pointing to the left. Perhaps it meant *go this way* or simply *leave this cave.* The next three runes said nothing to him; they were just squiggles, completely unfathomable. But the final rune was clearly what looked like the opening of a cave.

He had thought about it and thought about it, and could only think of one other cave: The Cave of the Six Arrows. Queen Rhynt had mentioned it to him, not as a source for solving the problem of the runes, but for a sight he should see if he had the time. She mentioned the wonderful paintings on its walls and how delicious the rats were.

And it was the prospect of tasty rats that had tipped the scales and prompted his journey. He walked inside, lit one of the torches that stood ready just inside the entrance, and began walking along the wall, holding the torch high to see the many wonders the queen had described.

The wonder of it all took his breath away and it was difficult to take it all in. When he reached the back of the cave, he turned and walked back along the wall again. There was the young woman and her tigers running away; it did indeed look like Queen Rhynt and her hill tigers. And there were the gods, each in their colorful robes.

And then something made him stop. Three runes centered just below the picture of the gods. He pulled out his parchment and held it up next to the runes. They were identical.

He moved his torch around, looking for more runes, finally spotting them just to the right of the running woman. His three runes were there, again and again, in different combinations, joined with other runes. Their meanings seemed to flash like lightning in his head. Words began to appear, then phrases, then sentences.

They spoke of trials and battles so horrific they sent chills up and down Orthor's spine. He wondered how anyone could have survived what was written here. And then came the biggest shock of all.

A single combination of runes made him gasp.

All that was depicted on these walls was not about some past events, as the queen had told him. The date revealed by those runes made it all too clear to Orthor. The Great Unraveling was a lie.

All these events were yet to come!

He slumped to the ground and looked over to the caged pigeons Bookins had given him to notify the queen of any findings. They cooed back at him.

He started to reach for the cage, but then he remembered the words of the Red God, who had insisted the only way to save the queen from harm was to tell the Red God of his findings first.

He had only to say three words.

Part Last

"Yes, of course there's more. There's always more. Did you think I could end my tale with my tail between my legs, outwitted by a nitwit? No, this story is not at its end, but it is a good place to stop and refresh ourselves. You've heard about the rats in the Cave of the Six Arrows. I happen to have some here, spitted and roasting before you now. They'll make us a fine dinner. Don't give me that look. No, they aren't rabbits or molfrumps. They are big, fat rats and quite delicious, sweet and succulent, at least if you get the seasonings right. Besides, if you don't eat now, you certainly won't want to eat once our tale resumes. Now, hold out your bowl. What's your pleasure, a leg, a breast, or—if I might make a recommendation— brains?"

Other Books by Len Boswell

Fantasies:
Barnum's Angel
The Cave of the Six Arrows

Simon Grave Mysteries:
A Grave Misunderstanding
Simon Grave and the Curious Incident of the Cat in the Daytime
Simon Grave and the Drone of the Basque Orvilles
Simon Grave and the Sons of Irony
Simon Grave and the School of Casual Invisibility

Other Mysteries:
Flicker: A Paranormal Mystery
Skeleton: A Bare Bones Mystery

Memoirs:
Santa Takes a Tumble
Unboxing Raymond

Nonfiction:
The Leadership Secrets of Squirrels
Stick Figures: The Life and Art of Len Boswell

About the Author

Len Boswell is the author of thirteen additional books, including the award-winning *Simon Grave Mysteries*. He lives in the mountains of West Virginia with his wife, Ruth, and their dog, Cinder, a speedy rat terrier known affectionately as "The Blur."

Note from the Author

Word-of-mouth is crucial for any author to succeed. If you enjoyed *The Fool's Gambit*, please leave a review online—anywhere you are able. Even if it's just a sentence or two. It would make all the difference and would be very much appreciated.

Thanks!
Len Boswell

We hope you enjoyed reading this title from:

www.blackrosewriting.com

Subscribe to our mailing list – *The Rosevine* – and receive **FREE** books, daily
deals, and stay current with news about upcoming releases
and our hottest authors.
Scan the QR code below to sign up.

Already a subscriber? Please accept a sincere thank you for being a fan of
Black Rose Writing authors.

View other Black Rose Writing titles at
www.blackrosewriting.com/books and use promo code
PRINT to receive a **20% discount** when purchasing.

9 781685 131371